Keep
Walking.
Rhona
Beech

Keep Walking, Rhona Beech

KATE TOUGH

ABACUS

First published in Great Britain as *Head for the Edge,
Keep Walking* by Cargo Publishing, 2014
This edition published by Abacus Books in 2019

1 3 5 7 9 10 8 6 4 2

A CIP catalogue record for this book
is available from the British Library.

ISBN 978-0-349-14365-1

Typeset in Caslon by M Rules
Printed and bound in Great Britain by
Clays Ltd, Elcograf S.p.A.

Papers used by Abacus are from well-managed forests
and other responsible sources.

Abacus
An imprint of
Little, Brown Book Group
Carmelite House
50 Victoria Embankment
London EC4Y 0DZ

An Hachette UK Company
www.hachette.co.uk

www.littlebrown.co.uk

*For Ken
and for Glasgow*

One

I step off the bus and stand there, planted; no part of me ready to go home. I watch the bus continue into the distance, start to pick up speed, stop to let someone off, start, stop. All that curbed potential.

A woman in leggings walks by, supermarket bag on one arm and yoga mat rolled up under the other. That's one way to spend your evening. But is it a life – a job, a hobby and dinner at nine o'clock at night?

My mind searches for things I could do at this time on a Tuesday. Realising this might take a while, I move inside the bus shelter to perch on the pole that passes for a bench. I scroll through my mobile looking for a companion, someone without children or an early start, who could meet me for coffee. Names flow up the screen and the thought of holding another conversation wears me out. *That woman's voice says things . . . I don't know where she gets them from.* Since the split, I've been out in public as her, yakking, or home alone as I don't know who, silent. What I really miss is being quiet in the company of another. I need to be quiet. I don't need to be alone. Nor do I need to foist this on anyone else.

I put my phone away and stare up the street.

～

I get up. I go to work.

I spend the whole day there.

～

Emerging from the underpass something cold and sudden hits my legs. I look down and my thighs are wet; soaked through. Brain whirring: *Am I supposed to walk home like this? Is it water? Is it piss? Was it deliberate? Are they laughing? More to come?*

On the ground: tattered balloon skin.

Look left, right. Up.

A collection of boys at the wall, a phone camera pointed at me. 'Very funny you wee pricks! Is it not past your bedtime?'

I bring out my phone and raise it towards them. They scatter. One stays.

Look away. Look back.

He's about thirteen, in his customised school uniform of shortened, fattened tie, un-tucked shirt and no blazer, no jumper.

'C'mere and say that tae ma face,' he goads. 'C'mere and say it.'

～

2

I get up. I go to work. I spend the whole day waiting for the words on my screen to make sense.

In the commuter broth of the carriage home, tears run in hot lines to my jaw and for a minute or so, I let them.

〜

I don't even take off my coat. I beeline for the walk-in cupboard in the living room. Moving a portable heater to one side, I can access a large cardboard box to reach inside. Both blind hands are required to lift out a smaller box placed there in July, when I swore I'd never do this.

Cross-legged on the rug, my coat seams cut into my armpits as I hold him.

My lungs remember air.

I slip-stop through the glossy stack: him alone, me and him, headshots, full-length, family groupings. Set against: landmarks and landscapes and sun loungers and celebrations.

Today has been a subway train rumbling towards this – I have to hear his voice. Just for a moment. The sound of it. I need to. I must.

I can't.

I don't have his new number.

I know I don't. But maybe I do. I reach for my bag and rummage to retrieve the phone. As soon as it's in my hand I feel a little better. Like I've fulfilled at least part of the craving that clawed at me all afternoon, from below the place where I know who I am or what drives me. I click the contacts icon: M ... Mark. There he is. With his old number. The one he no longer uses because it's a UK mobile.

I hold the phone to my ear. I imagine it ringing and him

answering. I feel sick and stupid for calling him. I haven't actually called him. I imagine we are talking, telling each other what happened today. Laughing before punchlines are delivered because we can second-guess what they will be. The phone is him, in my hand.

I may never hear him again.

The phone drops on the rug and tears trail hot, again, to my jaw.

If I can't hear his voice I will drink. I'll sit here, forget dinner and drink until bedtime.

I can't. I know what that would lead to.

Opening the wine would end in me phoning his mum to ask for his new number and she would a) not give it, and b) phone him and tell him I asked for it.

My number is the same as it always was. My number used to be his number. And he hasn't phoned it since he left.

~

I wake up. I am wearing my coat. I'm surrounded by photographs – remnants of the geek who didn't trust cloud storage and printed a copy of everything worth keeping.

As I gather and neaten them into a pile I notice it's easier to look at them now. Why? Studying the uppermost image it's apparent that I'm not the person I am looking at. Her static existence is not mine.

Mark, too, may not be the man I am holding onto. Putting the photographs back in their box, I'm untempted by the items littering the bottom – birthday cards, Valentine's cards. Envelopes with my name, in his handwriting. Little packets of temporary truth.

I bury the box back inside the larger box in the cupboard, so there will be no evidence in the morning. The phone screen displays his name. I delete his redundant number and go to bed.

~

I get up. I go to work.

Passing an entire day there, I'm subjected to the ritual call-and-response of colleagues as they leave the office ('Cheerio' > 'See you tomorrow'). When I notice I'm the only person left I look at the clock and it's seven forty-three. I won't cross the 8 p.m. boundary so I turn off the computer, gather my stuff and decide to walk it. Perhaps I'll feel like being at home by the time I get there.

Not long into my stride, the phone rings. On the screen: **Hilary**. After a salutation she says, 'It's the annual alumni dinner on Saturday. They sent me an email.'

'Thanks, but it's a no.'

'You don't know where it is yet.'

'Who cares?' I am using the background traffic noise to my advantage.

'What?' she asks.

I raise my voice. 'I have plans already,' I tell her. 'An alum*nus* dinner at home. If you want to go husband hunting, take Tania.'

'You just managed to get Tania and husband in the same sentence. Prize for the grumpy lady. Tania can't go, she's not a graduate. Just *come*. It'll be good for you, for us, to mingle.'

'New rule,' I say, loudly. 'No parties till I stop yammering with the brittle zeal of the recently dumped. I see it in their eyes, "Who brought her?"'

Hilary peddles her usual angle. 'You weren't dumped.'

'As good as.'

I wait for the red man to turn green beside the twin exhausts of a motorbike.

'I can't even hear what you're saying,' she yells. 'Phone me later.'

~

I get up. I speak to my cereal.

'Maybe it's time. It must be. I have to get used to doing things on my own.'

I go to work and manage small talk at the kettle. At lunch time, I ping round the internet like a pinball: **'What's on in Glasgow?'**

~

The 'musician' wears baggy garb, topped off with a hard hat. Not worn to deflect missiles sent towards the stage, it is an instrument. Tubing is glued to it which trails to her mouth (I conclude 'she' from something in the shape of her lips) and she blows through it to produce nothing like music.

Tightly surrounded by a set of objects found in any self-respecting back lane – bike wheels, bed frames, rusting white goods – she seems furious about this, hitting, scraping and banging them with the frenzy of someone on the wrong side of talented.

Metal strings connect some of the objects. She rubs the wires feverishly with flattened fingers and the audience is enthralled but I can't hear it. I just can't.

Easing myself to the end of the row and then out, I wait

for a bus while rain rushes at the vandal-proof glass in violent, percussive waves.

A short, shabby man teeters towards the bus stop, hand resting on the open can nestled in his pocket. Not judging distance too well, he sits down next to me so our upper arms are touching through the bulk of our coats. I wait for his uninvited, incoherent ramble. The half-cut, half-arsed attempt at conversation he will make and I will be expected to invest myself in, in case he causes a scene or stabs me or something. Conversation that he will apologise for starting, 'Sorry, hen, sorry to bother ye,' but will proceed with regardless. Conversation that will quickly move into the realms of the personal, 'Yur a lovely lassie. So y'ur. Where's yur husband the night, hen?' And I will have to shout my answers (because he'll be drunk *and* deaf) so passers-by will hear me say, 'I'M NOT MARRIED,' and he will reply, 'Lovely lassie lik you? Courtin then, aye? Boyfriend, then.'

'I DON'T HAVE A BOYFRIEND.'

'Och. That's no right. Come oot wi me, hen.' Does he honestly think? 'See when ah wis younger? Quite a looker. So ah wis. Aye. Ah'll take y'oot, hen. Up the dancin ...' at which point he will get up and step from side to side, turn in methodical circles with his arms out, all the while smiling and carrying a pretty decent melody of a sixties' song. And I will sneak off, leaving him to it.

But this is not what happens. Our upper bodies rest beside each other and I can smell his sour skin and breath but because he doesn't say a word, doesn't even look at me, I don't feel the need to shuffle along. We sit in our silences. I contemplate what he might be contemplating and realise I have no idea.

I start to like him for this; his courage to reject the coherent world and inhabit his own.

He sees a bus approaching and reels to his feet. Assuming that he wants to get on it, I face the rain to stick out my arm on his behalf. As the bus slows I hand him my day pass to use for his fare, thinking, *I'll walk off some of the antsiness, then maybe I'll be able to go through my front door.*

~

Cradling a mug of tea, I scroll through a screen of 35- to 45-year-old males (who live within five miles of my postcode, have an 'about average' body type, work in an 'executive/ management' occupation and 'no way' smoke). I pause at one. Continue scanning. Pause at another. My forefinger tendon twitches beneath the skin: if my laptop goes in for repair, will the shop staff know which sites I've been on? I remind myself it's not porn – but being caught looking at porn would feel slightly less humiliating.

Clicking the profile of LionRampant, I struggle to compute this realm of online romance. The last time I was in the market, occasional success depended on a blend of kismet, alcohol and making the effort (to get out the door, to look half decent). Now there's this strange internet shopping – with unwashed hair after a long day at work. No pheromones. No danger.

I read what he's written. Normal enough. Yet he hasn't met a woman at the pub, or a party. Do people not speak to each other any more? I look at his photos again. *Would we hit it off if we met?* I ask him. *Would I know how to function again if I hooked up with you?*

8

I can't imagine knowing what to talk about with Lion-Rampant. I can only remember knowing Mark so well that we didn't have to talk.

My eye focus has drifted during the reverie and I'm aware of my face reflected on the darker areas of the screen. Drooping where it didn't use to, it is not a face to offer on a dating site.

The ramifications of the choice I made in July pitch up and bed-in for the night: I let him go at an age when no one else will want me. I was reckless with my best years. I have nothing to show for them.

~

For several satisfying seconds, the blade hits a rhythm of back and forth.

The adenoidal breaths of its serrated edge come in quick succession.

Then (due to the angle of my arm, or the grain of the wood) it catches. The sides of the cut hold fast around the slim metal but I keep tugging at it, as though it's the teeth which have become embedded, when I know it's something else entirely: some law of physics I have no patience for.

As always, it comes free again and obliges me; rasping back-forth-back-forth-back-forth.

It's only when the blade is almost through the far edge that I notice.

I am sawing the branch that I'm sitting on.

~

I get up, I go to work. I'm hit on the ear by scrunched-up paper.

The boss has left for her holiday, and the others appear to

9

be doing as little as possible. A cheer goes up when I roll my seat over to join them.

One explains that I got in the way of the target. I look over to where I came in and there's a printed photo of the boss tacked to the door. 'Ten points for her nose,' he says.

A joy on Monday, by Wednesday, the inanity has back-fired to the point where I want to top myself. At midday, I say that I'm taking a long lunch hour, '... because I can, ha ha ha ...' but actually because I need to do something, anything, with a point to it. What I have in mind is the shops: stocking up on toiletries and replacing the gloves I couldn't find when I looked for them. What occurs is an impromptu decision to board a bus which comes to a halt as I'm passing its stop. *As long as I stay on it for less than half an hour, I can be back from wherever I am by one thirty*. My luck is in; the traffic is light and after twenty-five minutes I disembark in a village that would have been isolated before the suburbs came out to greet it. There are a few shops up ahead. I wander towards them.

The woman behind the bakery counter is from the genera-tion which considers it a female's duty to herself, and everyone else, to look as groomed as she is able before leaving the house (even if it's to serve sausage rolls to pensioners and off-course office workers).

Observing her, I can only conclude that her generation is right. The care she has taken over setting her hair and tying her neckerchief extends to the way she has the Empire biscuits arranged – also the way my sandwich is placed into its paper bag and the corners twisted with a dainty turn of manicured fingertips. She can touch nothing without nurturing it.

Handing over my money, I wish I'd made more of an effort this morning. 'Is there somewhere nearby I can eat this?' I ask.

She thinks for a second. 'There's a viewpoint behind the park,' she replies. 'Don't go into the park, mind. Go up the track at the back of the cottages. You'll see the signpost. It's a climb to the bench, but the views go all the way to the reservoir.'

For the length of time she smiles at me, I forget to speak.

'Will you be warm enough?' she asks.

'Be fine,' I say, making a 'tipping my cap', 'good day to you' gesture with my sandwich bag. This excruciating display of masculinity bewilders me. I make myself leave though what I want to do is wait there till her shift is over, go home with her and live in her house.

At the bench I imagine how the bakery lady might sit and I do my best to emulate it. Gulls and crows are fussing in the distance, each group determined to claim a field as its own.

Watching the black and white shapes rough and tumble, I stand to sweep crumbs from my coat then sit down again, wondering, *Does the bus go as far as that loch? Could I get off there another time?*

Edging in from around these musings comes the sense that something, somewhere, isn't right. It accrues momentum. Things are not fine. But what isn't fine? The feeling swells till it's loosened my moorings. The sandwich is on the ground and I am bent forward in a gaping-mouthed, perfectly silent howl.

I can't hold him. I don't have him.

Spit trails from my lower lip.

All the things I've lost . . .

I don't know how long I'm like that – seconds? minutes? – before I manage a drink of water. Thank God no one could see me. Thank God it happened here. It can happen anywhere; the acute, occasional human pain that stops your stride, robs your breath and sends you into the nearest alley, the nearest toilet, because you can't cry in the street. Who in their right mind cries in the street?

~

At the base of the track sits the village war memorial, a chunky granite needle engraved with names. I quash the usual curiosity to see if my surname is among them, given the risk that I'd see his – the heavily carved permanence of it is not an image I need to carry back.

Disco music builds inside my bag, signalling the life I have away from this place. The screen says, **Tania**. She's been in touch more regularly since I ceased to be a 'smug married' (her words).

When I locate the phone there's scant chance to offer a greeting.

'Thank God you answered. Where are you? Can you talk?'

Tania's grasp on the timetables of regular people is slight, ever since she left the service sector courtesy of a crippling anxiety disorder (full range of symptoms researchable online). She sells her NHS pills to a local dope dealer, and boosts her benefits by listing her flat on Airbnb. We're not sure where she sleeps.

I tell her I'm on my lunch break and ask if she's okay.

'I need surgery.'

'When? *What?*'

'It's shooting out my nose, Rhona. Oh it's nasty.'

'Put your head back.'

12

'Not *blood*. God. If only. A hair. A bionic one. It's dangling right out my nose and I don—'

'And you think you need surgery?'

'To cut out the follicle, so it never grows back. And I'll need some hormone pills. I'm turning into a man here.'

She's turning into something ... Let's see if I can coax her back.

'Tania, everyone gets a rebel hair now and again.'

'I don't. I think I should get it checked.'

'I wouldn't bother the doctor. *Really* wouldn't do that.'

'What am I supposed to do?' she whines.

Get a job? Do a bit of voluntary work?

'Set to it with nail scissors,' I suggest. Adding, 'And don't look at your big toes.' Cruel, maybe, while she's still in shock about her nostril but she'd have found out sooner or later.

～

On the journey back (me, three OAPs and a chihuahua in a jacket) my conclusion is, *I am not taken seriously enough at work, they have lost respect for me.* Reflecting on when this might have happened, I can conjure no evidence that they ever had any. Not in two years of compiling their rotas, reconciling their wages, making good their customer service blips and not telling the boss when their call times were out. If I stay any longer I'll be in danger of a personal best.

My desk isn't overlooked by anyone so I spend the afternoon updating my CV and surfing job websites because things can't go on like this ('It's not fair on either of us.').

～

I get up. I get to work at five to ten – within the bounds of flexi-time (just) but I've to reach the sixth floor still, and put my computer on.

The lift doors close behind me and the guy who's already inside raises his head. 'A'right?'

It's a rhetorical question. An awkwardness-easer. He doesn't need an answer. Why do I feel compelled to answer?

If the lift hadn't stopped on Level Three, if he hadn't got out, I'd have told him.

'Yeah, all right,' I'd have said. 'Though I woke up alone, again, to come to work, which has descended into a zoo this week, with me as a performing seal. I know what you're going to say and, don't worry, I'm already looking. Where d'you work? Do they need a Section Manager? If I could just shake this pervasive malaise ... everywhere I go, there it is. *Plus* I'm going to be logging-in late 'cause I was in my pyjamas Googling a cervical procedure. My appointment card arrived. Colposcopy – heard of that? I'll spare you the details but I don't fancy it. At all. Didn't have time for breakfast in the end. So yeah, all right. You?'

~

Hilary and I laugh behind our hands like Japanese women, shielding each other from the food that may be lodged in our teeth. I'm telling her about the Facebook account the guys at work set up in the boss's name during her holiday – and the insulting (or plain insane) messages they sent to the old school buddies who 'friended' her.

'You should've seen the replies these people were sending back,' I continue. 'Outraged and full of personal stuff – what she's supposed to have done in the toilets in 1982.'

'That's awful,' says Hilary, frowning. 'I wish I hadn't laughed. Is she married?'

'To a German Shepherd, in a humanist ceremony.'

'Not her "relationship status", Rhona. Married in real life.'

'... how can you marry a dog in a *humanist* ceremony?'

'Because I wouldn't like to be there when her bloke finds out.'

'... unless they meant an actual German, who keeps sheep ...'

Hilary claps her hands in front of my face.

'They've taken it down,' I tell her.

She studies me for a second before reaching into her bag.

Bringing out her diary, she clicks a pen into 'ready' mode and hovers it over an open page. 'Note to self,' she dictates. 'Email Rhona's boss with details of Facebook prank. Suggest Rhona is sacked.'

'Me!'

'I can't believe you joined in with that,' she says, laying the pen down (but not un-cocking it).

'I didn't know they'd done it! Until the replies started coming in and the hilarity went up a notch. You don't understand what it was like in there. I was tuning it out most of the time, trying to concentrate.'

Hilary shakes her head in slow motion. 'Never lose your authority,' she says. 'If I taught you anything I thought it was that.'

I raise my glass. 'A toast to October half-term and Miss Marshall being out on a weeknight.'

'And to you, Ms Beech, for being single and free to come out anytime.'

'Every cloud ...'

I get up.

At work, I remember to block off a morning on my calendar for the colposcopy clinic. Try saying that when you're drunk. I'm whispering it to myself repeatedly as a tongue-twister, when a text interrupts. Hilary's message says she wants to make the most of having no homework to mark and do I want to see a film this evening?

Top hole, I text. **Shall we meet somewhere first?**

At six o'clock, there she is, in a hangar-like bar close to the cinema. As I approach, she gets up from her seat and does a quick twirl, drawing my attention to her shorter hair.

'Classy,' I tell her. 'Suits you.'

'Spur of the moment,' she says. 'I phoned up and there was a three o'clock cancellation. This new do is *destiny*.'

I pick up her empty glass. Buying two large wines at the bar, I remember what she said last night and sitting back down I ask, 'Did I never come out midweek, when I had a bloke?'

'Made no difference to me,' she says. 'I don't go anywhere on school nights.'

'Tania must have commented on it, then.'

Hilary's expression doesn't change.

'If I went straight home during the week,' I tell her, 'it wasn't to snuggle up with Mark.'

'Tania doesn't understand six o'clock exhaustion,' Hilary says, which suggests she may have defended my corner when Tania was moaning.

'I looked forward to getting home,' I say, re-experiencing that congruent sensation between where the body wants to be and where the body is. 'Now I take as long as I can to get there. And I can't even cook a meal because serving it onto one plate makes me cry.'

'After how many months?'

Two (and three quarters) but to say this would be evidence of counting.

'If I can't get used to being alone, maybe I'm not meant to be by myself,' I say, to appear solution-focused, less of a wallower. 'I should meet someone else and then I'll feel normal again.' I don't mention that I got this idea from browsing a dating website.

'Do whatever you think you need to.' She's not looking at me, she's primping her hair in a metallic wall panel by the table.

'But?' I offer, because there is one.

'But ...' she concedes, 'why would a man take you on, in such a fragile state? That wouldn't be fair on someone who's ready.'

'What does that mean, *ready*? I hate being alone therefore I'm ready for a boyfriend.'

Hilary turns away from her reflection. 'It's because you hate being alone that you're *not* ready for a relationship.'

'I hope you don't teach this to impressionable children.'

'I think it makes perfect sense.'

'What? That if I'm a couple-y person, who feels happiest with a boyfriend, I need to transform into the kind of person who's happier with my own company, and that's how I become ready for pairing up? Plus, if I went to all the trouble of becoming an ecstatic loner, why would I bother getting into a relationship at all?'

'It's the conundrum at the heart of romantic love.'

'Or you're drunk.'

'On a Wednesday! Praaaise Jeeesus.'

'The conundrum at the heart of love,' I say, 'is that losing it is harder than grieving a dead person.' She can scoff at this, too, if she wants but I will say it. 'When someone dies, there's no ambiguity. You can't talk to them ever again and you have to accept that they're gone. The person I want to speak to is still alive, but I'm not allowed to make contact. I have to *act* like he's dead when he's not. The pain of that, at times, is indescribable.'

'You only think you want to speak to him,' Hilary says.

'Ease off, teach'.'

'Rhona, if I'd realised you were still at the ugly mess stage I'd have intervened sooner. The pain you're playing with is heady stuff. As addictive as love, in fact. You have to nip it in the bud.' Her Rioja-fuelled fist dunts the table, annihilating the bud. 'You want to speak to Mark again. Explain to me – what purpose would it serve?'

'We might get back together and I could stay at home on weeknights, not be out getting abuse from a drunk school ma'am.'

She emits a whoop-screech, leans across in a fumbled hug and carries on. 'You'd got into the *habit* of existing as a couple; of having him around. But that twosome habit will fade.'

'How long are we talking?'

'There's no set timeframe. You haven't been single for what, a decade? It'll take as long as it takes.'

'I need figures.'

'Welcome to my world. Sometimes you're a solo operator,

sometimes you're another half. You need to learn to move between them, to survive.'

'If you're suggesting I could be single for years, Hilary, I don't have years. I'm already past the beeps; I'm on the long continuous tone before the burglar alarm goes off. I need to shut the front door.' This bamboozles her. I will clarify. It's worth saying. 'You know what I realised this week – and I can't believe I never thought of it *before* waving Mark off to Canada – I realised that any guy my age wanting a family has no interest in starting to date me, at thirty-four, then trying for a family at thirty-six or thirty-seven.

'And what's more, an older guy would go for a proper "younger woman". A pert one. I am already surplus to requirements and you're suggesting I wait however long it takes to be *ready*?'

Hilary doesn't have a response to this. I thought it was quite revelatory, myself. After a substantial slug of her drink, she speaks. 'Tactful as ever. We're the same age.'

And both single.

'That's true,' I say, 'that *is* true. But *you're* ready. That's the difference. If you meet a nice guy tomorrow, you can get on with it. Plus you've been eating dinner every night since July. You're more fertile than I am. You, Hilary, have the eggs of a *twenty*-four-year-old. You'd get pregnant from a blow job.'

〜

I get up. At work an email arrives mid-morning thanking me for my application and inviting me to interview. A dragging feeling accompanies it, *What did I go and do that for?*

I remember the energy it takes to change jobs: write

handover lists of what I do and how I do it; say goodbye; say hello; learn where the stationery is kept and the procedure for 'non-standard item' requests; sit through the induction training, equalities training, health and safety training, IT training; learn what your predecessor called his/her file names and how far along he/she was with certain projects; and have no clue, for the first few months, how the photocopier works or who you are talking to.

I search for my saved application form, to remind myself what I would be interviewing for. This one is ... an Office Manager with ... a small firm of business-stroke-management consultants which has ... opened a second office, in Edinburgh. My role would be in the Glasgow office, to relieve the Director of HR tasks and other day-to-day stuff plus oversee the scheduling of concurrent projects. And ... it's a new post.

No predecessor, no pre-existing files and no spreadsheets with illogical column headings. For this reason alone, I block off my calendar under the heading 'flexi-time' and accept the invitation.

Two

The woman behind the desk extracts my file from the day's stack. She opens it and scans a finger down the first page. 'Is your GP still Dr Gillespie?'

'Yes.'

'Address still Heron Crescent?'

'Yes.'

'That's fine. Take a seat till the nurse calls you through.'

I'd been looking into her eyes, to gauge the gravity of the situation, but she could have been behind a supermarket checkout. Is this serious or not?

The L-shaped waiting area of the colposcopy clinic is as close to a B&B patrons' lounge as an NHS budget will allow. Why the special treatment – because they're softening us for bad news or because women need 'nice' waiting areas? I'm glad of the broad, padded seats. My legs are wound round each other.

In my world, routine smear tests had routinely clear results, until the letter which said I was being referred to the colposcopy clinic (the *what?*) to assess the degree of cell abnormality on my cervix and, in the meantime, I was to read the enclosed pink leaflet (is men's bad news explained in a blue leaflet?).

The appointment letter suggested that I wear a skirt and I bring someone with me. Almost a wedding invitation.

Who would I share this morning off with? Besides, I'm only here for a biopsy: a pinhead cell sample. Not for treatment; there might be nothing worth treating. I did read the leaflet. By definition, I suppose precancerous cells could *become* cancerous, but it's a misleading term, implying an inevitable connection and according to the internet there isn't one. Cervical abnormality progressing to cancer is rare. One dodgy smear result is exactly that.

The stresses of the past few months aren't the norm. Nor have I been eating proper meals. Now my body has responded to the hiccup, which confirms what Hilary was saying – it's time to get a grip of the grief. Time to take better care of myself.

A nurse appears from behind a pastel patterned curtain. 'Rhona Beech?' She smiles to the room. I pick up my bag and follow her through to what looks like – a second waiting room. Mother of *God*, the interminable suspense. She guides me to a cubicle and says, 'If you'd like to take off your underwear in here. Not the skirt. When you're all sorted, have a seat. I'll come back for you.' The metallic curtain rings slice cleanly across the rail.

To take off my underwear, I first want to remove my winter

boots but she didn't say anything about taking off footwear. Where's the wall chart showing the correct way to disrobe for a vaginal probing? Can I have my feet in the stirrups in a pair of knee-high, leather boots? Reeks of porn. The boots come off.

I take a seat, again. Cellulite assaults me from a tatty magazine cover with an invitation to guess which celebrity it belongs to. My lower leg mimics a pneumatic drill. I tell it to stop. I glance sideways at the other women. There's a respectful two seat distance between each of us. How can they read that crap? How can they read full stop? I try to work out why they've ended up here. *Do you smoke? Because I don't. Had more than a dozen sexual partners? Because I haven't. Eat nothing but junk food? Not me, love.*

The nurse returns. I walk behind her over the linoleum floor in my socks, no pants on under my skirt. Like I'm five and I've wet myself in the classroom.

~

We enter a small room cluttered with a treatment table, a storage bench, a consulting table and a consultant. Dr Carr stands to introduce herself. 'Former hockey captain' is suggested by her sensible hair, her breeze-block boobs and bottom. She's dressed in green walking trousers and a pink polo shirt with its collar raised at the rear. A feminine touch? Or the public school affectation? This is her golfing outfit, I surmise, during our seated conversation where she asks what I've got planned for today and reciprocates by saying she is playing golf; that she only works mornings. *Well isn't that nice*, I think. The advantages of earning ninety grand a year, pro rata. The advantages of making good choices at the age of 16. Burning, cutting and scraping cervixes before lunch, striding fairways in the afternoon.

'A routine visit today,' she says, readying herself to stand. 'As you know already, your smear test showed signs of atypical cells, which has resulted in us needing to take a closer look. Thousands of biopsies are performed every year, so, not something you need to worry about.'

Nor you, I imagine. Cervical abnormalities arise in women who've had sex.

'A simple procedure' – she is standing now; should I stand? – 'to obtain a sample of tissue about the size of a sesame seed from the surface of the cervix. Most people don't feel a thing.'

The nurse takes over. As instructed, I leave my things on the chair and walk between the stirrups of the treatment table. I turn and lie against its half-upright back. With my legs parted on the elevated rests, she tells me to wheech my bum down to the edge of the table. This pushes my skirt up around my hips, where it needs to be. She places a length of paper towel across my pelvis.

A thin attempt to protect my modesty, my bits are now visible to anyone in the room except me. Do some women find the sight of themselves offensive? Maybe it's seeing someone else fiddling around down there that's traumatic.

The nurse is standing by the table in silence. I know she'd smile at me if I looked at her. I look up at the line where the wall joins the ceiling.

Dr Carr starts asking about my job. This is not the hairdresser's. I need to concentrate, to follow what she is doing; to be ready for when it will hurt.

A speculum with curved blades slathered in lubricant

disappears under the paper and finds its greasy way in. Its mechanism is adjusted and my vaginal canal is held wide.

A white metal head off to the side cranes its hinged neck and the black circle of its single eye is aligned with my fanny. Dr Carr looks down binocular-style eyepieces on the rear of the box.

Because I haven't answered her question (I didn't even realise), she starts telling me about *her* job. Not in general, but moment-to-moment. 'You won't feel this, but you might smell it.' I can't see what her hands are doing below the shelf of paper.

'Recognise the smell?' she asks. 'That's right, vinegar. Sometimes you don't need anything more hi-tech than what's in the larder. Though here we call it acetic acid.' She says this by spelling out each syllable. Well, why wouldn't she? People who didn't get all As at high school have limited mental capacity.

What's going on inside me? I can't feel it properly. I don't want something happening inside me that I can't see or feel. I want to ask her to stop. I want a healthy cervix. I want Mark holding my hand. I want an easy life. I want my old life. I get the message. If we could make this stop now, I will be grateful for all that's mine and not squander it ever again.

My incapacity, my inability to bolt, my ignorance relative to the two women running the show are about to send me into meltdown. I can't cry here. Keep. It. Together. Keep. It. Together.

'The properties of the vinegar react with any abnormal cells and make them more visible,' she is saying. 'Cough,' she instructs.

I'm expected to participate?

After the cough, she places the sliver of cells in a sterile

25

container and the speculum is unclipped and retracted with a light suction sound. She drops her rubber gloves into a bucket, saying, 'There can be a little spotting, from the biopsy site, so I popped in a tampon.'

I look at her through my spread legs. I have a tampon inside? That you put there, without asking? You didn't check with *me*? You presumptuous, Thatcher-ish, doctor-knows-best, once-a-head-girl-always-a-head-girl, bossy boots. I may be less qualified but I know my body better and I decide, me, I do, if it receives a tampon or it doesn't. I happen to hate tampons. The dry boak sensation when the lumpen stodge of it slugs its way out with blind tugs on a blue string. Ugh. Don't exert that all-girls-together crap with me.

'The tissue sample will go to the lab,' she says, diligent about eye contact, 'and the results will be posted to you, in about two weeks.'

When she finally moves the colposcope out the way, and moves her brick-stack body towards the door, there is room for me to repossess my legs and stand up.

The nurse invites me to 'get sorted out' but I will not struggle in a corner to pull on pants, socks and boots. I go straight to the toilet in the waiting area, sit down, catch the blue string and drag the fibrous bullet along my vaginal walls.

Retch.

With my sleeve pulled down over my thumb, I dab at the tear which trickled into the crevice of my ear.

～

Tania doesn't answer her phone when I call it from my sofa at seven o'clock. She does answer when I call her again at seven thirty. I tell her I need a pick-me-up. I suggest the pub at eight.

'Can't. Sorry.'

I wait a second in case there's any more in that sentence.

'Plans already?' I ask.

'Mm, sorry.'

A personal life she doesn't need or want to talk about – the joy of being Tania.

~

I get up. I get on a bus. I try not to let a single particle of my coat touch the damp-day-plus-bus-heater sweat on the window. The traffic is light. I remember it's still the October half-term.

I text Hilary: **You are still sleeping, lucky lady.**

I text Tania: **Who are you sleeping with, lucky lady?**

I'm rummaging inside my bag for a packet of tissues to soak up the moisture that's collecting in the window rim, when the phone beeps in my hand.

Hilary: **No I am not. I went to bed early cos was still hungover at 9pm.**

I reply: **Ah, sensei. So wise . . . yet so mortal . . .**

Hilary: **I could hardly swallow my dinner last night, thinking of you crying into your single serving. Fancy a decent meal after work?**

– **No thanks. Am now wildly happy with own company. Don't need companionship.**

– **How about meaningless sex?**

– **Thought u'd never ask . . .**

– **Tart. It's Friday – wanna go dancing? The men of Glasgow await.**

– Who could resist those specimens?

– Woo! That's the spirit! Call me when you finish work ☺

I put my phone away to prepare for my stop. There's a gash in the window condensation. I feel violated.

～

Four of us sit round the table of a staff kitchen ('Sorry, the shared meeting room was already booked.').

I was welcomed, my hand was shaken and, so far, only one person is doing any talking. 'Many, many people, Rhona, told me to change it *but* you don't get anywhere in this life doing what people tell you. Otis kept sittin' on the dock of the bay and I kept the name. You need to stand out in business – maximise every asset. It's what I tell my clients. I'd be a hypocrite if I didn't take my own advice. And you can't be a hypocrite, in business. Integrity is paramount.' My application form has crumpled in his impassioned grip.

'You clearly have an enduring interest in commerce,' he continues. 'A degree in Business Studies from Strathclyde. Not an honours degree, I notice, but experience counts for more in this game, eh? Theory is all very well for, for, a *physics* guy, but business people operate on instinct and street smarts. Am I right?'

I remember to eyeball all three of them during my reply. 'When I was at university, an honours year wasn't considered essential.' *Especially by students who had no interest in their subject.* 'It was more for those who wanted to specialise and, as you say, I was ready to put what I'd learned into practice.' *And take a year out before it was too late.*

'Yes,' he says, gesturing towards my form. 'I see you

volunteered in South America. Canny. Business is international. We ignore other economies to our detriment. Muffin Management may be Glasgow based but we're outward looking. If someone from Bolivia phoned looking for business advice we'd offer it, same as if they were in Blantyre, eh guys?'

'Si,' says the other bloke, under his breath. The woman forces a deep inhale through her nostrils. 'Can you tell us about your time there?' she manages to ask.

'It was a sustainability initiative. Creating capacity within the local community for a viable enterprise trading cocoa with Western companies. I'd spent the previous six months in Ibiza ... learning Spanish, so I was able to offer basic translation and research skills. The project is still going. The people involved are training other communities to do the same. It's amazing what they've achieved.'

The other man on the panel lists the 'range of industries' I've worked in, including recruitment, local government, telecommunications – *all right, all right* – and asks why I've never focused on one sector.

'That's my priority now,' I tell him. 'In this position, I could return to the fundamentals of business in a company which combines expertise with good old-fashioned nous.' I look at Donald Muffin. 'Helping businesses in their times of need – I know how good that feels.'

'What is it about your current role that you're not happy with?' asks the woman. At last, a question I can answer truthfully.

'As a smallish firm, specialising in teleconferencing, in my view, they retain a top-heavy management structure. So the Section Manager role lacks challenge. I've re-organised the shift system, streamlined procedures for international conference calls and accommodated some tricky demands from the pharmaceuticals, our bread-and-butter, but I see a role in your business consultancy as better suited to my untapped potential.'

The boss responds, 'I don't think "top heavy" is a criticism that could be levelled at Muffin. There's me, as Director, two business consultants in Glasgow, two in Edinburgh plus one senior consultant. The Office Manager is a new position, Rhona, at a time of expansion. The role is there to be defined. It might not be client-facing but doing the job well would mean we could do ours more effectively. And that shows.'

'Have you got any questions at this point?' asks the other guy.

'No, you've given me a lot of helpful information already.'

'Well, there's one last thing,' says Donald. 'Go with me on this ...'

Oh not one of *those* questions. What's my favourite animal and why? I haven't prepared anything. What's the last film I saw?

'If you were shipwrecked, Rhona, who would you rather be stranded with – the director of the CBI or George Clooney?'

Does it matter, seeing as I can't populate an island with either of them? George Clooney is happily married and the CBI director has the same equipment as me (she was pictured in the *Metro* today, advocating investment over austerity).

'I'm nothing if not a pragmatist, Donald – may I call you Donald? I'll have to say George Clooney, as he's the one most likely to trigger an international rescue effort.'

This elicits the charmed guffaw I hoped it would.

~

We've eaten two courses in a jumping pub.

'I hope I wasn't too harsh with you the other night,' Hilary is saying. 'It's difficult being alone. Nine years is a long time. But I meant what I said about not overdoing the doldrums. You were the one who gave him up, remember?'

'That's debatable, *remember*?'

'I think,' she continues, 'your boyfriend leaving the country has been such a shock because there's nothing occupying you in his absence. If you had more going on in your life that meant something. If you liked your job—'

'I had an interview today actually, so—'

'Your usual, is it? Rhona's annual job swap.'

'Leave me alone! You sound like my brother.'

She is glancing at the Italian biscuit on the edge of my saucer. If she wants it she should just ask. Keen to change the subject, I say, 'I'm worried. About the vagina.'

'What's wrong with your vagina?'

I don't know yet, I'll find out in a week or so.

'Nothing,' I say, 'except maybe under-use. I'm worried about *the* vagina.'

'I'm worried about you,' says Hilary.

I continue, 'It occurred to me yesterday that even in this day and age there is a campaign against the vagina, and women are colluding in it.'

'What happened yesterday?'

What *did* happen? I still can't revisit the clinic memory.

'Erin's sister had her baby,' I tell her, 'by Cae—'

'Oh lovely! What did she have?'

31

'A boy. Girl. I don't know, anyway, she had it by Caesarean. What is the obsession with Caesarean deliveries if not a mass bypass of the vagina?' I am slouched over with sadness for all the undervalued, forsaken birth canals.

Hilary is systematically gathering the crumbs of her Italian biscuit onto the pad of her finger. Licking her fingertip, she says, 'Erin's sister met her husband online. Maybe I should try that.'

'Which site?' I sit up. But then I remember we're off topic. 'Women's anatomy is not superfluous to the birthing process,' I say, leaning on my elbows.

'You actually look depressed about this,' she says, her forearms outstretched, fingers resting beside my biscuit.

'Doesn't it bother you?'

'I never thought about it. If anything, I thought Caesareans were a means to preserve the vag . . . do we have to keep saying that word? You know, preserve the pelvic floor muscles, tautness, pleasure.'

'Yeah, men's pleasure.'

'Oh, here you go, getting into one of your moods.' Why is her cleavage on display? Why has she come to meet *me* for dinner showing full cleavage? 'I get upset about something I have a right to be upset about and it's "one of my moods"! You sound like a man!'

'No, *you* sound like a man, after one pint too many with a bit between his teeth over something he won't care about in the morning.'

She's right. 'I do, don't I? It's still true though.'

'Okay then, let's do something about it. I know,' she says, straightening herself and raising a fist in the air, 'Vagina Day! There must be a day in the year that's free – between

Hug-an-eejit Day and Bring-back-hanging Day. We could have T-shirts printed. I could hand them out to my Primary Fives.'

I'm laughing but at the same time I'm thinking Vagina Day is not a bad idea. I keep talking to distract myself from this. 'Everything is still skewed in favour of men.'

'May I?' Hilary asks, as her fingers sweep the biscuit from my saucer to her waiting mouth. Crunching it, she says, 'But look at us. Two women – in a pub, no less – eaten our dinner with no chaperone. What more do you want?'

If she'd started this conversation, I'd have done the same as her. This is what we do – take it in turns to be the riled and the flippant.

'Look at magazines, look at advertising,' I add. I have to shake the contents from this piggybank, now that I've begun, or it'll be the next person I meet who gets it. 'And don't even get me started on TV dramas, there's only one storyline: woman gets raped, woman gets murdered, or woman gets raped *then* murdered.'

'Isn't that three storylines?'

'We're pitted against each other on the basis of how good we look, how desirable we are to men, and while we're distracted by this, they're running away with the pay packets, the promotions and the political agenda.'

'I'm not giving you the response you want, am I?' she says. 'Get yourself along to Glasgow Women's Library.'

I can't think of anything less appealing. 'Just 'cause I can spot the problems, do I have to be the one to fix them all?'

'What you need,' Hilary says, winking, 'is a good night out.' She lifts her chunky scarf off the back of the chair and gives me a look that says, 'Ready?'

Hilary's gone to the loo. I sit facing the dance floor, stabbing my straw through the stack of ice in my glass with semi-hypnotic determination. I look around at people I don't know and make assumptions about them. What else is there to do?

There's the square kid at school who turned trendy late in life. Looking like a Topman mannequin come alive, the clothes have borrowed his body for the evening. But with his jeans one half-inch above the trainer tops, he's clearly good husband material masquerading as a bad boy. What I would give for some good husband material; many contented years with a man who pulls his fair share of the weight. Once I got to know the guy better I'd have to say something though, or maybe drop a hint. Like the wife who brings home a beautiful negligee for her closet transvestite (showing him that she knows and she's okay with it), I'd buy my awkwardly trendy good husband a golfing V-neck and slacks and let him relax into the person he was born to be. Maybe I'd make the M&S conversion myself – ageing while pretending not to looks like a load of hard work.

Ooooh! Ooooh! This song! My song! Where's Hilary? She's just coming back through the archway. I trot towards her, moving my arms like I'm already dancing to indicate that's what we'll be doing now. She smiles, walking and wiggling her arms too. Yay! She wants to dance! It takes my body parts a minute or so to find their rhythmical assemblance but we get there, turning arms above the head, feet planted hips moving, feet moving mouth shaping the lyrics. Smiles! And now we are three. A short, mature, Mediterranean-looking man has joined us, stepping from side to side, smiling, nodding, 'Yes yes?' says his facial expression. 'No no,' we respond, silently; turning slightly, trying to mask our enjoyment, tone it down, attract less attention, pretend we are lost in the music, interested in nothing else, especially not him. The transaction takes mere seconds and he's woven himself back into the general mass.

You always hope for two good songs in a row and that's what we get. Hilary and I make eye contact to check we both want to keep dancing. We do! The music has jumped two decades but not my dancing. Hands slightly elevated and out to the sides, mouth open, face to the ceiling, torso pulsing. Smiles. Oh hello. The return of the little interloper. Bless you for not being northern. Bless you for showing what you want and believing you can have it. But look at me – I'm so carried away by the music that my eyes are closing and my legs are turning me round, away, away. I would chat some other time, somewhere else. Tonight is not about effortful small talk in an onslaught of music. Tonight is unfettered.

'Drink?' I mime to Hilary, and we go together to the bar. I feel we should get priority service over this row of nineteen-year-olds. 'Move aside, sonny,' I say, to an insouciant youth who fails to make room, 'might be the last night out we ever have ...'

It's not that funny but Hilary and I laugh like bastards. Clubbing at this age – best time for it. Okay, gone is the turbo-charged anticipation for the night ahead, and self-defining significance of the night as it's happening, but also gone is the deep doubt about the wrong outfit or whether the guy you snogged last time will acknowledge you.

We take our drinks and stand at the railings of the two-tiered club.

'What about him?' Hilary says, pointing to a crowd of about two hundred dancers. 'Left side, three pillars down. See the red T-shirt? Yellow logo, skinny jeans.'

I can barely be bothered to follow her directions but I pick him out. 'He's a mere boy,' I say.

'He's lovely though. Look at the hair falling over one eye. Gorgeous.'

'Okay, he's gorgeous. But does he have anything new to say? Can he spend more than a fiver on a bottle of wine?' What's making me crotchety? 'Yeah, not bad,' I contribute, 'but what about him?'

As I extend my arm sideways to point, I strike a young woman approaching the railing. She's heavy on the make-up and hair streaks. I start apologising as soon as I get my mouth in gear. 'Sorry, sorry,' I say, crinkling my face to show how unintentional the blow was. We hang there between my apology and her response. She grips the handrail and barks through her teeth, 'Fucksake! Wantin to start somethin?' Of course not. It was an accident. But she's being such an arse I think maybe she deserved it. Sensing I might continue a dialogue with this bacchante, Hilary steps in. 'Sorry. She didn't see you coming. Really, really sorry.'

It seems all the woman wanted was more pandering to her pride because she turns and moves away with her posse, albeit slowly; the eight-inch stilettos have them shunting along like zombies.

After downing my vodka, I ask, 'Were we nearly in a fight?'

'Well, you were.'

'We can't go to the toilets again, she might jump us.'

'Fine by me, we can use the men's.'

I'm starting to relax when a large figure in a black, puffy jacket emerges from the throng, walkie-talkie in hand. 'Had a report of harassment. Know anything about it?' he asks us.

'Yes, we were just harassed by a woman and her mates,' I answer, helpfully.

'The way she tells it, you punched her. Unprovoked attack.'

'Punched? It was an accident. I stuck my arm out and didn't see her. I said sor—' Trying to hear and be heard over the music is wearing me out. I turn to Hilary to let her know she's welcome to take over. It's not like her to be so quiet. She looks self-conscious. Guilty even. What have we got to feel guilty about? Why is she blushing?

～

I get up. I leave for work. I meet the postie in the stairwell. 'One today,' he says, holding out a brown envelope with a window.

I see part of an NHS insignia sitting above my name. In the subway station, I take myself to the quieter end of the platform to open it.

The recent biopsy taken from your cervix has shown an area of abnormal cells, also called cervical dysplasia, graded as CIN 2. A full explanation of this and the treatments which could be used, are given in the enclosed leaflet. Please telephone the clinic to confirm the following appointment.

I enter a state of contained panic – an anxious hum rising to a buzz; bluebottle in jar.

The pink leaflet is the same as last time. Except last time it didn't apply to me. They weren't going to find anything. It feels as though each treatment it describes is occurring as I read about it.

If it's a case of having the lady golfer cut me with an electrified metal loop, burn me with a below-freezing probe, or doing my own research, I'll do my own research, thanks.

Three

Paraphernalia on the morning pavement; workmen up to something or other. A pathway through it has been created with cones but it's single file only. Amble amble. Not in the mood. A wolf whistle sings out behind me. Sod that. A split-second decision to turn around.

'Piss off!' I shout, blood pushing my heart walls to capacity. 'You're not paid to give me marks out of ten.'

'Calm yer jets, darlin,' one of them calls back, through laughter. 'Wisnae whistlin at you.'

A couple of micro-skirted schoolgirls brush past. Mortified, I fall in behind, cursing their pace. Just because I'm trying not to get there early doesn't mean I want to walk in late. Nine thirty for ten, I was told. I'm aiming for nine-fifty-nine. Why sit around drinking coffee with people I've never met and, with any luck, never will again?

We're the recent intake from various workplaces, turning up

to fulfil our corporate IT induction from an outsourced provider on the fringes of nowhere. It's my first week in the job.

A voice behind a metal plate releases the door into the single-storey, burgundy brick box. A whole day in this windowless head-fuck. The receptionist asks me to sign in. Following her directions to the coffee lounge I hear her say, 'Waiting for one more.' I instruct God to punish whoever's had the bad manners to turn up late and mess with my plan to avoid the holding pen.

Walking into the room is like walking into a toilet cubicle that smells of someone else's jobbie – alien, repellent. As expected: strip lighting, catering urns and stilted chat. Ten or so people are dotted around. To avoid having to deal with the where-to-sit situation, I buy some time at the water dispenser, decanting a cupful. Then I head for the corner where nobody else is, but they're not far away – six or seven feet at most. I recall the phrase 'the average person' and feel this must be who it refers to. People who can live without agonising over it. Necessary people. Lucky people. It's not them I dislike – it's corporate training courses and days with no daylight and needless self-revelation ('Where do you work, then?') to strangers. I feel for the only two who know each other because the rest of us are listening in to their conversation.

'The roast beef was cooked pretty well, but the Yorkshire pudding—'

'You could've stoated it?'

'Aye. But no bad for his first attempt at a Sunday lunch. My wee Jamie in his own place.'

'Wee Jamie nothing! What is he now, Moira, twenty-seven, twenty-eight?'

'Twenty-nine. I don't half miss him. You know it yourself, Irene, it's harder to let go of boys.'

I picture six-foot-something Jamie shutting the door after Maw and Da yesterday and sinking into his Ikea couch to suck on the fat joint he'd been rolling when they rang his buzzer. 'Oh yehhh,' he'll have told the plant-in-a-cellophane-collar left on his coffee table, 'home sweet hooome.' You might miss him around the place, Moira, but it'll be another five or ten years before he has the capacity to miss you. And I hate to break it to you but the dirty roasting tin is still by the sink.

Jesus I'm tired. I reach for the three-in-a-pack biscuits on the table and I'm opening them when the woman from reception pops her head round the doorway. 'Okay folks, everybody's here. Head to the Mandela room. Last door on the left.'

As we sit down at PCs – three rows of four – the trainer welcomes us. She's a large lady whose height doesn't help her carry it off the way her friends probably tell her it does. I think she's been to the dentist first thing because she's having trouble talking out of the left side of her mouth. I'm having trouble concentrating on what she's saying, so fascinated am I with how she's saying it.

The gist of it is that we need to learn to manage email using the two-bit mail system our companies use because they won't pay for Microsoft. Rather than ask us to say something about ourselves (small mercies), she just asks us our 'firsht naymsh' and writes these on the whiteboard next to our generic names for the day: User One, User Two, User Three and so on. I am User One.

She sits at a desk facing us: the content of her monitor projected on a pull-down screen behind her. Previous experience of any email system would make it easy enough to use this one so it doesn't matter that she's almost unintelligible. After demonstrating how to create a new email and send it to one recipient, or a group of recipients, she sends us all the same message.

Sender: Trainer
Subject: Travel
How did you get here today?

She explains how to send a reply and these start to arrive on the big screen behind her (the top half shows the list of emails she's received, and the bottom half shows the content of the latest mail to arrive).

Sender: User Four
Subject: Re: Travel
Car then train then bus.

I think we can assume that if I'd had to endure User Four's epic trek I would not be sitting here.

Sender: User Seven
Subject: Re: Travel
Underground.

I picture a mole in the back row, propped on booster cushions, eager for IT training. As moronic as it feels, I too am obliged to reply to her mail to show that I'm keeping up with the training.

Sender: User One
Subject: Re: Travel
I walked.

'Oh you dihd noth!' she says out the side of her mouth.

'It wasn't far. About twenty minutes.'

I can tell from her expression that she thinks twenty minutes is very far indeed but she resists saying so. While she was speaking, I noticed the dental impediment had moved to the right side of her mouth and was sounding clackety ... a boiled sweet.

'Play abouth for a whee while,' she tells us. 'Shend a few mailsh and I'll whalk around and shee how you're gething on.'

The training-induced Tourette's in my head is on full throttle, 'fuckinwasteoffuckintimethisisforfuckindunces,' but to ensure my eventual release, I comply and start sending a few sparse messages.

There's an older guy two desks along who must have come from a manual job, or an office where managers had secretaries, because the trainer is pointing at his PC and answering his many queries.

A mail arrives on my screen.

Sender: User Ten
Subject: check the size of that arse

I stop breathing. Whose arse? *My* arse? Who sent this?

There's no way I'm turning round to find out. While I debate whether or not to open the full email, I hear a muffled, 'Shit!' and stifled laughter. When I look at the big screen the mail is sitting in full view.

Sender: User Ten
Subject: check the size of that arse
shes really enjoyin those sherbit lemons man. no even ofered them round, nae manners.

Presumably, the lad at the back meant this for the guy next to him but unfortunately he's clicked 'send all'. Now they're both too panicky-giggly to function. The trainer, like the rest of us, can hear their hysterics. 'C'mon now, vhoysh, conshentrate.' She straightens up. Oh God. And turns to the back of the room. Oh thank God. And tells the boys, 'I'm helping Alberth at the moment. I'll vhe whith you in a minute, okay?' And turns back round. And glances at the big screen. Oh good God.

Sender: User Twelve
Subject: test mail
blah blah

'I know you're only practishing, Uzher Twelve,' she says, 'vhut you can vhe a vhit more imaginative than that with your emailsh!'

The group laughs loudly because we couldn't when we needed too.

Passing my PC, she tells me to retrieve all the emails from

my trash folder because I'll need them for the next exercise. There are no emails in my trash folder. I barely care enough to converse with her on this but if it's going to affect my ability to progress to the next exercise I suppose I have to.

'I haven't deleted any emails,' I tell her. *Except one about your bum.*

'Where are they all then? Oh dear. Hash no one shent you any? That'sh a shame. C'mon guysh, shend shome mail to Uzher One.'

All I wanted was to turn up, do the training and go. I didn't care about being included, didn't even notice that I hadn't been – it's not playgroup, I don't need to beg to be let in the Wendy House. Now this irrelevant shower is feeling guilty for leaving me out.

Sender: User Four
Subject: oops!
Sorry, Rhona. Didn't mean to ignore you over there! ☺

Sender: User Six
Subject: Hello
Hey! Have a mail!

Sender: User Ten
Subject: phew
shit man! that was close a minute ago!!!

Sender: User Eleven
Subject: User One
Great training course, eh (lol). What's your new job?

Sender: User Three
Subject: Ahoy-hoy Rhona
Think I am getting the hang of this at last.

Some folk seem stuck on using 'reply all' because a few of these messages have appeared on the big screen. Everyone can see everyone else's pity for Rhona. And what, I'm supposed to be grateful? Well I am. Still, it's a relief when the flurry dies down and we can move beyond the incident.

A late arrival hits my inbox.

Sender: User Five
Subject: Fancy a curry??
Fancy a curry? Glasgow's famous for them . . .

I check the big screen to see if this is a group invitation for when we finish up today. Nope. I want to look behind me and see who User Five is, but I don't want him (or her?) to think I'm taking the invitation seriously. It might be test mail gubbins. The whiteboard states that User Five = Malcolm. Is that the name of a young guy or an old guy? A joker or a gentleman? Is Malcolm asking me out?

Contemplating the ins and outs of who he might be and whether there's potential for 'us' opens up a well of weariness; a feeling that whoever comes next will feel like the song *after* my favourite song on the album. The one I never listen to properly. The beginning of it kills the high from the amazing, buzzy song. You can never love that song.

'Now you've goth the hang of thath,' says the trainer, 'let'sh move on to mailbox management. Delething unwanted mail.'

She highlights about fifteen of her most recent mails, including the one about her arse, and sends them to her trash folder.

~

Making moves for bed, I go to switch off my mobile. It's showing one new voicemail. I forgot to take it off silent mode after the training. Dialling into the mailbox, Tania's Black-and-Decker vocals bore through the handset. 'I hear you were frequenting hostelries on weeknights. Why wasn't I told?' – *Because when I asked, you said 'Can't, sorry'* – 'I hope you're still feeling sociable. I need an excuse not to see the WB tomorrow.'

Winter Boyfriend: in the autumn, Tania's possessed by the need for a relationship – terrified by the thought of being alone at Christmas. Monogamy, though, is harder to cope with and once Valentine's Day has gone, the WB is never far behind. Her message continues, 'He won't have sex when Newsnight is on and I'm not standing for that.' – *Or lying down, or kneeling on all fours* – 'Plan is, to make him jealous. I need to be unavailable. You are my bit-on-the-side. Phone me back, Ms Bee-atch.'

It's too late to phone her (by my body clock) so I text:

OK for tomorrow. Come to mine at 7. Bring wine, I'll make food. Won't shag you during Newsnight, if that's what you're after. New job is fine, by the way. Thanks for asking ☺

~

Tania arrives twenty minutes before seven, with two bottles of white. Somehow, from a dinner discussion about the sexually absent Winter Boyfriend and the entirely absent Rhona

47

boyfriend, we end up on CatchMe.com looking at Tania's sister's dating profile.

'Look ...' says Tania, tracing her finger along the screen, '... "Spontaneous at heart, passport and travel insurance at the ready".' Tania shoots herself in the head, with sound effects. '"Just as happy on the couch with a wine glass. More kitten heels than killer heels. Looking for the Paul Newman to my Joanne Woodward." Beyond cringe. I hope no one knows she's my sister.'

'It must be impossible trying to describe yourself in one of those things.'

'Anyone on a dating site who calls themselves spontaneous is lying. Spontaneous people don't need screens and apps. Spontaneous people speak, spontaneously, to other people they meet in the big, bad world.'

'I thought internet dating burgeoned because everyone's so busy. You've forgotten what working full time does to your life.'

Even if I explain it, she won't care. The decimation can't be understood till you're doing it. Five days focused on getting there, being there, being presentable and well slept. Leaving two days a week – 30 waking hours – to shop, clean, do your banking, get a glimmer of daylight, a gulp of fresh air, go for a swim/hillwalk/massage, make love with the energy it deserves, cook a decent meal, have a haircut, see a doctor (that's a laugh), get an eye test, see friends, go to a gig, get steaming drunk, dance, sleep in, see a film, go to the dry cleaner, sell stuff online, buy stuff online, go to the post office depot to collect parcels, phone your family, see your family, stop and smell flowers, chill, go on a city break, have house guests, search house websites, job websites, holiday websites, health websites, change the sheets, put three loads through the machine and, if you have kids? Multiply the above many fold.

No wonder I haven't met anyone yet.

Tania responds to my 'busy people' dating theory, saying, 'Busy is the *best* way to meet people. Every profile we've just opened mentioned jobs, going to the gym, the pub, travelling, the cinema, eating out. If you're doing all those things, you're surrounded by other human beings doing the same. Why not talk to them? People end up online when they've lost faith in human chemistry and our natural, primal whatevers.'

'Have you told your sister this?'

'Bloody right. I told her the reason her profile will never work is that she's written the kinds of things chicks want to read, not guys. Again, here ... "hoping to meet a caring person who brings out the best in me and discovers the best side of himself, too, through being with me". She wants to meet a woman, not a man. Real men want to think for them-selves. And they respond to the shape, the sound, the smell of a woman. Not all this sappy, over-thought, electronic shite.'

'You've never been tempted to try it?'

'D'you think *this* needs to resort to the internet?' Tania gestures her hand down her body. 'Do I look like Bryony? I get men by normal means, thank you.'

'You could ditch the WB, get a pre-Christmas upgrade.'

'On CatchMe? I don't think so. It'd be like Scarlett Johansson putting a profile online. I mean – why? Sexy women turn heads. Everywhere, men ask you out – attracting too many is the problem.'

Tania scans me for a couple of seconds. Her face registers

49

a thought worth saying. 'You don't have to be a total stunner,' she adds, 'you just need to *think* that you are. It still works if you project it, Rhona.'

~

I'm entering contract details into project-planning software when Donald Muffin leans down level with my head. 'Putting your IT training into action, there?'

I laugh because I think I'm supposed to, saying, 'I'm a natural.'

'Time for a lunch break?' he asks. 'It's a policy of mine to meet team members monthly, for some one-on-one.'

I laugh, but don't know if I'm supposed to.

'Usually it's a roll in the kitchen,' he continues, 'but with new staff, I like to go out. Exeat, as they say. On me, of course.'

Donald tells me to swing by his room when I'm ready.

'I hear the Happy Meals are very good,' says Raymond, as I pass his desk. I rub my tummy with enthusiasm, then knock on Donald's door.

We eat macaroni cheese in a bygone-era tea room, complete with tartan carpet. By the time we finish our second pot of tea it's getting dark, and I've been led through phone photos of his wife and son. I have told him the not-entirely-edited version of what happened with Mark, and he has told me that two people being together requires a lot of sacrifice and that his wife deserves a medal, and I have said yes, I'm sure she does, and he has laughed and told me that he's sure the right person will come along and that, in the meantime, I can throw myself into my work, and he's winked, and I have laughed . . . to cover the feeling of rocks and shale skittering down my sternum, where nothing new can root.

It turns out that given a good immune response (and who knows what other factors) cervical cell abnormalities can resolve themselves. So when CIN 2 is diagnosed from a cell sample, there's no way of knowing whether it is on its way up to CIN 3 (and then cancer) or down to CIN 1 and then normal. This means my cervix has the potential to become healthy again all by itself.

Why leave it to chance? Internet research has also thrown up several options known to eliminate the human papillomavirus (which is responsible for most cervical dysplasia), including, an extract of aloe vera in capsule form or an extract of coriolus mushrooms. I will take the latter. And write a letter. If I boost my immune system with a clinically tested mushroom extract, I won't have any CIN.

Addressing it to Dr Carr, I type:

Further to the diagnosis of cervical dysplasia, CIN 2, I am
electing not to undergo treatment at this time. As cellular
abnormalities can return to normal without any intervention,
I would prefer to explore that option first. In addition,
I will take measures to boost my immune system and
eradicate HPV, and would gladly return for a check-up in a
few months.

What I don't say is, *I don't want you anywhere near me. I'd try anything before I'd allow that.*

'Hello?' I say, receiver clasped in a rubber glove.

'Oh good, you're home,' says Hilary. 'I wasn't sure if you had plans for today.'

'Neither was I. By lunchtime I decided that I probably didn't and got on with some cleaning.'

'I can't look at another nine-year-old's jotter,' she says, 'and if I lie on the couch now, Sunday will be over. Fancy a jaunt?'

'Do I have to be feeling jaunty?'

'It's not compulsory.'

Within half-an-hour the intercom buzzes. My walking boots clomp down to where Hilary is waiting on the steps. We share a quick hug. In the car, she hands me the road atlas.

'We're heading for that country park.' She points to it. 'Should take, oh, about thirty minutes? Keep me right.'

'Can't we use sat nav?'

'No.'

'Why not?'

'Sprawling open moorland doesn't have a postcode.'

'Everything has a postcode.'

She switches on the radio. 'Shout directions at me as we go.'

Hilary tells me about the film she watched last night as I rapid cycle through radio stations: Neil Sedaka, 'Ugh'; ceilidh music, 'Ugh'; radio play, 'Ugh'; competition winner mid-squeal, 'Ugh'; advert for beds, 'Ugh'; manufactured band, 'Ugh'; hymnal organ music, 'Ugh,' and end up back at the first (*Oh Carol! What do you see in him?*). I press the 'off' button.

'You weren't joking about not feeling jaunty,' says Hilary. 'Anything specific?'

'Och, textbook stuff,' I reply, thinking of what explanation I can give. 'I should be Christmas shopping by now but I can't get in the spirit. First Christmas as a single person since I was twenty-five, blah blah.'

With stage two precancerous cells on my cervix, blah blah.

She seems to buy it. 'I'm the opposite,' she says, adding hurriedly, 'I'm so used to single Christmases, I'd find the other way round weird!' She fumbles for the stereo 'on' button. 'Anyway,' she says, now adjusting the heater controls, 'we're heading into party season. Fabulous bird like you, Ms Beech? Anything could happen.'

~

I got up. I went to work. Heading home, I had my evening meal planned in my head. There were no missing ingredients. I'd come up the stairs two-at-a-time and through the front door smiling. I remember it, smiling.

Now I have a belly full of adrenalin and wrists weak with the weight of mail.

Not one but two of these letter bombs in the same delivery; Christmas cards addressed to both of us. Tell me it won't be like this all week, home to these glad tidings. Perhaps two is all there will be and the fact they have come together is a blessing.

I hadn't noticed that my ever-present heart pounding had eased off until it started up again. How many months till it trails away this time? Clearly, the redirect that Mark put on his post doesn't apply to items with my name on too.

I wanted dinner. I wanted lamb chops and rosemary potatoes.

I want to be back in the simplicity of a hunger that is satiable.

Is it wrong to open this mail without him? Worse to toss

them in the bin? I've told all my people. These must be from his people. I get left with this and he gets to go to Canada and reinvent himself and forget he ever had relatives and residual friends from university. Now it's *my* duty to tell them he doesn't live here anymore? What's the etiquette – disturb the silence with an email to tell him he has a couple of poxy cards?

If you're going to bugger off, do it properly and sort your Christmas card list while you're about it, agony merchant.

If I'm dealing with these, I'm doing so like a sane person. My coat meets the floor, I yank the stopper from a bottle of wine, grab a glass and sit at the table.

First envelope: red paper, black calligraphic script, indecipherable postmark. Inside: traditional Santa by a large tree covered in candles. Inside again: a message in the same ornate script. Names: Hannah and Gunter. That couple we met in Cuba, must be five years ago. The message I can't be bothered decoding probably explains why they are sending us a card this year. A baby, I bet you. Her address is on the back of the card. Fine. I can take care of this one.

Second envelope: yellowing-white. Infirm handwriting. Inside: pastoral snow scene at dusk. Inside again: just as indecipherable. Signed by: Aunt Gloria. Now I can't direct any anger at Mark because he probably did tell Gloria he'd moved – not his fault her memory isn't what it used to be.

Well, there's no need to tell her again. She wouldn't remember anyway and she'll be dead by next Christmas; she was half-dead last Christmas. Some capacity to rally, that woman.

And I don't know where my next thought comes from but it comes – am I going to get a Christmas card from *him*? It hadn't occurred to me. Should I send one? That's what Christmas cards are for, no? The people you have no contact with any other day of the year.

I wish my brain hadn't done this. I'm tormented by a problem that didn't exist a few seconds ago. What is the right thing? What if I do and he doesn't? What if he does and I don't?

If I don't get a card from him, he hates me; if I do get one he's thoughtless for not letting me move on. If I don't get a card, he's totally moved on and never loved me; if I do get one, he's feeling sorry for me alone at Christmas. If I don't get one, he's met someone else; if I do get one, he's met someone else and is feeling guilty.

Oh this noise. This nausea.

He let me go. Why can't he just let me go?

~

'Do you want to see them?' asks James. I'm not sure if I do. 'Come, I'll show you.' He leads me back out the front door, over the gravel and into the garage. I conclude that everyone who arrives tonight, before they can take a coat off, is being trooped out to see the day's spoils.

Laid out side by side on top of the freezer chest, tied at the neck with sky blue twine, his petrolescent green head resting on top of her brown one. 'Beauties,' says James.

'Yes,' I say, studying their sturdy bodies and implausibly precise patterning. Both beaks sit slightly agape. I stroke feathers I wouldn't naturally be allowed near.

'Feckin cold out here. Drink?' he suggests, reminding me where I am. I consider his suggestion – into the fray, evening propped up with the scaffolding of boozy chat, or here with these two, honouring their dignity? Again, I'm not sure I want to go with James, but I do.

I'm soon thawed by the fairy lights hung about the house and the general hubbub with its hale-and-hearty feel. The person I know best is Erin, but she's busy being the hostess. Sipping mulled wine, I wander the room, alighting on different huddles till I settle at this one.

'James was a decent shot,' says a short man whose shoes look bespoke. 'Not bad at all, for a first-timer.'

'Did he shoot the ones waddling along six feet away?' asks the woman next to him. She must be his girlfriend because she's clutching his upper arm and speaking to the group rather than him.

'Not allowed to shoot ducks on the ground,' he tells her. 'They have to be flying above a certain height.'

'You shoot regularly?' someone asks him.

'Two or three times a season. Always do a shoot before Christmas. Corporate thing. A thank you to the guys who've brought business our way.'

'No women?' I inquire.

'We did ask a couple, but they didn't come. Not really their thing I suppose; killing.'

Depends what the target is. 'Might be the "all lads together" atmosphere that puts them off,' I suggest.

'It's not a football supporters' club,' says his girlfriend.

'God forbid,' he blusters. 'Same banter, better accents!'

The household Labrador meanders past. 'Hey boy,' says one of the men, scratching the dog's head.

'He'd have been in his element today,' says bespoke shoe chap.

'I'm not so sure,' says the other bloke, pulling its ear. 'Looks pretty domesticated.'

'Just needs training up – don't you, boy?'

Erin passes by, carrying a tray of empty glasses. I excuse myself and weave after her to the kitchen.

'Mind if I help in here for a bit?' I ask. 'I feel like hiding.'

'Why do you think I'm collecting glasses?' she replies, white foam rising in the sink. She hands me a dishtowel. It's a familiar scene. We used to get a tenner each washing glasses at her parents' Christmas parties.

'You've nothing to worry about,' I say. 'Everyone's talking, booze is flowing and the decorations have achieved Architectural Digest. Sterling job, missus.'

'Damn, I knew I was forgetting something,' Erin says, reaching across and turning the oven knob. She opens the freezer, then empties boxes of pale, inedible pellets onto baking trays. 'You can help me hand them round,' she says. 'I know how you love to mingle.'

'I have been mingling!' I protest. 'Despite the tour of death when I arrived.'

'He's so pleased with himself. We're having them instead of turkey. And before you say it, I know, *it won't be the same*. If I've heard that once tonight I've heard it twenty times.'

Erin is back at the sink, pulling an apron over her head. 'I thought I'd know more people here,' I say. 'Where's Hilary? Where's Tania?'

'Tania never RSVP'd. I don't know where she is. And I thought Hilary and Gary would have been here by now, but you know what new couples are like, can't get anywhere on time.'

'True,' I say. *Gary? And he would be . . . ?*

'Tonight's their first public appearance. What's he like?'

'I don't know . . . we arranged to meet up but I had to work late,' I manage.

'Well, she seems very keen.'

'Can those trays go in the oven now?' I ask.

'Oh bugger, please, yes. Set the timer. We'll keep our ears open for it.' Erin removes her pinnie.

'I don't trust either of us to hear it from the lounge. I'll stay and dry the rest of these.'

'Would you? I have to get back out there.'

She picks up a tray of clean crystal and walks out with careful steps. The tray is like one my mum had in the seventies – circular with a gold, plastic fence around the edge, large faded roses in the middle and small feet of green felt. I smile. It must be trendy again.

Opening and closing drawers till I find fresh dishtowels, I select the thinnest; the wine glasses look as though they'd crack like winter puddle ice. Holding one by the base, I carefully rotate it between my towelled thumb and forefinger. Why hasn't Hilary told me about Gary? At least no one else has met him yet but why hasn't she mentioned him to me? Must be a recent thing – must have got together in the last couple of weeks. Thank goodness for the heads up. I can be ready with my happy face when they arrive. I *am* happy for her.

I lean against the sink to watch the pastry bites revive in the oven while I'm drying the next glass. Pondering where Hilary and Gary could have met, I become aware of someone in the doorway. The figure starts to sing a Laurel and Hardy-esque ditty in a cutesy, faux American accent,

'All good parties have a pooper,
And tonight the pooper's you,
Mrs Pooper,
Party pooper.'

Bold, considering I have never met this person.

'I didn't know whether to come in or not,' he says. 'I thought for a second you were crying. Honey, I'm not far off it myself – that Christmas compilation is a *travesty*. It's not a party without the Ozzie princess of pop. Never mind.' He manoeuvres around me. 'Don't let me interrupt. Only here for a glass of water.'

'I'm not sulking,' I reassure him, 'I've been left in charge of the ov—'

'Is that sausage rolls I smell? Do *not* let me near them. Ron'd kill me. I'm not even allowed wine tonight. It's hell, sweetie. *Hell*. Only two thousand calories a day till the wedding. Oh that's right! *I'm getting married!*' he squeaks, and waves his ring at me.

'Our going away outfits are fabulous – Versace – but totally unforgiving. I've lost ten pounds already, feel this.' He yanks hold of my wrist and pats his belly with my limp hand. 'You should come. Come to our party! I'm sure the hotel has a lobby you could sit in looking glum.'

Luckily, it's not the kind of conversation where I am expected to join in. I wouldn't have the first clue what to say.

'Ten more days till W-day and then I can eat whatever I like. His mum's doing a turkey when we get back from honeymoon. There's no *way* I was waiting a whole year for my Christmas dinner.'

The oven timer goes off with those high-pitched, alarm

clock beeps that cause the rudely roused to beg for death. 'Duty calls, Cinders. Enjoy,' he says, leaving with no parting glance.

If I know Erin, the serving dishes will have been warming in the drawer below the oven. Bingo. I lift out two large plates and shake the mini pastries onto them. What else? A sprinkling of parsley. Napkins? I place a pile between my hand and the underside of each plate, and head out to give Erin one of the dishes.

Progress through the busy room is slow. While I attempt tiptoes to locate her, a hand reaches towards the plates. 'Wait,' its owner says, 'my wife missed out on the nibbles.' *I'm not officially serving yet, I'm looking for Erin, we're a team.* Oh fuck it. I stand and smile while his wife, and the group, help themselves. When their pincer activity lulls I carry on, moving a few paces before another set of hands reaches in; Hungry Hippos for grown-ups.

'Runty little savouries!' says a voice I recognise. 'About time!'

I try to move on but there is no free space to move into. 'Oh you're *staff*,' says bespoke shoe chap. 'Nice of James to let you join the party earlier.' He turns to his girlfriend. 'Just like James, isn't it? The incorrigible socialist.'

I offer the tray to his girlfriend, though she looks like she only eats every third day. 'Nipples?' I ask. She declines. Another few feet through the throng and the dishes are empty.

Coming out of the lounge into the hall, I bump against Hilary. She has her coat on, and the man next to her has on his puffy jacket.

'You're here!' she says, but we can't hug because I'm holding the plates. 'I was hoping you would be,' she adds. 'I see Erin's got you hard at it.'

'I volunteered.'

'Rhona, this is Gary. Gary – Rhona.' Hilary doesn't offer anything else by way of introduction, such as, 'Rhona is my best friend' or 'Gary is my boyfriend'.

'Hi,' we say, smiling but unable to shake hands because of the dishes. 'Nice to meet you,' I add. *I've heard so little about you.*

I'm content to stand in awkward silence for a few seconds because it's not me who's caused the awkwardness.

'Is Erin around?' asks Hilary. 'We've brought something.' She elevates a festive bottle-bag.

'Haven't seen her for a while. Take your coats off, though, before James sees you. He's been frogmarching new arrivals to the garage to see the ducks he shot on some corporate jolly.' Hilary and I catch each other's eyes. 'Not so jolly for the ducks!' we say together.

'In other words,' says Gary, 'he'll take us for a gander at them. Geddit?'

I produce the most natural sounding laugh I can.

Hilary and her ornithology whizz head through the rabble in the hall. My arms ache from the weight of empty serving plates. I sit on a stair for relief. I am eye level with a lot of bottoms. 'Nice view,' says Erin, coming down the stairs and I oblige by pretending to grope the nearest buttocks.

'The hot bites went down well,' I tell her. 'I left a couple of trays in the oven for you.'

'Sorry! I forgot – of course. Mindy woke up. I had to read to her till she fell asleep.'

'No problem. Like you said, it gave me a chance to meet your friends properly. They think I'm staff. It's marvellous.'

61

'I'll pour you a large one. You've earned it.'

'Actually,' I say, 'I have to get going.'

'You can't go!'

'Getting up early for the train. It's my brother's turn to host Christmas.' I hand her the plates. 'Hilary's arrived, she'll keep you company.' I give her a one-armed hug and we wish each other a good Christmas.

There are so many coats piled on the spare room bed – bulky winter ones – that I give in to temptation and lie down, burrowing in. Who's going to know? It's as comfortable as I imagined. Every muscle in my body lets go. Minutes pass. But knowing this has to end – and could end when I am discovered rather than when I choose – makes me scrabble up, smooth out the coats and find mine.

At the front door, James is standing on the step having a cigarette. He's watching his Labrador running up the lawn to retrieve a toy being thrown by bespoke shoe chap.

'Leaving?' James asks.

'Train to catch, first thing.'

In a tone that blends pain with amusement, he says, 'The Christmas Eve getaway. With snow forecast? It's a recipe for cannibalism in a railway siding.'

'On that cheery note . . .'

'Have a good one,' says James.

'And you,' I say. Shoe chap is glancing over so I raise my voice, take James's hand in both of mine and add, 'Oh, Gawd bless ya Mr James sir, most generous of ya. Upon my soul. An angel from above, you are, an angel from above.'

As I crunch down the gravel drive, I see the toy being flung up the garden for the dog is a duck.

Waking up, I remember what day it is. Silly with excitement, I turn over and look at him for a moment. I squeeze his hand to rouse him because that's the rule; whoever wakes first wakes the other.

He doesn't open his eyes, just unfurls his arms and draws me to him, holding me there while he surfaces more fully.

'Morning, lovely,' he says, with half his voice.

'Morning, you,' I reply, fitting a bare leg between the warmth of his.

'Ding dong merrily on high,' he says, showing me what's under the duvet.

'For me?'

'Santa said you've been a very *good girl.' His fingers come to life over my skin.*

On my way to the bathroom, I fill the kettle and switch on the tree lights. Back in the bedroom, I put on my dressing-gown and chuck his on the bed.

We sit in the light of the tree beside two piles of presents. Having thought I was keen to get into them, I don't care what's under the wrapping, I just care that this is. He's stalling too but somebody has to go first, so he hands me a gift. We take turns. He knows better than I do the things I'll like and each time I'm surprised by what he's chosen and how much I like it. After each one we say thank you and share an emotion-filled kiss. By the fourth, it's a struggle to unwrap another because we can't feel any more emotion than we already do and we don't need anything more than we already have. He stands and extends a hand. I take it and follow him.

After I've showered, he comes into the bedroom holding two polished brogues. I see him in jeans, I see him in suits, but this 'smart casual' apparel is an occasional occurrence (slim-legged wool trousers and a neat fitting V-neck over a shirt). It's a treat to encounter this version of him. It elicits a full-face smile from me.

'Yes? Can I help you?' he asks.

'I'm allowed to ogle my boyfriend.'

'You don't look too bad yourself,' he says.

I'd forgotten that I, too, have put on Christmas Day clobber; shimmery-and-a-bit-impractical-but-who-cares-because-I'm-being-taxied-from-A-to-B-and-staying-indoors-all-day.

Outside his parents' house, the cab drives away. We hold hands and kiss, as if to cement who we are now before we turn into who we will be with them.

After the main course, I go to the bathroom and when I emerge he's there, motioning me back in. He locks the door behind us and we stand in a tight, silent hug.

'Let's do this again later,' he says. 'Seven o'clock?'

'Seven suits me,' I say.

During an all-family game of Trivial Pursuit, he catches my eye and throws a glance towards the clock. I laugh. His aunt looks at me. 'Ian Botham,' I say. 'No,' she says, sternly, replacing the card. 'Joan of Arc.'

'Shall I make a pot of tea?' I inquire.

'That's a nice idea, Rhona,' says his mum, 'I'll give you a hand.'

'You've done more than enough today,' he tells her. 'I'll go.'

We stand in the darkened kitchen, waiting for the kettle to boil; resting on each other, just resting.

～

Waking up, I remember what day it is. *Today doesn't have to feel a certain way*, I tell myself, *it's not the law;* and I must fall back asleep because when I open my eyes again time has moved to 8.24.

Not twitching as much as a toe, I lie there calculating how much time will be used up in showering, dressing and eating breakfast. Twenty minutes for each? Which takes me to … 9.30. An hour-and-a-half short. I'm not needed anywhere till eleven o'clock.

I won't go to a hotel gym on Christmas morning. It's not right. There is a line.

With a multi-course meal being eaten later, there's no point in extending breakfast. And dressing can only take so long. The task I will have to eke out is the shower. Bathe instead. That thought engenders the closest thing to happy I've felt for days. A brimming container of hot water, in late dawn light, with complimentary products to test. Brain off, body on.

Heading to the bathroom, I switch on the wall lights and pick up the one-person kettle to fill at the basin. I set the bath taps going and pour in the thumb-sized bubble bath. In the bedroom again, I connect the kettle, pull on my dressing-gown and chuck myself on the bed.

I won't watch TV alone on Christmas morning. It's not right. There is a line.

The clock has a built-in radio. And I'm in Yorkshire; there could be stations I've never heard. Little gifts, like emptying the Christmas stocking before the main pile. I turn the volume and tuning dials all the way to one end – no chance of a sneak preview. I want to encounter each station fresh, in its proper order.

Restoring the volume, I move the tuner carefully in minuscule increments to catch every signal, however feeble; a safecracker listening for the click. Millimetres along, Bhangra music bounces out. This reminder that some people are having a day like any other is very welcome. Then ... Radio 2; I recognise the voice saying, 'Santa said you'd been a very good girl, Chloe.' Gently, between thumb and forefinger, the knob revolves and my ear strains for the smallest sound. The bedside telephone rings. I shout in fright. For a micro-second I think, *Is it Mark?*, but of course it won't be. It could only be Reception, or one of my family. I brace picking up the receiver; *Don't wish me Merry Christmas over the phone, don't wish me Merry Christmas over the phone.*

'You almost ready?' asks Mum.

'I'm not due there till eleven,' I tell her.

'I know but you could come along now, if you wanted. Save you sitting there on your own. Callum would love you to play with his presents, your dad and I are exhausted already.'

'Annie said eleven. She and David have got enough bodies under their feet. And I've not had my bath.'

At 11.10, I get out of the cab and arrive at my brother's front door. *Don't hug me and wish me Merry Christmas, don't hug me and wish me Merry Christmas.*

After the main course I go to the bathroom because the dining room has no air left, and my family at the table has become a scene in a snowstorm ornament that I'm holding in my hand.

During the all-family game of Trivial Pursuit, I can't remember which colour belongs to which category.

'Photosynthesis,' I offer.

'No,' says Annie's aunt, sternly, and replaces the card. 'Billiards.'

66

'Time for a pot of tea?' I ask.

'That's a nice idea, Rhona,' says Mum, 'I'll give you a hand.'

'You've done more than enough today,' I tell her.

Waiting for the water to boil, I stand in the darkened kitchen. My shoulders fall forward, my chest convulses and no sound comes out as tears smash to nothing on the Italian slate tiles.

~

After several mini-bar miniatures, if I had a number for Mark I'd bloody phone it.

Why wasn't one of them ever a small velvet box? I'd ask him. *YOU WERE SUPPOSED TO SURPRISE ME!* I'd scream.

~

I call out, 'What time is it?'

The WB looks at his watch. 'Shit, five to,' he says. 'Champagne, Tania. Glasses.'

Half-an-hour later, it's a case of 'as you were'; small groups sitting talking. An abandoned board of cheese and biscuits sits too close for comfort.

'I think menstruation is the answer to everything,' says a guy beside me. That gets my attention.

'Pardon me?'

'I said meditation is the answer to everything.' Too late.

Helpless giggles set in; slap-happy with the strain of confinement.

'What's so funny?' he's asking.

'Nothing ... misheard you ... thought you said ... *menstruation* was the answer to everything,' I say, reining it in.

'Amen to that!' says Faye, visiting from Bristol. Unfortunately, she doesn't stop there. 'I always feel so cleansed afterwards. Renewed.'

'Get the cigars out,' says Faye's partner. 'The ladies are ready to retire to the drawing room.'

'You don't have to listen, my love,' she says. 'Isn't it wonderful being cyclical?' she continues. 'Understanding you can't dominate nature because she dominates you.'

'Erm,' says Hilary, 'we certainly are at the mercy of our reproductive systems. More so than men.'

'Not what the philanderers would say!' Faye booms. 'Apparently they just can't help themselves.' She empties the wine bottle into her glass. Somebody has to puncture the 'men are this way, women are that way' conversation; it's a new year for goodness' sake.

'Resolutions, anyone?' I mumble.

Silence. The unresolved betrayals between Faye and her bloke have sapped everyone's sense that it's okay to be having a good time, to be having a good life.

Except Hilary. 'My New Year came early,' she jumps in. 'I had a fresh start in November.'

'Why, what happened n'November?' asks Faye.

'That's when I met Gary,' Hilary says.

Two months ago? She had a boyfriend I knew nothing about for two months?

'Aww, Hilary, thatsh wonderful. You enjoy it, girl. Squeeze every last bit out of th'early days. They're the besht.'

'This sounds like a real love story,' I say to them.

'Think we'll need a refill. Help me with drinks, Hilary? Back in a minute, folks.'

68

I hadn't planned what I would say when we got to the fridge. After I say it, I wish I had. 'You got together with Gary in November? You don't have to tell me these things. But I can't believe you didn't. I'm offended and I can't work out if I have any right to be.'

'We didn't tell anyone.'

So now I'm 'anyone'.

She continues, 'I might have mentioned it, if you'd asked me. You assumed I wasn't seeing anyone and I went along with it.'

She's right.

'You told Erin, though. It was her who told me. I was so embarrassed I pretended I knew already.'

'I'm sorry it was awkward at her party. I didn't know how to broach it by that point. I'd left it too long. It was nothing personal, honestly.'

'What was it then?' I say, thinking, *this had better be good.*

'Gary kept finding excuses to avoid my friends. Eventually I got it out of him – he felt uncomfortable, you know, different kind of job. Anyway, by the time we had that conversation it was mid-December. You wouldn't believe how nervous he was about coming to Erin and James's house that night.'

I am a horror sometimes. 'How's he doing tonight?' I ask.

'Oh fine. He realised he'd been making a deal out of nothing.'

'What's this job he does, that's so different?'

'He's a bouncer, at Trampoline.'

The puffy jacket. 'He's that guy! The walkie-talkie man who came over when that scary bint picked a fight!'

'He said he might need to get back in touch if she wanted

to take it further. It was an excuse to get my number. Quite sweet, I thought.'

How many times has he used that line?

'Seems like a nice guy,' I tell her. 'Aren't *you* the dark horse, Marshall.' And I seize the chilled bottle from her hand.

Four

The detritus of party-making is evident on our desks. Who were the people in this room that day? What demonic jollity possessed us?

'Chocolate snowman?' I offer, when Mr Muffin appears through the tinsel curtain across the doorway.

'Lousy services in this building,' he says, taking off his raincoat. 'If we could grow the business a little, we could get our own cleaner.' Walking towards his office he casts his hand around, adding, 'You wouldn't mind, would you, Rhona?'

Pause for effect.

'If we got a cleaner? Not at all. I can add her – or him – to the payroll. Give me a nod when the business has grown enough.'

~

I'm entering credit card details into a website, because thirty quid is a small price to keep that consultant's cauterising probe away from my privates, which she no doubt wields like a sand wedge.

Unlike her, I know what my body needs. When this second batch arrives, I will change from four mushroom capsules per day to two. A high dose to start with will have cranked my immune system into gear. A maintenance dose for a month or two will take care of any remaining papillomavirus and abnormal cells.

A name for this sensation pops to mind – smug. Making the doctor redundant, doing it better myself.

~

Donald likes the Glasgow and Edinburgh teams to meet every couple of months, alternating between the two locations.

Walking into the Edinburgh office for the first time, I am drawn to the full-length window view of the Castle, the townhouse rooflines, the sea.

We talk about the train delay, we help ourselves to coffee. Around the table, we spend a few minutes feeding back to each other about the last two months. Donald greets each update with whole-body pride and eye contact smiles which say, 'Isn't that *great*, everyone? How fantastic is *that*?'

At the last meeting, I'd thanked them for helping me settle in and find my feet. This time, I say that I've mastered the project planning software. I hand round a timeline for each team's contracts and say it's stored in the shared drive. I tell them that the council with the outstanding invoice has now settled and mention we had an inquiry from a school in the same local authority. They know there's wastage in their spending and they want to identify it, diverting any savings into extra-curricular initiatives.

'Usual story, not worth it, no budget,' says Donald. 'Tell them we're too busy. Martin, your pitch to the insurance company yesterday for a management review. How did that go?'

'They were interested in our promise that we could have the review completed in a matter of weeks, with recommendations by Easter. It's hand-holding during implementation they seem to need most. They won't admit it, of course.'

'Okay, see if you can dress it up another way and keep at them.'

Martin nods. Donald sits back in his chair, allowing silence to gather around us. 'Now,' he says, 'the item I've been waiting for. Any – other – business.'

Petra speaks. 'Glasgow Chamber of Commerce is host—'

'Me first,' says Donald. 'One word. Manchester.'

Nobody responds.

'One more word. Third office.'

Sodden with self-satisfaction, he gives us the details. Ann-Marie, who relocated from Glasgow to lead the Edinburgh team last year, has been putting feelers out in the north of England. There is a sniff of a large construction company wanting a thorough look at how it finances and manages developments. If she gets them to bite, she'll stay down there and if the climate's right, scout for more projects and recruit another consultant.

On the train back, Petra talks to Donald about the project she worked on a couple of years ago for Parkinnon Homes. 'I'll give Ann-Marie a call. The sector information I gleaned will be useful in developing her pitch.' Petra leaves her seat. Striding to the sliding doors she has purpose in a way I have never experienced.

Petra and Ann-Marie. Donald and Raymond. Martin and Paul. They're so . . . *invested*.

Is that what I lack? Passion. Immersion. The train whips across the waistband of Scotland, passing slag heaps shaped like Uluru. I didn't end up this way intentionally. I hadn't aimed my arrow. Was doing day-to-day stuff. Wasn't unhappy. Had Mark. Had holidays. Had a lot to do in my two days off a week. Hadn't twigged that thirty-something wasn't the same as twenty-something.

Raymond is listening to his iPod and gaming on his phone. Donald is drinking water from the teat of a bottle he bought from the trolley. Freud would have something to say on the product design. It's all I can do to stay looking at the oversized infant of him while we converse.

'Donald?'

'Hmm?'

'If Ann-Marie needs help in Manchester . . . if she secures more contracts . . . I could go down and work with her.'

'Oh. Um. Well, your remit sits better in Glasgow, in head office so to speak. Don't you think?'

'I was meaning I could go to Manchester as a – a business consultant. Be on Ann-Marie's new team, if she's looking for someone.'

'Nice of you to offer, Rhona, but we're not quite at that stage. AM will be scoping the terrain, but first she needs to get this construction gig she's pitching for. And do a good job on it. A laudable show of team spirit, though. Write that down, would you? Team spirit, so I remember to mention it at your appraisal.'

~

Hilary's so pissed her night's not going to end till someone tells her it has to, and the last of the others has jumped ship. I'm still here because I'm happy to hang out till the lights come up. It's been a good night. That rare occasion when a few folk meet for a drink and hours later the night's still going; pulling each other about a dance floor amongst the mixed bag of randoms packed into the only club that's walk-able for home.

Some women are frightful when they've had a few: brash, biting, or spoiling for nonsense. Others, like Hilary, become adorable: gently earnest with a flush about her face, oblivious to how endearing she is.

Hilary leans her shoulder against mine and dips her head. 'Hey. It's just us left,' she says, 'we can catch up properly.'

Treading an unsteady line, she takes us to a couch, asking, 'How's Rhona doing? How's life treating her?'

Treating. Treatment. Colposcopy. How *is* life treating me? I can't see the dysplasia to gauge its progress, but I feel relief that my cervix is a site of healing rather than stealthy cellular mayhem, thanks to the mushroom capsules.

'Good,' I tell her. 'Life's good.'

'Has it been okay, you know, starting the year on your own? Turned a corner?'

I know the best thing I can do is not pick at it but New Year wasn't the line-in-the-Mark-sand I assumed it would be. I welcome this opportunity to say so out loud.

'Not quite. More like parallel lives. One version, where I'm getting on with things. And the other version, when the old feelings are there, strong as ever, and I can't believe I have to exist without him. Days when I don't know whose life I'm living because it doesn't feel like mine.'

'Petal,' says Hilary, pulling me into a hug. 'You're doing amazing. Better than 'mazing.'

'It's been that way since July. Free of it, not free of it. D'you think that's normal?'

Hilary's facial concentration is not in response to what I'm asking her. 'Hold that thought,' she grimaces. 'Bursting for a pee. Back in *one* minute.'

Music, strobes, bass, bodies. The hyper-stimulation shuts my senses down. The dim anonymity sucks me under.

I took it for granted I'd be over the split by January 1st. And that's the thing, most of the time I *am* over it. Except on the days when I bang up against the absence.

God knows there were some things he and I couldn't pull off but love was never one of them. Like spilled beads, I'd no idea how long after the break I'd still be finding bits of love to be cleared up. And do what with? I come across ways in which I still miss him and at best I'm sweeping them into a pile. How does one dispose of love?

'You're miles away,' Hilary says, sliding along the seat. 'Check it. Cute guys at five o'clock.'

'Is that so, Hilary Tank Commander. Where *is* five o'clock?'

Glass in hand, she gestures towards two blokes on the half-empty dance floor.

'Nice,' I concur. 'That one on the left is a nifty wee mover.'

'Shall we?' she asks.

'Shall we what?'

'Go over. Say hello.'

It wouldn't be that big a deal. It's a club. It's the time of night when striking up a chat is almost expected.

'I'm not sure,' I say.

Why can't I match her impish impulse, her conspiratorial grin? She's suggesting this for my benefit. I know how to get out of it.

'Are you meeting Gary when he finishes work? How's that going – it's been, what, three months now?'

She's off. Away on the trail of how lucky she is and I try to listen but am mesmerised by the blizzard of mirrorball light flakes swarming over the red couches. A feeling comes to visit, like I'm a teddy on a turntable, passively revolving to the laughter of the brat who put me there; my sewn-on expression masking my perennial tension about whether the speed will get thwacked up to 78 and send me flying.

~

Evidence of my existence accompanies me home: heel-strike bouncing round the tenement-lined street. It would be nice to walk more slowly, to enjoy ownership of this 3 a.m. quiet; a notion that's overridden by the habitual efficiency of my pace.

Rows of unlit windows dully puncture the sandstone. Rounding the corner, I pay scant heed to two guys walking up ahead. I don't notice, till I'm almost there, that they've stopped at the bollards of a no-through street beyond the bridge. 'S'cuse me,' says one. I adjust my course to the outer edge of the pavement. 'Hey,' says the other one. I continue on, wishing they couldn't hear my progress. And I don't look back, to give off an air of confidence. Slipping a hand into my bag I get my keys ready. I want to open the door with no faffing. On the top step I look both ways to check I wasn't followed. I wasn't. They're probably back there waiting for a woman more drunk; someone who'll stop in response to their prompting, someone

77

who smoked her last cigarette outside a club and wants the one they're offering.

What can I do but hope nothing too ugly happens out there before dawn?

Just sober enough to care about cleaning my teeth, I do it, and fill a cup with water for the bedside. When I lie down, it's apparent I'm not sleepy. I listen to a high ringing sound in my ears and wonder what's happening on the inside to cause it; the aural hangover of loud music, gone when you wake and the other kind is kicking in.

Here I lie, a few weeks into the new year.

And how is Mark spending his weekends? Who is he lying beside? Who's harassing him on the way home?

I could phone him and ask. Nope. No number. And it's the middle of the night. Where I am. I don't know what time it is where he lives. Would I want to be living somewhere I didn't know what time it was? I can't imagine liking that ver much.

Though I can't say I'm loving it here either, where I always know the exact time. 3.37. See?

Would I want our old, cosy set-up? Life A? It's no longer an option. I haven't exactly been drowning in declarations of 'I miss you', or calls pleading 'Take me back'.

But Life B. This is a never-ending eye test; a seven-month appointment in the optician's chair, looking through the viewfinder thingy at the letter chart while she repeatedly slots in a lens and removes it again, waiting for a response to her question, 'Is it better with the lens? Or better without?'

'Better with? Or without?'

'Slotting it in again . . . With? Or without?'

I don't know but she won't stop asking me till I make up my mind.

⁓

Antiques Roadshow forms and re-forms on the screen with the sound turned down. Twisting the cap off a bottle of wine, I miss the struggle with a cork; the fair fight to the contents. A screw top feels like medicine. The new lamps illuminate from choice positions, the CD playing is the Mercury Prize winner and this charade of a life has to stop.

If Hilary is mostly occupied with Gary, and Tania is still with the WB, and Erin is at home with her husband and daughter, I will take matters into my own hands.

⁓

Subject: Bob-a-job40 has winked at you!
Subject: NakedInTheRain has winked at you!

Wink, wink, wink. I'm not superhuman. I'm as curious as the next person.

⁓

What makes me accept? In his emails, he comes across as not one of the herd. And he's damn funny.

When I get there, I can't see him and I have to walk the full length of the place to check, though I'd rather not. At the far end, I turn and saunter back towards the door. That's when I spot him, absorbed in some activity with his mobile phone (or pretending to be). He's chosen a booth built into an alcove.

Not embarrassed at all then, about web-dating. Suits me; I'm not gung ho myself.

We introduce ourselves and I notice no physical spark but I'm happy to hang out, expecting an evening of belly laughing and offbeat banter. I'm not expecting the ex-wife-is-a-bitch-from-hell-and-even-kept-the-dog routine.

'Started calling herself a "feminist", the way other people say "diabetic". Sad cow. Didn't stop her tapping fifty quid every week to get her hair done. Money well spent. Was bad enough listening to that lesbo crap – couldn't have her looking like one.'

I am not on this date. I cannot be on this date.

'Took my house, my car and my beautiful wee girl, like a true effin feminist.'

By the end of an hour I'm in a daze on my bar stool, thinking, *If I ever meet the woman who rescued herself and her daughter from you, I will pay for her next two haircuts.*

'You wanting another?' he's asking.

'No thanks, work tomorrow.'

We walk to the taxi rank where we say goodbye and I continue on foot.

⁓

The second man I arrange to meet persuades me with his photos; he looks happy and has incredibly blue Catholic-boy eyes. Reading between the lines of his blurb, he's ready for something committed.

I feel like wearing heels. On the main road I flag down a taxi. Riding the short distance to the venue, I wonder when I turned into a woman who could internet date. It occurs to me

I'm able to do this because I haven't told anyone about it. No one knows, therefore it's not really happening. I push aside any parallels with domestic abuse and pay the driver.

Craig is there already, on a brown leather sofa, preoccupied with his phone.

Having spent today alone, I find I can't shut up. Nor can he. A classic Glasgow raconteur, he strains through his own mirth to tell one tale after another; me throwing out rejoinders like I'm this funny all the time, spraying my 'ha ha has' everywhere when he chips in.

After his third trip to the bar, he returns and sits on the same couch as me. I get the next round on my way back from the loo. We notice our glasses are empty again and he says, 'What d'you fancy now, Miss Rhona?'

His finger toys over my thigh while he speaks. It's a long time since this happened; since a man I was hoping would make a move (but didn't know so well that I had to bloody ask) goes for it.

'Film?' he asks, circling his palm over my jeans. 'Go for something to eat?'

His touch is not what I'd grown used to. This 'groping-by-numbers' almost makes me hoot. I don't though, in case he retracts his optimistic fingertips. It wasn't expected but d'you know what, bring it on. I might get some tonight after months and months of nothing.

'What I fancy,' I say, turning and manoeuvring a leg so I'm sitting astride him, 'is taking you home for a late supper . . .' The older I get the worse it gets: I am a beast when I'm ovulating. I tilt my pelvis forward till it makes contact with his.

'I don't go home with strangers,' he says, his knuckles stroking the fleshy areas above my hips.

'Wise man. Allow me to introduce myself,' I say, lowering my mouth slowly towards his (and making a mental note never to show my face in this bar again).

A few evenings later, Craig invites me round for home-cooked food. He looks almost as I remember, though he hasn't changed out of his work suit which makes him look his age. Suddenly, the idea that this is an acceptable way for grown-ups to behave bothers me. We don't know each other. Our computers connected us. Who is this guy?

At home, he is less of a blether. After clearing the empty plates to the sink, he stands behind my chair, brushing his lips against my neck. 'No Viennetta?' I quip, and he snorts into my hair.

'This is Glesga,' he says, exaggerating his accent, 'we're no posh enough fir they fancy desserts.'

'A scoop of raspberry ripple?' I ask. 'Wee squirt of Ice Magic?'

More hair snorting. 'If madam would be kind enough to bring her raspberry ripples this way,' he says, pulling my chair out, 'dessert will be taken in the bedroom.' Such is the mediocre banter one tolerates for a bit of afters. At least he resists any pun about squirting his Ice Magic.

After a while of being naked and into all sorts, I must mishear his strained voice because it sounds as though he's saying, 'Like it's a gear stick.' I don't ask him to repeat, I just keep moving my hand up and down, up and down.

'Put it in first, baby,' he cries out, 'and come for a ride!' Oh Lordy. 'Over and up . . . over . . . and up!'

I haven't dated for ten years. This might be bog standard behaviour. I don't mind helping him to reach his destination – but I've never used a gear stick. What to do? Pretend?

He grabs my wrist. 'Shift it, lady, give it some *revs*.'

I take my mouth off his earlobe to explain. 'Thing is, I, um, don't drive. You could . . . give me my first lesson?'

He palms himself through the full 'H' of gear changes, with instructive commentary.

When he's breathing normally again and not like a walrus, he says, 'We'll do clutch control next time. I'll teach you the *biting* point.'

In my head I'm wondering how to block a number from a mobile phone.

~

Several days later, I'm out with Tania for a drink and who else should be there but him – on another internet date by the looks of it. The woman is someone I used to work with.

I consider whether to go over and say hello, to which Tania responds, 'Vroom, vroom!' I can't resist. Arriving at their table, I say, 'It's times like these that remind you how small Glasgow is.'

'Rhona . . .' he splurts.

'Hi, Caroline,' I say. 'How's things?'

Realising she and I know each other, he looks petrified by what I'll say next. I don't think it occurs to her that I know this guy for the same reason she does.

Caroline and I catch up. Her voice is instantly familiar with its shaver-that-needs-recharging quality; not ideal in a conference-call mediator. She's telling me she's given up booze for Lent, pointing to her mineral water, and I say, 'Typical Craig, eh? Happy to have a few drinks and let someone else do the driving.' I train my widest grin on Craig's frozen face.

Caroline smiles awkwardly. She doesn't know him well enough to know if this *is* typical. Ah, she'll find out soon enough.

I can't be bothered any more, so I excuse myself. The conveyor-belt vibe of internet unions is not something I'd bargained on. I'm not sure I'm comfortable with it.

Tania tells me to get out of the 1950s.

'Maybe I'm just not ready,' I tell her.

'Dry those misty eyes,' she says. 'Still missing someone is not the same as still being compatible. Of *course* you're ready! Any idiot can get over a broken heart. If that wasn't true, the whole world would be single.'

~

The solitude has gone on for so long I'm forced to count back and see how long: it's Sunday and I haven't seen anyone since two Fridays back (if I don't include colleagues).

I'd forgotten life could be like this when you're a yeld: barren spells when everyone you'd usually see has other plans. It's years since I spent two entire weekends by myself. I'd ridden it out pretty well till yesterday, when, *That's the way it is sometimes* became something altogether more tragic.

It was a test and I failed it and life pushed me to it, knowing I'd crack first. The flat had been cleaned wall-to-wall and I was loading the washing machine, singing along to the radio; then I was hanging on to the counter top, sobbing.

I'm being punished but no one will tell me what for, I remember rasping.

Day nine. It takes the full length of my breakfast to loosen my attachment to a thoroughly hacked-off feeling. Sunday will be a loss if I don't. I make the effort to recall previous weekends when there were so many options I'd had to choose.

And if I had kids and a husband, I'd be desperate for time to myself. It is with this perspective (that at least I'm having someone's ideal weekend even if it's not mine) that I head out for the next few hours, moseying from place to place.

In second-hand furniture shops down tenement lanes, polished walnut surfaces reflect my outline on the tones of endurance. Along the river beyond the point where I usually walk, the ancient beat of heron's wings thumps through the bridge arch. Back along streets I'm not usually on, I feel unsettled by row upon row of windows I didn't know existed; by myriad lives that tick along unlinked to mine. To a retrospective at the Kelvingrove Galleries; massive canvases of winter landscapes, where either side of the horizon is the hopeless grey of a cold afternoon.

Around two o'clock, in a tub-chair of a coffee shop, light breaks through dissolving cloud. I can see that my specs are grubby and take them off to wipe them. The lenses are spattered with tiny, crusted dots: today spent looking out through yesterday's tears.

～

Subject: Someone who likes cycling has emailed you!
Subject: Someone who likes films has emailed you!

Two unspectacular humans have emailed me!

~

Hungry as I am, I can't eat a meal in front of him at this tiny table. My gullet closes over at the thought: heavy, stocky smells, cutlery clattering, sauces polluted by straying mush, bullying food onto a fork and chewing, chewing.

Together for an hour already, I feel able to say something. 'I don't think I could do a full meal but please, order whatever you want.' Confessing aloud takes the sting out of it. 'I could do chips,' I decide, imagining picking one up between two fingers, biting half.

During our meal we are reduced to the very small talk. 'What did you get up to today?' he asks, slipping his knife between his lips to harvest some mashed potato.

'I went to the Mitchell. There was a lecture on.' I smile, knowing this comment is ripe for exploitation. He makes the fingers-wiggling-from-the-chin gesture whilst saying, 'oooOOO, a *lecture*.'

I have to laugh because he pulls it off. 'Yeah, so, what did *you* do today?' I ask him. 'Read the *Sun* and play with your XBox?'

'I play with my XBox every day, darlin. Side effect of not having a girlfriend.'

'Careful.' I raise an eyebrow. 'You can damage your eyesight doing that – sitting too close to the screen.'

'You're the one wearing specs,' he says, wagging his finger. I laugh.

'Women don't wank,' I remind him. 'Surely you know that.'

We can have this conversation, sober, only because we don't fancy each other. Like, yes. Fancy, no. If we fancied each other we'd be skirting around the baser stuff, to make

86

a good impression. And we'd be drinking more, to facilitate contact.

'That's right,' he winks, 'I forgot.' He is scooping up potato like his fork is a trowel.

When he's done with eating, his cutlery sits like snow-ploughed skis. I reach over and bring knife and fork together.

'Woah! Proper little madam.'

'Years of experience – I waitressed through uni. It lets the server know you've finished. Therefore letting her know she can clear the plates.'

'*Therefore*,' he mocks, 'you can go home.'

I don't have to answer because the waitress appears and starts clearing the table. 'Dessert menu?' she asks.

'No, ta. Just the bill,' he says. 'My date isn't enjoying herself.'

She laughs then stops abruptly, unsure if she laughed with him or at him. Hands laden she retreats.

'Why keep the discomfort to ourselves,' I say, with a big smile, 'when we can share it with everyone?' He grins and holds my gaze. The waitress makes her way back with the credit card machine.

'Can I pay for my chips?' I ask.

'Embarrassing.' He waves me off with his hand and deals with payment. Transaction completed, we lift our coats. I add pound coins to the saucer. He ushers me ahead then stretches an arm round to open the door for me. On the pavement there is a stop-and-look moment, which I break by indicating the direction I'll walk in. He is parked beyond the corner where I'm turning, so that's where we say goodbye. I'm glad I don't get to see his car. If it had been high-end and comfortable, I might have found it harder to walk away.

~

Erin's on my couch, asking, 'So *then* what did he say?', 'What did *you* say to that?'

Technically, nothing was 'said', it was all done by text. Two days of messaging with some guy who popped up online last week, and somehow weaselled my number from me when it's my policy not to give it.

He'd sent a suggestion to meet, which I didn't grab, and things evolved into a lobbying campaign, insisting he was worth seeing in person.

Tania's doubting my final message (the only excuse I could think of short of, EFF OFF!!!).

I don't think I'm ready for a relationship.

'Rhona. You sweet and precious simpleton. He isn't looking for a relationship. Your mistake was answering his first text. If you're not interested, don't answer.'

'That feels impolite.'

Tania's looking at Erin, like *Can you believe this?* 'You're so right,' Tan's saying, ''cause good manners were his top concern, too.' She's faking hysterical laughter. 'What did you type – you "don't *think*" you're ready? No wonder he kept texting. You let him think you just needed persuading. Do *not* reply again.'

'Lesson learned. I got it all out my system on a three-screen draft.'

Tania grabs my phone, fiddles to find the Draft box. Frowns. Taps her finger down a few times. 'Your phone's so confusing!' She hands it back. 'I finally get your message open and it goes and sends itsel—'

'Nooo! Shit, no! He's going to see what I thought of all his texts. And send me ten more.'

'And you'll ignore them. You need the practice. This *dating* or whatever it is you're doing, is less complicated than you're making it. You *care* too much about these guys. You all do. That's your problem.'

'Eh, excuse me,' Erin's saying with her hand up, ready to defend her corner, but Tania's in full flow. 'Sod the lot of them, it's not your job to protect their feelings – they're not thinking about *your* feelings, they don't even understand feelings. They're pursuing an agenda. Their own. Always. And you don't need them, so stop giving the impression that you do. They thrive on it. Put a *carrot* in a condom, if you're that desperate,' – Erin spits her sip back into her glass – 'you think they're indispensable, but they're *not*.'

~

Licking a damp bus window holds more appeal than another internet meet-up but when a stranger emails fluently and doesn't appear to have mental problems and does appear to be keen – who could say no? Who could forgo the possibility that he might, just *might*, be the guy you're supposed to have been with your whole adult life?

Part of me wants to phone Hilary, so she can talk me out of it, but I haven't told her anything about my internet activities.

I open the office window for a weather check – colder than earlier because darkness has crept down. The will-it-won't-it threat has settled into smir. I don't have a brolly but I don't have far to go either. Down the steps, onto the oily pavement,

I walk to the bar at wolfish pace and fight with its heavy door. He's already there. As it should be.

I don't stall or pretend I haven't seen him. We shake hands.

'Nice to meet you,' we say over each other.

'What would you like to drink?' he asks.

'Maybe a coffee. Yeah. A latte, thanks.'

'Sure?'

'Yup, it'll take the chill off.'

I put my coat over the chair, sit down and take in the surroundings. I haven't been here before. I'm liking it. It has the natural brick walls and vaulted ceiling of whatever it used to be, and the ash floor, wall art and careful lighting of what it is now. It's large enough that the nearest table's conversation can't be heard. He walks back from the bar. He merely resembles his photographs but that seems to be the way of it. Whether a guy puts up one photo or a dozen, the real-life version is always a surprise. It makes you realise, when you're looking at a photograph of someone you know and love, the extent to which your memory completes the picture.

'Well,' he says, raising his Guinness, 'cheers.'

'Cheers,' I say, raising my cup. 'To Thursday,' I add, hoping he knows that I mean 'because tomorrow is Friday' and doesn't think I say pointless things in an attempt to be kooky.

The chat is pleasant enough. I can't decry him on the basis of it, nor can I say we're hitting it off. Still early, though. We're on favourite holiday destinations.

(*Internet dating topics, delete as appropriate: what you think of the meeting place; what kind of day you've had; how often you do the thing you were doing today; where you lived before you lived here; if you live in a flat, what your neighbours are like; if you live*

in a house, how little time you have to make it a home; if you're a
wanker, how much your flat/house is worth relative to what you
paid for it. Where you've been on holiday; where you'd like to go on
holiday; whether you prefer dogs or cats; how many children you –
or your siblings – have; how many weddings you went to last year;
how many times a week you go to the gym; preferably not work. As
a last resort – work. If you're really struggling; topical news items.
After a couple of drinks: when your last relationship ended; how
you can't believe you've resorted to online dating; how much your
colleagues ragged you when they found your profile. After another
couple of drinks: why your last relationship ended; how much you
miss sex; how much you owe on your credit cards and how much you
love some mothballed band who, if you had any taste at all, you'd
know had been derivative at best.)

'I've been to Oslo too,' I interrupt, 'a few summers ago. Loved it.'

'We didn't see enough of it. The best man had the itinerary pre-planned. Bars, mostly. Nursed a major hangover at the waterfront. That was quite refreshing.'

'We ate lunch at the water,' I say, memories kicking in. 'Supermarket picnics.' I remember how good I'd felt in Norway. How I'd craved protein at every meal from the miles we'd been covering with our rucksacks. 'The postcards we sent had finger marks all over them.'

'Same again?' he asks.

'I'll get them,' I say.

'You can get the next one,' he says.

'Okay then, vodka tonic, please,' and I stand up with him, to go to the loo.

Coming out of the cubicle, I check myself in the mirror.

How fetching. There's a rain-curled crown of crazy fuzz around my hairline; Mrs Rochester before she sets the house ablaze. I undo my ponytail, tame the frizz back into the bulk then pull my hair into the band again, using the merest smear of lip balm on fingertips to marshal any remaining wisps. Should I say something? If I mention that I sorted it, and he hadn't noticed it in the first place, I'll seem like an appearance-obsessed, girly girl. But if he *has* noticed I've dealt with it and I *don't* mention that, I'll seem like an appearance-obsessed, girly girl. Fuck it. Some things have to be sacrificed at the altar of unfamiliarity. I sit down, abdomen tingling. Butterflies? On an internet date?

It's amazing how much a couple of minutes apart can revive one's enthusiasm. 'So, Alan, what made you want to meet up with me?' I ask, but don't give him time to answer. 'I wanted to meet you because you can spell.'

He looks nonplussed. I have to rescue this comment and make it the compliment that was intended. 'It was always such a pleasure to get your emails,' I tell him, 'correctly spelled and punctuated. Compared with the others, they really stood out.'

He sees I'm not joking and risks a smile.

'I bet you got an A in your English Higher,' I say, wondering why I can't let go of this.

'Got a B,' he replies, 'second attempt! All I do is apply basic rules. Read what you've sent me, reply to any questions, add a couple of questions of my own and finish off with something cheerful . . .'

Now I don't know whether *he's* joking.

'The black and red differentiation helps,' he adds.

'Black and red differentiation?'

'In Word. I paste your emails onto a Word document, in black. And I write my replies below, in red, so I can see who's who and keep track of the topics. And that lets me use spell-check on my messages, before I paste them back on to CatchMe and send them.'

Kill me now. I can't bear to think of this charlatan speller, home alone with his red-and-black Word document. I am not one of these people. I will not have my words cut, pasted and pored over by these people. I decide there and then my profile is coming offline. I stare with dismay at the new drinks.

Five

Midday sunlight penetrates bare trees to the woodland floor, though there's not much heat in it. Donald is beside me, shouting, 'Man down! Man down! Yesss!'

'I'm right next to you,' I remind him, making a 'calm down' motion with my hand.

'Blasted another one!' he booms.

'Who was it?' I ask, holding aside the fake foliage on my helmet.

'Blue Team. Male operative.'

'*Which* male?'

'Mmm.'

'You still don't know their names,' I say.

'The enemy only has one name.'

I shake my head. 'How many casualties is that?'

'Depends,' he says. 'How many have you killed?'

'None.'

'None! We won't win if you don't kill people.'

'I can't pull the trigger with these gloves on.' I hold up my hands.

'So take them off.'

'It's too nippy.'

'Christ on a bike. Nippy? Some soldier you'd make. This is *important*. You want the team from the new office to feel welcome, don't you?'

'Remembering their names might achieve that. Or being on the same side as them.'

'It made sense to put the Manchester staff together. Chance for them to bond,' he says.

'Maybe you should have sat this game out then.'

'Sat it out? I'm the best man on the field.'

'They're letting you win.'

'I don't think so! Twelve years in the TA, Rhona. I did learn a thing or two about combat.'

'All I'm saying is, if I'd started working somewhere new, I wouldn't be kicking the Director's ass at paintball.'

'Yes, well . . .' Realising he's lost awareness of his visibility while talking, Donald quickly steps behind a tree. He's waving at me to move in.

'Why do you think *I'm* still alive?' I ask, wandering around in full view. 'And don't even try to credit this camouflage outfit. It's because I'm on your team.'

'How do you explain Petra then?' he counters. 'She's on my team too, or *was*.'

'She texted an hour ago from the café. She promised Raymond a pint to shoot her.'

'That's what she wants you to think.'

'Yeah, 'cause having to admit she got caught off guard by a splodge of paint would be too humiliating.'

'Are you going to be this narky all day?' he asks.

'I'm not narky, I'm cold. Hurry the massacre along so we can stop for lunch.'

~

The assault course is bloody murder but I draw on resources of unknown provenance to get me round. The effect of being outdoors, perhaps. The connection to the time of day, the time of year. The full focus on each task.

From glancing at people ahead, my brain assesses how best to approach each obstacle – which movements to make, what pace to go at. From glancing at Donald, my brain notes how not to set about it.

On the rope lattice, I know where each foot and hand is and where they need to go next. Under the ground-level netting, I know the open air will come again if I repeat my elbow-after-knee tummy-shuffle and don't get freaked out. When a little voice suggests that I give up, I only need to recall my usual day – eight hours on a chair in a strip-lit box – and I surge with the energy I need to carry on.

On the zip wire I'm aware of nothing except the tops of trees and *Wheeeeeee LUCKY ME!*

At the end I want to go right back to the beginning and start again. I almost do, but make the mistake of telling Donald where I'm going and he says, 'What? We're leaving in half an hour.' Which means it must be four o'clock. It baffles me how the last two hours were compressed into twenty minutes. Four o'clock?

In the changing room, the instructors take back our safety gear and announce how long we each took to complete. I out-performed the other women and a couple of the guys. Donald sidles over, saying, 'Who enjoyed herself after all? Fitter than you look, Beech.' Then he adds, 'You should think about the TA.'

'Still got your sense of humour, despite your dismal ranking.'

'This has been an unqualified success,' he states. 'Don't you think? I'm going to bring us here every year.'

I don't want to leave today, never mind wait a whole year to come back. Donald picks up on this.

'Never mind, Rhona,' he says. 'When you have kids, you can come here as often as you like. Chesney would have me here every weekend if I let him.'

～

'We're having a child,' I'm telling him.

'We are??' His forearms clamp below my butt, lifting me in the air while turning us round.

'Children, to be precise.'

'Twins!'

'I don't know.'

'You must know.'

'He never said.'

'The doctor didn't tell you how many children you're carrying?'

'No, my boss.'

The circling comes to a stop. 'You're having your boss's child?'

'Children. He said I'm having children.'

My head bumps against Petra's car window. By the time

I'm awake enough to realise that Mark was here, he's slipped away. The more effort I make to recall him, the more irretrievable he is.

~

Maybe it was talking about Oslo, maybe it was being outside on the assault course, but the idea of being very far away for a few days hooks me. Tania'll come. It's not like she's doing anything else since the WB was dumped.

I phone her and leave a message, reading aloud an online description of a Canary Island resort, ad-libbing a line about bronzed, attentive pool boys meeting your every need, ensuring a trip you'll never forget (though with Tania, it's more likely the pool boys who'd find it unforgettable. She can reduce even the sluttiest of men to quivering amateurs. We'll book a room each – what do I care?).

Checking my mobile after a meeting, Tania has left a reply. She can't come on holiday. Something about a new year's resolution, and a dozen applications, and fingers crossed, and she has an interview. A *job* interview.

Welcome aboard! I text. **Details later, please** 👍

Deciding I'll still go somewhere, I start Googling for ideas. By bedtime, I've booked a guesthouse on Orkney for the following week. When it occurs to me that no one will know where I am unless I tell someone I'm going, I phone my mum. We spend ten minutes establishing that, yes, I am going on holiday by myself and, yes, I'll be fine and may even, believe it or not, have a nice time.

'Are you sure, Rhona?' she asks, again. 'What will you *do* all by yourself? Will there be enough for you to *do*?'

'I canvassed a few people at work for advice,' I tell her. 'Raymond said that before he was married, he got through solo holidays with long hikes, red wine and masturbation.'

'Oh for goodness' sake', Rhona. Shoosh. Not in a public place.'

'Don't panic, Mother. I've never enjoyed hillwalking.'

~

On board the ferry, many faces are familiar from the coach journey all the way to John O'Groats; it's almost like we're holidaying together. No harm in enjoying the familial feeling while it lasts.

For the most part, the passengers are the types to make use of midweek prices – retirees and parents with pre-school children. I'm in safe hands. I can relax.

Out on deck, I hunker down in a seat weathered from red to pink. Fleecy collar zipped around my chin, hat down over my ears. We pass a crop of seal-sprinkled rocks. Catching eyes briefly with an adult, there's a flicker of something, like recognition. I wonder as to their intelligence and whether or not they have teeth, but there's no one to bounce these queries off.

It's an easy crossing, spent numbed by exposure. When harbour shop signs become readable, people begin moving to the railings and soon the ferry has slowed right down. With an abrupt lull in sound and speed – for better or worse – we have arrived.

Travelling alone is easy; the time is fully occupied with travelling. What will it be like every day now that I'm here?

~

Wet, tempestuous gusts batter about my old window frames in the late afternoon and no bastard to have sex with. What a sad waste of a storm.

Though it doesn't have to be, I suppose.

A wee while later I acknowledge that taking care of business wasn't an overwhelming success. Masturbate, cry. Masturbate, cry. It's been like that since he left.

~

We sit in the wild grasses at the edge of the coastal path. 'That seal was flirting,' I say.

'Put this on,' he says, taking off his cap and handing it to me. 'You've had too much sun.'

'All that tumbling around and looking up at us. It knew exactly what it was doing with that lengthy eye contact.'

'Whatever you say, dear,' he answers, in a sitcom husband voice.

'I was tempted to jump off the cliff and join it. Live happily ever after in the North Sea.'

'More likely to be the Atlantic, on this side of the island,' he says.

"Tis my destiny to be a selkie wife.'

Mark points out that I couldn't be a selkie wife – that selkies are seals who shed their skins to take human form. 'He'd have to be your selkie husband,' he says, 'as long as you were out of the water.'

Reminded of how pedantic he could be, I stare out to sea with a sensation of deep fatigue coupled with urgency. Something has to happen in my life, but what?

If he wasn't here I would cry. Head for the edge and keep

walking. At a small table in a visitor centre café we lean our heads towards each other, so we can read from the same laminated menu.

'Have you decided?' I ask.

'Let's keep it light,' he says, 'there's a lot to do this afternoon.'

I don't want to respond the way I'm about to, but I'm powerless to halt it. 'What's this premium on doing? What about seeing how we feel? We can rush round visiting dug-up villages but will we be different afterwards? We could sit here instead. Spend the afternoon eating lunch and staring at the sea. That's if they even serve anything after three o'clock.'

'Oh oh. What's got you?' he says, taking my hand.

I was sure it was something to do with losing him. But it can't be because he's right here.

'I've been so tired,' I tell him, 'all year. I can't stand feeling this wiped any more. I know what triggered it – things happened. But enough already, you know?'

He keeps hold of my hand.

'It was you leaving and a health problem and changing jobs. Nothing that other people don't deal with.'

'Hey,' he looks right at me, 'just because you don't see folk bawling in the street doesn't mean they're not struggling.'

'The silliest things I can't deal with. Summer's on the way. I know it's coming and I'm railing against it. Making the adjustment.'

'Give it time,' he says. 'It'll get easier.'

We're sitting in his car and he's started the engine. 'Watch!' I tell him, as he almost hits a boulder, but he already has us going backwards when he replies.

'I was only creeping forwards an inch before I reversed. For luck.'

'What?'

'An old salt at the harbour was telling me about his time on the fishing vessels. Always start a journey forward. That's what he said.'

~

As nice as it was to have a change of scene, I can't say I feel revived. And it's more than just returning to metallic, urban air.

I concede, though I'm loath to, that I might *have* something; might be suffering from a thing with a name. How did it get to this? Why didn't you snap yourself out of it, woman?

I don't want to have depression – to be so far down a road of mental health issues that they're official and need treating.

~

'What's brought you along?' asks Dr Gillespie.

'A classic case of time wasting, probably.'

She smiles tolerantly. 'What are your symptoms?'

'That's the thing. I'm not sure. It's more like, when I look at how I used to be, say a year ago, I see I'm not like that any more.'

'What's different?'

'I don't have the same oomph. I can't be bothered with much.'

'Sleeping okay?'

'Yes. It's not that kind of tired.'

'How's your appetite?' she asks.

'Fine. Same as usual. I might have lost a few pounds last autumn, but I'm back on three square meals.'

'Are you crying a lot?'

'Not particularly.'

'More than you were a year ago?'

'Goes with the territory after a break up. And I was feeling stressed around that time with the cervical clinic, and the cell changes.' I've mentioned it before remembering I shouldn't have.

She clicks into my notes on her desk monitor. 'Ah, yes, the referral to colposcopy, last November. It says here the biopsy showed CIN 2.' She moves in and out of screen pages like she's searching for something. 'You had laser treatment on it, did you?'

'No.'

She's searching around the screen. 'Should be a record here ... Cold coagulation, then? You'll be due for your six-month follow-up in May.'

Nope – not if I didn't go for the treatment.

'What would the follow-up involve?' I ask.

'It's a standard smear test. To check the cells of the cervix. They'll write to you soon with an appointment.'

It occurs to me that if I had a smear test and it came back normal, then I'd know the mushroom extract had reversed the dysplasia. I wouldn't need to go back to the clinic, or that woman, at all.

'Couldn't we do the smear test here? Now, even?'

'The follow-up test is done by the colposcopy service. That's how it works.'

I don't want that to be how it works. Crossing one leg over the other I catch sight of my socks; navy wool to my shin. Sensible. Mannish. Shameful.

I rub at the wet tickle that slipped down my cheek.

'Try not to worry,' she says, sliding a box of tissues across the desk. 'The smear is to gather information. Nobody enjoys a smear test, but they're something us gals have to put up with, mm?'

I have an internal debate about whether to own up; tell her I sent a letter to postpone my treatment. But if I do, I'll have to mention the tampon-popping hockey captain and the mushroom cure.

And whether I own up or don't, I'm headed back to the colposcopy stirrups. Why bother?

'You – you don't think I've got depression then?' I ask.

'Do *you* think you've got depression?'

'I don't know what's going on,' I tell her.

'I think you had a difficult year. Emotional upheavals are tiring. Put some fun back in your schedule. Draw on your support network. If you don't feel better in a few weeks, by all means, come and see me.'

~

The doctor said much the same as Hilary and Tania. Get over it! Get on with it! But the advice packs more of a punch when someone I hardly know had to go to the trouble of giving it. And with a stranger there was nowhere to hide; the only part of me she could see was my broken part, the only thing in the room was my problem. With Hilary and Tan, I can hide it behind all the other bits of me that they know.

The NHS has it on record. I've been 'outed' to myself as a grief hogger.

Just do what the woman suggests and put last year behind you.

~

Multi-coloured light spots swirl over the polished floor, across our bodies and up the walls.

'We call thees thee quiet samba,' whispers the Brazilian dance instructor into his mouthpiece, while gyrating his speed-hump buttocks. Tania, Hilary, Erin and I mimic his minimal foot movements, keeping our bent arms in at our ribs.

'We call thees thee LOUD samba!' he sings out, and forty or so people pump spread-eagled fingers in the air, throwing one knee up and down, like he is.

His syllables of instruction hit the carnival beats filling the mid-evening club. 'Shh–shh, qui–et, now, woo–OO, LOU–OUD!'

Gary is pacing the shadows in his big jacket, throw-catching a bunch of keys. 'On yourselves!' he calls over, laughing.

'Want some?' Hilary calls back, and the four of us synchronise in a hip-circling twirl, just for him.

~

I remain supine while the landline ring-ring-rings and then stops. My mobile starts and I rub cheesy Wotsits' residue on my pyjama top before answering. There's a number showing but no name.

'Hello,' I say slowly, so my head doesn't move.

'Thees ees the quiet samba, shhh,' whispers a man's voice. Oh *shite*, I gave him my number? Familiar laughter breaks out, hurting my hair roots.

'Bog off, Gazza.' I curb my own laughing because it seems I could puke. I moan while it passes.

'Feeling delicate?' It's Hilary's voice, now.

'Mmm.'

'Is he with you?' she asks softly, because she must really think there's a chance that he is.

'No he is not. He tried to get out the taxi at mine, but I told him my boyfriend was inside asleep.'

'You two-timing hussie! Are you seeing him again?'

'How little you know me.'

'Go on!' she says. 'He could wear his little headpiece and give your neighbours a running commentary. Thees ees the LOUD shag, woo HOO!'

'Winching the samba teacher,' I say, with no strength. 'Textbook singleton.'

'Call it a step in the right direction – you're groping strangers. We'll go out next weekend to maintain your momentum.'

~

I get up. I'm late for work. I open my post on the bus. Bank statement, charity newsletter and:

Our records show it is almost six months since you wrote to the clinic, to postpone your colposcopy treatment. Please contact the clinic receptionist to confirm the appointment time enclosed.

I'll be glad to get the all clear. It'll be worth going back, even just to explain to the consultant how I cured it.

~

Logging in to the email system, I see there's one from Donald. He wants to bring us all together, briefly, at eleven. That's got to be an announcement. Whatever it is, I want a part of it. This could be life conspiring in a fresh start.

I have two hours to come up with something to take in with me. Something that shows I have a business brain.

'Morning, Don,' I say, sunnily, arriving in his room on the dot. 'Coffee anyone? Ray?'

'Petra's gone out for some,' Raymond says. 'She's getting your usual.'

I have a usual? We don't know what the new Rhona likes to drink.

Donald turns back to Raymond and says something about the interim report due on Friday, for Direct Claim. This is filler chat, while we wait. This is my chance.

I interrupt, 'Remember I mentioned a school that wanted to bring us in as consultants?'

Donald actually scratches his head trying to remember. He has learned all his habits from cartoons.

I remind them both about Denburn's inquiry, a while ago, seeking efficiency savings to fund extra-curricular initiatives. I say the Head got in touch again last week.

'If we tell them what the services of Muffin cost,' I say, 'they'll see they don't have a hope. But,' I continue, 'we could, for a few grand, offer them this level of input.' I hand out sheets I've prepared. 'With the emphasis on educating them, excuse the pun. After a rifle through their budget headings, we could examine best-practice case studies and tool them up to make their own changes. Instil the confidence to do it themselves.'

'That's more than a few days' work,' says Raymond, handing back the sheet.

'Well spotted. We wouldn't be charging the usual rate

though, because it's a school. And our junior consultant would be working on it, which allows for more days.'

'We don't have a junior consultant,' says Donald. When the penny drops, he looks intently at my project sheet to avoid eye contact.

The bustle of Petra appears. 'Sorry! Queue out the door.' She distributes cups from a cardboard tray, muttering, 'Fifteen minutes of my day I won't get back.'

Once she's seated, Donald announces two big contracts, one in Manchester, one in Edinburgh. After forty minutes of ins-and-outs have been covered, I let the other two leave the room ahead of me.

'I've picked up a lot since I started,' I tell him. 'I could develop my role, have client responsibilities. With more experience, I could go to Manchester, or Edinburgh, as a business consultant.'

Donald tosses his coffee cup in the bucket. He smooths his hair into place.

'I'm not saying no, Rhona. But this is new information. At short notice. Staff training and covering your current job – those things take planning. Preparation.'

'But it's not a no?'

'If you're serious, let's talk at your six-month appraisal. When is that? Next month?'

'Week after next.'

~

Turning up for my postponed appointment, I'm unaccompanied still; numerator with no denominator, but it's the last time I'll have to go through this. My bag holds a sanitary pad. No repeat of the previous violation.

I am waiting. There is nobody else here. Why am I waiting? I reach for the nearest magazine, *Homes & Gardens*, skim through and toss it back. Maybe I should give Hilary and Gary a housewarming present. But they haven't moved house – he's moved in to *her* house. Present required? No present?

'Rhona Beech.' A nurse holds the dividing curtain to one side. She shows me to a cubicle in the second waiting room. I go through the pants-off, shoes-off, skirt-on, socks-on routine then sit back down. Not long till I'll see Dr Carr's reaction to my healthy cervix. *Ha!* I'll be able to say.

'If you'd like to follow me,' says the nurse. She enters the treatment room ahead of me.

The doctor seated at the table is not the matronly lady I met last year. This is a boy-man; no more than 26. I sit down across from him, boots and pants in hands. 'I'm Dr Kitson,' he says. 'Dr Carr retired recently.'

Or maybe she was sacked, for leaving wee gifts inside people without asking.

He is looking at my notes rather than at me. 'I understand you were here last November, but you didn't want treatment.' He talks quickly. The pressure of his next appointment is at the table with us. What about *my* appointment? This one. Whatever direction the discussion takes, this unformed adult is getting nowhere near my anatomy. Is it legal for a man to do these procedures? Why didn't they warn me, in the letter?

Against a wave of malaise, I start to retell my story. 'I knew that cervical cell changes could get better by themselves so I was keen to explore that route first. There was a lot going on ... I didn't feel up to a medical procedure. Not if things could resolve naturally.'

My longer than necessary reply is causing his face to contort in mild agony. Probably best if I don't mention the mushrooms I ordered online, for their immune-boosting properties.

'The first thing to do,' he interjects, 'is get you up on the table, see what we're dealing with. Then we can chat. I'll come back when you're ready.' He stands and leaves the room.

The nurse guides me backwards onto the treatment bed and places a paper sheet across my naked pelvis. Splayed and ready, we wait for the doctor. It occurs to me he's in another treatment room, talking too quickly to another woman. Is a rushed appointment a competent one?

I'd prefer it wasn't him, but I want proof the CIN 2 has gone. How else can I get it? I'm realising this follow-up visit isn't simply a smear – it involves a second look with the colposcope.

'Been at work today?' the nurse asks. *Oh spare us*. Don't ask questions you don't care about the answer to.

Dr Kitson comes through the door and sits close, on a stool. I remember to say, 'Don't put a tampon in after, I brought a towel with me.'

'I don't put tampons in,' he answers. Is there a right way to do this or not? My eyes brim hot. We should be following a set procedure.

A sudden smell of vinegar. He must be painting solution on my cervix and I haven't felt a thing. He swings a UV light below the paper-line: that'll show how the vinegar has reacted with any abnormal cells. It's the second time I've been through this so, while I know he is poised with his scalpel, I also know it won't hurt. He instructs me to cough. My cough morphs into a long exhalation of pain. The pain continues to echo as this clumsy fucker pushes back his stool.

'Right, that's you. I'll come back when you're dressed.'

~

After I've put my pants and boots back on, I sit at the consulting table. I imagine the poor love coughing in the other room. I realise the fact he took a sample from my cervix means there was something to take a sample of. The solution revealed abnormal cells. Fewer, though, since last time. I know that much.

Dr Kitson enters the room and sits opposite. Fat-fingered youth. What do you know of women's pain? He has the cheek to doodle on his pad while he's talking.

'Last May, your cervix showed changes in the cells, graded CIN 2,' he is saying. 'We'll have to wait for today's results to come back from the lab before we know what level of dysplasia is present now but, from what I saw,' he turns his pad to me, 'I'd say the area of abnormal cells has increased to CIN 3.'

I look down at a pen-and-ink cervix with a large shaded patch. No one else has done this – illustrated what we're dealing with. This is what young men bring to the process. I am grateful. Shot with helpless desperation, but grateful.

I fire questions: If CIN 2 increased to CIN 3 in six months, how long till CIN 3 becomes cancer? Do I have one of the more aggressive strains of HPV I've read about? I mean, can we afford to wait three weeks for the lab results?

'I can't tell you which strain you have because we don't test for it on the NHS. We don't treat the virus, just the dysplasia caused by it.' He sweeps his pen nib around the ink patch. 'When you come back, I'll remove that area with loop diathermy.'

'The hot loop that slices away part of the cervix?' I ask, fighting the downward pull of my bottom lip. 'I read that weakens it.'

'Another Googler,' he sighs. 'You don't know how deep a lesion is till you start treating it and with the other method, cold coagulation, you can only treat the surface layer of cells. It's more efficient, I think, to take away several cell layers.'

Even if they're healthy layers? 'Which risks weakening my cervix, if I was pregnant.' My lip wobbles freely. I'm no longer trying to mask my upset. This lad will know that he's not just dealing with a clutch of my cells.

'The cold coagulation procedure – technically, burning with a hot probe – carries risks too, of inflexible scar tissue,' he offers.

'What does that mean?'

'That the cervix may not be able to stretch sufficiently during labour, requiring a Caesarean section. I have to emphasise how small these risks are. Things heal fine, usually.'

Am I having children? I don't know but it makes sense to preserve the option. A Caesarean birth is better than not sustaining a pregnancy. I see his agitation returning. He'd wanted to conduct a short seminar, not a discussion.

'I'd prefer to let it get better itself . . . but I tried that already. I can see it does need treating. Some time maybe . . . to get used to the idea of having the treatment.'

'The results should come back in a week or so,' he says. 'I'll see you again then.'

After I've been to the bathroom and stuck a sanitary towel to my underwear, I shuffle my way through the automatic doors and down the hospital drive, past A&E and the Maggie's Centre.

Six

The ironing board is six feet from the TV and I'm leaning on it, distracted by Tibetan foxes hunting small, defenceless things through their stony domain.

When the landline rings I reach to answer the iron, realise this is wrong and walk to the phone.

'All right squirt?' says the caller.

A rare phone call from my brother. Not 'bad' rare, just 'brother' rare.

'The Boy David,' I reply.

Older than me, he mostly sat in his room with the door shut; occasionally leaving joke-shop turds in my bed, or Ken and Barbie in flagrante on the stairs. His wife has turned him into someone with social skills. Almost. I can hear the tip-tap of his keyboard while he talks.

'Mum says you've got a new job. You going to stick with this one?'

'It's the same new job I had at Christmas, David. I haven't started two new jobs in six months.'

'Just as well. It has been known.'

'When are *you* getting a proper one? Grown men don't tinker with bikes for a living.'

'Exactly. Grown men pay people to do that, while they order shiny new ones for their two-shop empire.'

'Whatever. Are you phoning for a reason?'

'I am.'

'Don't tell me – you had your ponytail cut off.'

'Nooo, I found your real birth certificate and it turns out you *are* adopted.'

'Thank God. Why else are you phoning?'

'Annie wants to know when you're coming to visit your nephew.'

I hear Annie in the background saying, 'David! I never said that!'

'What I'm supposed to say is it's Callum's fourth birthday party this weekend. Mum and Dad are driving down on Saturday. First thing. You could get a lift.'

I sit, to assimilate the out-of-the-blue joy on offer.

'Thank Annie for the invite,' I tell him. 'I'll go and phone Mum.'

For most of the weekend, I crawl, piggyback, play fight and feign death to accommodate the joy being offered.

～

The results of the second biopsy arrive from the clinic.

The letter confirms what Dr Kitson had sketched on his pad – CIN 3. To my huge relief the cell sample hasn't shown

115

cancer. They've scheduled me for next week, to dig out the dodgy bit with a hot wire loop. Next week's too soon and it's not soon enough.

~

I thought TV scriptwriters had invented it – the scenario where, if you mentioned 'women's problems' to a man, he would cringe, stammer and leave the room.

But when I'm telling Donald I need a day off, not just a flexi-morning, and he asks why – that's exactly what happens.

~

I stock up on painkillers and sanitary towels as suggested. I shop for comfort items: mashed potato, chocolate-flavoured custard and a five-quid magazine. I worry about getting myself through the automatic doors tomorrow morning. I have to go, I can't go, I have to go, I can't.

I should talk to someone.

Why haven't I discussed this with my friends? Because none of them has ever mentioned cervical treatment. They might gripe about having to go for a smear but I've never heard mention of a result, dodgy or otherwise; certainly never been told of dysplasia. Why am *I* defective?

The head chatter continues through dinner, which I'm finishing when the phone goes.

'Hi Rhona.'

Lizzie! We phone each other every few months for a long catch-up. 'Liz, great to hear you! You well?'

'Very well,' she says. 'We're just back from the Lake District.

116

The boys stayed home with their gran. We sat by the fire, did a couple of long walks. It was lovely.'

Wild, peaty miles in spring light.

'Rhona?'

'Yeah,' I muster. 'Still here.'

'What's the matter?'

'Ach, nothing.'

'Frazzled? Work is it? Bloody knackering going to work. Still gives me shivers thinking about it. Jump on a train and visit me! Come on, throw a sickie and come to mine!'

'I'm already taking a sickie,' I say, tears beginning. 'I'm going to the hospital tomorrow.'

'Everything okay? Want to talk about it?'

Apparently that's exactly what I want to do because I don't stop for ages: this test, that test, this appointment, that appointment, this herb, that herb, CIN 3, Caesareans and several cell-layers deep.

'I don't smoke. I eat fruit. This isn't supposed to happen,' I state. 'I don't want high-grade cervical dysplasia and I don't want hacked at by an adolescent. I'm fed up with all this. If it can resolve itself naturally, why didn't mine?'

'It happens, hon. Bodies misbehave. Tying yourself in knots won't be helping. What if minor surgery was the simplest way to cure it. Then you put the whole thing to rest. Imagine the relief.'

'But they said I could bleed for a fortnight.'

'Could. Probably won't.'

'Hmm.'

'You don't have to do it on your own.'

When she says that, I weep again.

'What time's your appointment?'

'Ten thirty.'

'If I get on the eight fifteen, I'll be at yours for nine forty-five. I could stay all day. On a *Tuesday*, what are the chances, be just like the old days, hey?'

We make our plans and I hang up the phone, knowing I can turn up the next day and go through with it.

~

Having done what he had to, the doctor has left the room. The nurse remains. Slowly I pull on my underwear, and ankle boots. I tug down the hem of my wool dress. I'm unable to hurry; arms enfeebled (sort of hollow from trauma) coupled with a need to demonstrate self-care. I'm the child who's been treated harshly and told it was for its own good. And I have the same dependence on the perpetrators.

I can only go through the curtain if this doesn't come with me.

Lizzie smiles with all that she has when she sees me. She reaches out her arm and draws me in. She doesn't ask. After a minute, I say, 'It's not painful. More of a deep ache. Maybe when the injection wears off I'll know all about it.'

She rummages in her bag with one hand. 'Want one?' She passes me a packet of painkillers. 'It might not get painful if you aren't worrying whether it will.'

I press out a pill and swallow it with a swig from her water-cup.

'I asked at the desk,' she says. 'There's a taxi rank round the corner. No rush, though. We can sit here till you're ready to go.'

'Now's good,' I tell her.

Lizzie puts a mug on the coffee table and asks what I fancy for lunch. I know immediately. 'Scrambled egg.'

'Buttered toast, baked beans?' she asks.

'Yes, please.'

'Kitchen table or on a tray?' she asks.

'Kitchen's fine.'

'I'll shout you when it's ready.'

Lying on the couch, head on the armrest, I reach for Lizzie's folded newspaper. The crossword is facing up. It's showing a couple of unanswered clues but I don't read them. The pointlessly obfuscated riddles, the barricaded solutions, would put me back in a funk.

The high-ceilinged tenement kitchen is an amplification chamber for clanging pans, alongside tuneless bursts of Lizzie's singing. She's amusing herself; this concert is deliberate.

We'd met when she was lying beside a pool in Ibiza with her eyes closed and headphones in, singing so loudly and badly that people around her were laughing and mocking. I'd felt protective of this nutty lady and tapped her shoulder.

Turned out it was our mutual day off – she worked in holiday lettings, I worked in a bar. We shared many Tuesdays after that; by the pool, or hiring mopeds, or hitting the wine with lunch. I remember thinking it was strange that someone had got to her age, thirty-three, without being married or having a kid. HA.

Honestly, twenty-one-year-olds don't know a damn thing. At least, not that twenty-one-year-old. Late in the season I left for Latin America, and she rented a villa to a forestry manager with pre-school twins (and a year later married him, pregnant).

An *X Factor* reject with startling melisma is letting me know, 'It's REEeeEEeedeee'.

In the kitchen, we sit with two plates of perfect lunch. At the first mouthful I put my fork down and look at her. 'So tasty. How did I forget about scrambled egg?'

'Because you don't have kids.'

'Yet.'

'Oh? *Yet* is it?'

'I don't know where that came from. Must be delirious from the medication.'

'One Nurofen?'

'What's for pudding?'

'I didn't think about a dessert. What have you got?'

'Don't know. Oh yes I do. Chocolate custard.'

'All that's missing from this lunch is toddlers to eat it,' she says, then rests her cutlery. 'You do know your procedure was minor, in the scheme of things. What I mean is, it won't affect you getting pregnant. If you're worried.'

Her delivery is a 'we who know the sacred sacrifice of birthing and rearing' oil slick, minus the pity smirk. She's not that kind of woman.

I touch her hand and say, 'I know,' because that's what will comfort her.

She lifts our plates to the sink.

Lizzie is right. Treatment for dysplasia doesn't threaten pregnancy. Other things do that: day dreaming, game-playing. Pride. Waiting for your boyfriend to propose while he waits for you to come off the pill.

A feature in my five-quid magazine referred to the shortest story ever written. Not hard to remember: 'For sale. Baby shoes. Never worn.' I'd counted the six words by Hemingway, thinking, *I know a story with only four*: 'Healthy womb. Never occupied.'

Lizzie wipes her hands on a tea towel. 'Hey dozy, I said I brought a film. Feel like watching it?'

'Aye. Perfect. What is it?'

'*Terms of Endearment.*'

'Very funny. What is it?'

'*Who Will Love My Children.*'

'Stop it! Tell me what film you brought.'

'*The Man With Two Brains.*'

'Really?'

'Really.'

Settling back under a shared blanket, Lizzie takes my hand and says, 'I barely sit down during the day – cleaning and shopping and washing and cooking. This is some treat.' She gives my fingers a squeeze and releases them onto my knee.

Whether it's the pill she gave me, or her sing-song laughter at the film, the pain never materialises.

～

I wake up with clear April light punching through the curtains. I can't wait to get to work.

I'm cleaning my teeth, thinking, *It's gone.* I'm putting a banana in my bag, thinking, *completely gone.* I'm walking to the bus stop, thinking, *I've things to be getting on with.* I claim a double seat to myself, thinking, *onward and upward*, thinking, *this is the point I will look back on*, thinking, *this is the day I point my arrow.*

At my desk, I listen to messages while my PC comes to life. One is from Donald. 'Rhona, quick call from the train. I'll be in Manchester till Friday. There's a *situation* with County Constr— em, best not say, in public. Raymond can tell you. Hope your, eh, thing, went fine. Speak later?'

My arrow sets itself between the string and the bow.

Donald's absence frees up time to prepare for my appraisal.

There's mileage in the school idea, I know it.

By Thursday, I can't wait any longer and email him something to read on the return train:

As you know, a barrier to efficiency savings in the public sector is a prevailing culture of resistance. In Denburn's favour, the Head is keen. If he can re-deploy the Deputy Head's teaching commitments for a couple of months, that's two designated staff members leading the reform agenda which, previous examples suggest, make it likely to succeed. Leading change from within etc.

Couple that with Muffin's expertise on integrating streamlining into strategy and it couldn't fail.

Granted, we don't make our usual percentage, but we don't lose either. On my figures, this is still profit-making. Two days per week of my time, for two months. After that, you can decide if it was worthwhile.

Don't say no before we've tried it.

Let's talk, at least.

After pressing 'send' my mood's too high to focus on

anything mundane or work-like. I must discharge this zippity energy in web surfing.

—

By mid-afternoon, FerrisBuellerSenior has sent a reply. And he continues to reply for a week.

Thanks for the wink ...

... it's made an old man very happy ... and I totally agree with the comment in your profile about a distaste for endless emailing. When should we marry? Actually that is the LAST thing on my mind. Re your cat – do you ever play the eye narrowing game with cats? That's fun. Lovely photos RBGlasgirl

Mr Bueller x

Re: Thanks for the wink ...

A proposal! Wait till I tell my mum! Oh at last! A proposal!

I phoned the registry office and they had a cancellation, so it's all set for Tuesday!

(Probably shouldn't make jokes like that to a man of your years – blood pressure and all that.)

Joking aside, thank you for replying to the wink. 'Old man' you said? Pshaw. You've still got all your hair. Unless it's a wig ...

Re: Re: Thanks for the wink ...

My life is complete – I never thought it would be this easy. Tuesday can't come too soon. You don't feel rushed into things do you? I'm so glad. Yes, all my own hair, teeth, limbs – just the one eye though . . . in my forehead. Can't wait for Tuesday – regards to Mum.

Ferris.

Mrs F Bueller

My dear Mr Bueller,

Just to let you know, 'Hi There' magazine would like a few photos afterwards and wondered if we'd mind posing with some Aztec Bars. I didn't think you'd mind at all! Then Wetherspoons is expecting us at 3pm. We will be met there by all 57 members of my immediate family (where your cycloptic eye will pale into insignificance, trust me . . .). Mum can't wait to meet you. She wants you to call her 'Maw' straight away. You're like a son to her already. Till tomorrow.

Re: Mrs F Bueller

My cherub – I too have been busy and have managed to attract interest from Paisley's premier freesheet 'Hullorerr'. In a joint sponsorship deal with Greggs it seems we will be awash with steak bakes and fudge donuts!

Your mother must be on the brink of ecstasy – I imagine it will take all her concentration to lance her boils tonight. Bless her. Until tomorrow then my cupcake . . . when I hear your familiar foot slap gait coming up the aisle, see the faint outline of your hump against the stained glass windows, and inhale the whiff of Mycil foot powder mixed with Tweed Eau de Toilette . . . sweet dreams my mail-order princess.

All I remember from the letter is the term 'negative margins'.

They needed them. They didn't get them.

I think it's referring to my biopsy tissue but it could be a budget report from my in-tray.

~

He habitually raises his hands out in front of him when he speaks. A representation, perhaps, of the fact he is delivering information. My attention is taken by the way he hooks his third fingers around his pinkies while his other fingers point straight ahead. I've never seen anyone do this. It looks effortless. I move my own hands under the table to emulate his digital posture. I can feel I'm not achieving it and look down at my hands to see where I'm going wrong. The third and fourth fingers will not move independently of each other. Maybe his abilities are genetic. Maybe it's like tongue rolling. I manipulate my tongue inside my mouth, to see if I can still do it.

'I can see this is upsetting for you,' he says. 'It will be, without doubt.'

Am I showing any signs of being upset? Am I crying? 'There are things we can do to enable a pregnancy in the future,' he continues. 'A purse-string stitch is the usual method. What's important right now,' he goes on, 'is your well-being. And we've identified it early, which helps. Like I say, a cone biopsy is successful in the majority of cases.'

I raise my eyes, meet his gaze and smile. He has an unfinished feel about his face. Not in the common very-fair-eyelashes way, but in some other way. I count his features. They are all there. He reminds me of raincoats I sometimes see in rush hour, with belt loops but no belt.

I nod my head, indicating, 'Go on.' Tell me what you have to tell me, Mr Medicine, so I can leave you to it. We are both busy people.

'The surgeon would like to operate next week. I know that's short notice but we don't recommend waiting. Usually people find their employers very sympathetic.'

My face bunches up in an effort to hear better but he carries on, not adjusting his volume to compensate. Can he not hear this high pitch? This keener's wail banging around my skull?

'The things in your schedule – you'd be surprised how many of them don't need doing, or can be taken care of by someone else.'

The things in my schedule, Dr Death, are how I orientate myself in the world. They're how I know who I am.

'You'll stay in overnight after the general anaesthetic, but you'll be home the next day. The hospital has a cancer support team, to answer all your questions. They'll make sure you know any sources of assistance available. They should be your first phone call.' He holds a leaflet out to me, realises I will not be taking it and lays it on the table between us. I know who should be my first phone call, but I don't have one of those any more. *Are we done yet?*

'It's a lot to take in. If you need anything explained, or have any questions, please call the clinic and I'll phone you back as soon as I can.'

I smile again. Nod once. Then a few more times.

I'm not often in this part of town. On the walk through the small park to the station there's a long grassy slope to my left. It sweeps up, bright green and uninterrupted by tree or bench. It occurs to me I have never seen what's on the other side. Not in any hurry, I start up it and within a minute or so I'm at the brow.

Sometimes it's better not to know what's over the hill.

Sometimes, it's just more of Glasgow.

~

In the hallway of Tania's flat, at her sister Bryony's thirtieth party, I've been inching through to the bar for what feels like days but am further waylaid after visiting the loo by someone shrouded in a cloud of vape-smoke, asking if I enjoyed myself in there. 'Yeah,' I reply, 'Did a monumentally long piss actually. Can recommend it, quilted loo roll, scented candles, s'got the lot.'

'People put the fancy stuff out for parties, to impress their friends,' the guy retorts, in less time than most people need to formulate a thought. 'Worked, by the sounds of it.'

And it becomes my job to let him know, 'Tania doesn't need to impress me, she's in my inner circle.' At which the man grunts suggestively, and I continue, 'And for your information Tania's toilet roll is always quilted. Party or no party.'

'I never go near the toilet at parties,' he says, and lists various other shared spaces he avoids, finishing off with the subway. 'Subway seats are ninety-two per cent faecal contamination,' he is saying, and his inference that Tania's toilet, which I have this minute emerged from, is also ninety-two per cent contamination, isn't something I'm prepared to let this party non-pooper get away with.

'Hey, life and soul,' I snipe, 'says who? Where you getting

these fake facts? Your *brain* is ninety-two per cent faecal contamination, how about that statistic?' Shouting it now, 'If you won't go near the toilet then where've you been pissing all night, the stairwell? The world's ninety-two per cent contaminated 'cause of you!'

Tania's dragging me out of range of the response while I'm announcing, helpfully, to passing faces, 'No need to thank me, was nothing really, that's it, that's my good deed for today, everyone else can sort themselves out.'

~

The small, dark room smells of dust and the people staring at the screen look like lobotomy patients in the reflected light. We're standing at the back while silent footage of a desert-dwelling family plays on a loop – getting ready for the daughter's wedding CUT sitting around knitting CUT wandering in scrub snapping leaves from agave plants – why this is art, I'm unsure. Hilary is losing interest too. 'Remember that conversation we had, way back,' she whispers. 'You had a bee in your bonnet about something or other, and we joked that the solution to your gripe was to start Vagina Day? Remember?' She allows me time to catch up then raises a fist in the air, proclaiming, 'Vagina Day!' The audience isn't lobotomised after all.

'Yeah,' I whisper. 'What about it?'

'There already *is* a Vagina Day.'

'Shut up.'

'There is! It's a worldwide thing. This weekend. I saw a poster for it in the fruit and veg shop.'

'You mean International Women's Day.'

'I wish I did but it's Vajazzle Day. I know what I saw.'

'That could fair put you off your broccoli.'

'Pff, in the West End? Hardly,' she says, 'they lap that stuff up.'

A couple of beats of silence, then it's head-back hilarity. Hilary is pushing me out the room as I'm telling her, 'Not in my flat they don't but, you know, maybe soon, if I'm lucky.'

There's nothing to do but let the giggles run their course, drawing attention to ourselves in the echo of the main gallery.

'So where's it on?' I ask. 'Are we going?'

Hilary is no longer laughing.

~

Through the side entrance of the church, we arrive into a cacophony of kettledrums and shrill whistles. A female percussion group claims the stage in a fiesta of foot stomps and head flicks. I sense Hilary wants to turn back. I mustn't say anything that provokes her. 'I didn't think there'd be *any* men, but everyone here looks like a man.' Nerves are getting the better of me.

'We haven't paid yet,' she says, over the din. 'Shall we just go?'

'Half an hour,' I suggest. 'We're here now. I'll get yours.' I hand a tenner to the attendant. She gives me back four pound coins which I display to Hilary. 'Let's look for the home baking,' I say, employing the distraction technique that works on Callum. 'A church social without baked goods is against the law.'

I can tell she doesn't get why I want to hang about (I don't either) but I love her for seeing that I do.

At the first row of tables, we buy fairy cakes with glitter icing and eat as we amble. It's mainly promotional stuff for a range of groups we could join, none of which admit men. No use to me. The last 'stall' is a fabric booth with a sign stitched on: 'Say HI! to your vulva!'

'I don't know why you've stopped,' says Hilary, ''cause we are not stopping here. Nope . . .' She is tugging me by the sleeve.

'What d'you think they're doing in there, though?'

'Nothing that needs to be done, ever, by normal people.' Today's message is, 'Wimmin! Your bits are beautiful!' I wonder whether Hilary thinks hers are beautiful, but I don't ask.

'Seen all you want to see?' she says. I sense that I haven't, but don't have the specifics to offer.

She repositions her bag strap. 'Let's catch the shops before they shut.'

'And miss all this?' I ask. 'I don't feel like heading into the weekend crowds. You go.'

Her forehead crinkles. Her mouth gapes. I don't budge. She relents with a shrug. 'What time, for tonight?' she asks.

'Come about eight-ish. Just drinks, not dinner.'

She leans in for a cheek-to-cheek goodbye.

~

People can react badly to general anaesthetic. Some people never wake up.

I am making a list. Word of mouth would take care of most of those who know me, but there are people I keep in touch with who no one else knows about: from old workplaces and evening classes, from uni and my year out. How can my family let them know I am dead unless I leave a list of email addresses?

FerrisBuellerSenior hasn't been added. I hate to leave the guy in limbo but you can't have someone at your funeral who you've not been on a date with yet. Social networking has put social etiquette in flux but not freefall.

I missed our email wedding day. It was my turn.

He'll think I've fluttered my digital eyelashes elsewhere.

Moved on without the decency to mention it.

But how can I announce urgent cancer surgery to someone who doesn't know my name? And I can't email him a fib either ('I'd rather leave it, if that's okay') because it's not okay. I wouldn't rather leave it; wouldn't rather leave any of it. I'd prefer to keep my schedule, keep my job, keep my friends, keep my family, keep the tingle of anticipation when I'm checking my emails.

~

'Hey lady!' says Tania, giving me a hug as I hold the door open. In the living room she says, 'Let's line these babies up along the sideboard,' lifting bottles from a plastic bag and putting them next to the ones brought by Erin and Hilary. The high octave sound of women reacquainting themselves echoes up the hall as I go for another glass.

'My, you're a gorgeous bevy,' I tell them, taking my space on the couch. 'Whereas' – I look down – 'I would appear to have crossed some kind of line.'

'Och shoosh!' says Tania. 'You're at home for goodness' sake. If you can't look like shit in your own home ...'

I'm about to explain how I went to the bedroom earlier, to

change into something more 'Saturday night' and ended up in pyjama bottoms, but it seems irrelevant.

Hilary raises her glass outwards with a massive smile. 'Cheers!'

We all lean in to clink.

'Once more with feeling,' Tania says, looking at me and tapping our wine glasses. 'That's better,' she says. 'You know the rule – seven years' bad sex if you don't make eye contact.'

'Who told you that?' asks Hilary.

'I wish someone had told me sooner,' I say.

Erin puts her glass on the table. Clapping her hands and awkward with de-domestication, she says, 'Girly catch-up time! News please. Who's got news?'

Penny, pound: sheep, lamb.

'I've got news,' I say. 'It seems I've got cancer.'

In the following moments I become aware that I've forgotten to put music on. It's a relief. The only thing worse than this silence would be an earnest bunch of twenty-year-olds playing on regardless.

I can tell I'm going to have to speak first. 'I had to say it straight out, or I might not have said it at all.'

Hilary moves closer so she can link arms with me.

'I'm not surprised you're quiet,' I tell them. 'I wouldn't know what to say either.'

'Jesus fucking Christ,' says Tania. 'Cancer? Proper cancer?'

'I'm glad you've told us,' Erin whispers. 'I hate to think of this happening to you and us not knowing.'

'Same,' says Hilary. Her mouth is trembling. Why isn't mine? 'I don't know what to say.' She continues, 'If I'm being nosey, slap me but, I mean, how're you doing? Can we help? Do you need your shopping done? Is it that kind of cancer?

You look all right, which is good, but you're not all right, are you, no, course not—'

I quieten her by taking her hand. 'I found out last week and I've to go in on Thursday for ... for ... they're going to—' Continuing is proving difficult because of seismic tremors in my jaw muscles. 'Surgery ... to take away a cone-shaped portion from my cervix.' I try to keep talking because no one else is. 'Lucky, actually. Localised ... malignant cells at the margins of the bit they took befo—'

For the next while we are bunched up together on the sofa and I am crying and I think they are crying too but I am crying quite hard so I'm not aware of much except that I am being touched: there are hands on my legs and my shoulders and my hair.

～

A soap opera scene, I think, sitting by the telephone staring at the business card of a therapist I'm debating whether to call. The viewers know fine well I'll dial the number, even if I don't yet.

Sod it. I'll phone her. If she's a maniac I can make an excuse and hang up.

～

The plaque underneath her doorbell states her name, 'R Endicott', but not her job title. Brazen as you like about vulva introductions in a church hall, in the day-to-day world her business card calls her a 'counsellor specialising in the female experience'.

On a sofa, surrounded by embroidered cushions, it's her

skin that holds my attention; uniformly ivory-coloured and kid-soft, like an evening bag my grandmother let me play with.

'Most women have never seen that part of themselves properly,' she's telling me, 'which is odd when you think about how well you know your hands, or your face.'

That's because it's perfectly acceptable to look at your hands, or your face. You can even look at other people's.

'The aim is for you to leave here feeling connected to that intimate area of yourself, by welcoming it into your overall concept of your body,' she says.

Will we do it here or in the tent I saw? I want to ask. I hadn't realised I was attached to the idea of the tent. Associations of summer, maybe. Familiar faces reflecting the colour of the material.

'I won't show you by example, don't worry!' she laughs. My reality, though, is moving a few heartbeats slower than hers, so it's not until after her next comment that I realise this comment was a joke.

'You won't be able to see the cancer, if that's concerning you.'

'Ha!'

Behind a concertina screen, I recline on massive cushions, naked from the waist down. A large mirror is propped against one wall, and there are a few hand-held mirrors to choose from, offering different levels of magnification.

'It's your session. You're in charge,' she says. 'You can explore as much or as little as you feel ready for. It can be helpful to relay any feelings that arise as you become acquainted with yourself. But we don't have to talk, if you find it too strange.'

*What's strange about this? For all I know you're streaming it
live to a pay-per-view website.*

'You're in a safe space, Rhona.'

Sure I am.

'As you begin' – she presses play on some pan-pipe music –
'remind yourself why you took the decision to make this special
time for you.'

'I wanted to know what I look like,' I tell her, 'before I don't
look like this any more.'

~

With the rest of the day to fill, I walk my way home beside
the river that weaves below the network of streets. At points
the river and the bank are almost level, until the bank rises
steeply away and the footpath follows the incline. Midway up
is where I see it.

A grey-beige lump, fist-sized, sitting in the path. Chirping.

Its gaze squarely on me. Its elbows in some attempt
at motion.

'Look at you,' I say. 'Oh dear. Fallen out?'

The deciduous canopy overhead must be forty feet up.

I go in closer, masking my concern so as not to worry it,
beginning to wonder about ways I can help. I see, though, that
this is not a candidate for a cardboard box and milk-soaked
bread. This chick is in a different league of damaged.

The stodgy skin of the un-feathered squab stops halfway along its body. After that it's a bloody blue mess. And
it looks at me like it knows there's something wrong back
there. Looks at me like I'm the answer it was waiting on,
like I will explain. I act as though everything's okay, saying,

135

'It's going to be fine,' but it's a struggle because it's horrific – not the wound, the bird. An overgrown baby is a particular kind of disturbing. I didn't know a nestling could be bigger than an adult songbird. This burly, goose-bumped, grotesque baby needs me.

I step towards it, crouch down and there's a thud behind me, where I would have been standing. I turn.

A friend once mentioned that if a deer runs out in front of your car, watch for the other one. Same could apply to mutilated pigeon chicks. This one is more anxious, more animated with its stubby little wings. More intact at the rear, less intact at the neck and shoulders.

What on earth is happening here?

I look up and see a commotion of leaves and hear squawking that I now recognise has been going on the whole time, I just hadn't connected it to my situation. A large bird, black and white, is moving around a nest.

'Yaaaahhhh!' I yell.

I have to make it stop what it's doing. It's not even finishing a whole one. Taking a few bites before flinging it out.

'Yaaaaaahhhhh!' I scream. 'Stop it!'

Bastard bird. Why doesn't it eat what it needs and go?

Two half-open, wholly alive birds. Cheeping. Cheeping. With me as their solution. I'm the kind to stop and help – I don't know how to finish a thing off.

Drowning. Folk do that, don't they? It's kinder than leaving them lying on the path with their pecked, fleshless backs, for how long; hours? Till who finds them? Kids, a fox, no one, death, their mother?

Fifty yards down, where this path and another converge,

the bank sits at river level. I rearrange my bag cross-shoulder. Whatever I get on my hands and clothes can be washed off. I try to bend. My legs refuse. I wish the fall had killed them. This is a horror show.

Cheep. Cheep.

I want to walk off. Again, legs refuse. Such suffering cannot be abandoned. This is not their fault.

I hate each endless breath. It's not like waiting while an ambulance is on the way; comforting someone till it gets here. No one is coming.

A plastic bag is caught between twigs. If I can get the birds closer together, with the bag as glove, I can scoop them inside.

And this is how I go briskly down, with my butchered messages. And the dog walker doesn't notice. And the joggers don't notice. And the guy on the bike pings his bell so I'll move aside.

The bank is inaccessible with bushes and branches.

I may think I know about drowning but I don't know about weighting a thing down. I don't know, on this bridge, that mangled baby birds dropped from a bag into a flowing river float on the current, so you have to watch them undulate away, till you can't hear their confused, grateful tweeting any more and eventually, eventually ... can't see them, when the river at last rounds its bend.

They were meant to sink and suffocate. I will run after them to a spot where it's shallower. Wade in and rescue the ripped-open cold mess of them. Phone the SSPCA. Confess.

I didn't know what to do. I made it worse.

I could fall on the ground and sob at casually murderous birds and mutilated bald babies and bewildered bereft mothers and lonely paths and why was it my feet they fell at? Why couldn't someone else have seen them first?

If I let my knees go from under me, some meddler like me will ask what the matter is. Who could understand what I'd had to deal with? Who could I say this to, except . . .

It's not just another person who leaves when it ends; it's part of me that goes. I am without that place where everything's okay because it's heard, where the terrors of life can't drown me because they're shared, with someone who has chosen me as the one he will take time to listen to.

My legs can't support the weight of this. I sit on my heels, to appear less collapsed, and folk continue past.

Seven

The surgeon waits for an anaesthetist. I feel we could start now. Awash with stress chemicals and pretty much out-the-game already, blinking is a thing of the past; gone, along with fully formed thought. I appear to be in the room with these people but not in the same way. They move around a lot. I will let this post-menopausal female hold my hand. I have no other use for my hand at this time.

This moment is what I was rehearsing for yesterday at the Maggie's Centre, with a woman whose zen-ness made my scalp tingle. Being near Andrea reminded me that some people are more than just alive. They exude life; are on good terms with it. I matched my breathing to hers. Then she told me to put my attention – all my attention – on the cool air entering my nostrils and the warm air leaving. '*Be* your breath,' she said.

I did as I was told and became the circular flow, growth and retreat.

'Your stress, your cancer, your treatment – they hover in front of you, separate from you. Stress, Rhona, is a temporary, physical experience. The real you exists beneath these passing states. Take your breath behind your stress, under it. Find the space around the problem.'

As instructed, I moved my breath under my stress. Then I took the visualisation one step further and moved my whole self under a bus, which pretty much took care of the stress and the cancer.

～

On the table is a drawstring bag. I reach in and bring out a small, bird-egg-blue card. It has been signed by everyone: David, Tania, Donald, Dad, Mum, Hilary, the lot.

'For luck' says the message.

I reach inside again and bring out a black, enamel box. Lifting its lid, there sits a grey, lumpen object attached to a key-ring. Turning it round I work it out – it's a hand-crafted pudendum made from clay.

～

I do not want what has happened to have happened.

Something's happened.

To make a person fear for her own survival; to surgically trim her motherhood – I do not want what is happening to be happening.

～

I will let these people sit by my bed every afternoon and every evening and I will thank them for coming, when I am able.

I'm not trying to cause the worry I see when they're leaving but I have no words for them.

~

I am a patient. My job is to lie in this bed. I do my job well. Who I would be at home is less clear. And nobody would be there, beside themselves with relief that I am back.

I'd have to do things, necessary things – plus other things I would have to do just to be seen to be doing something.

Doing things makes me tired.

Doing things leads to other things, and things have a habit of changing when you'd got used to them being a certain way.

My heart broke. My body broke.

The bailiffs came for a cone-shaped piece. What exactly do you people want from me?

~

I didn't have obsessive compulsive disorder when I came in but might well have it by the time I leave (an okay trade?). There is precious little to do but notice things and how often they occur.

Times per hour I assess how my wound site is feeling: about seven.

Times per day I remember to visualise a healthy wound site: maybe one.

Number of days with a Tupperware lid of cloud cover outside: six.

(The sheets, the walls, the sky – all the colour of bone.

Am I that colour too? I have no mirror to tell otherwise.

Maybe everyone who goes under anaesthetic wakes up in

this world of bone, while their previous lives continue somewhere else.)

Minutes per day the nurses listen to a facile breakfast DJ: 120.

Minutes per day I am now able to breathe behind the radio and tune it out: 40.

Times per day I imagine being outdoors for hours on end: one, but it lasts awhile.

Times per day I notice that my left foot sits higher under the sheet than my right: about a dozen.

Times per day I speak: zero.

Times per day I make eye contact with the parent who has come to visit: on arrival only. (I will not cry in a room with a half glass wall, with a person who has to leave afterwards.)

Times per hour I remember what other people have to cope with in life: one, if I make myself.

Times per day I imagine a year from now, when things could be very different: zero, initially, now up to two or three.

Times per hour the perma-grin nurse sings out to the woman opposite, 'Feeling okay, Nancy?': too many. (I am waiting for Nancy to be discharged or die.)

~

If he'd told me he was leaving if I didn't, then I'd have had one. Jesus.

I never left *him* even though he wasn't marrying me.

I wouldn't have taken it that far.

Silent negotiations were ongoing.

~

If he hadn't left last summer, he'd have left anyway, after this. He would have left when my equipment failed. He wouldn't have wanted his progeny held in by thread.

~

I make eye contact with my seven o'clock but it's not my mother, it's Hilary. She looks away before I do.

'Your mum phoned and asked if I could come. Said she'd been held up at an appointment but frankly, I think she needed a break.'

Hilary handles her coat buttons like they're children who're taking too long over something. 'I've been calling her, you know. She kept saying that you didn't want to see friends yet, but your "yet" was lasting a long time.'

She begins to sit, then straightens up again. 'Today she admitted that you've not said a word to anyone. I think she's got me along to see if a new face'll make a difference.'

She leaves a gap. I don't fill it.

'They're only keeping you here because you won't talk. You do understand that. Of course you do. You're here because you want to be, Rhona Beech,' says the woman who will never be 'Auntie Hilary' to my kids. 'Just show them you're fine and you'll get home. How can you like being here?'

I wholly, deeply do not like being here.

She has placed her bag on the chair, which she stands behind. 'I watered your plants on Tuesday. You have post, Rhona. Piling up. If this is what you think you need, fine. But they'll turf you out because they need the bed. You'll end up with a social worker or a mental health visitor or something. Is that what you want?'

I just want to lie here.

'Whatever it is, we can sort it out. Come *home* and be mute. This is no place to be.'

She grabs a greetings card from my side-table and puts it down again.

'Bloody hell! I bet I'm not supposed to say anything harsh, anything *sensible*, but this is *craziness*! You said it yourself, you were lucky, it was superficial. And you can still carry a baby with a stitch to keep you shut. Worse things happen. What *is* it?'

She is looking at me. I am looking at the bedcovers.

'You have us,' she says, re-buttoning the coat she never took off. 'We have a rota drawn up. Leave here, and you'll be the dedicated project of several people who care about you.'

She softens into her first smile. Perhaps I have missed her.

'My freezer is full of soup,' she says, leaving the room with her temporary childlessness. '*And casserole*,' she shouts from the corridor ... kadunk-dunk of imagined saloon doors swinging in her wake.

~

After twenty-eight 'Nancys', while I'm looking out at a Tupperware sky and imagining a year from now, a bouquet is delivered, complete with vase. The card reads:

I forgot to sit down. And the worry made me say too much.

You know I hate hospitals. Missing you – a lot!

Don't make me come back there ... Hilary x

Half of the lilies are still closed, elongated pods tucked amongst the dark sheen of leaves. The flower heads which are open span my hand, their curled-back petals a bruised

144

bluish-pink down the middle. The rusty bars of pollen smell of weddings. I lie back and let the flowers happen because a nurse will amputate the sheet-staining stamens as soon as she sees them.

~

A trolley is wheeled in and the aroma of pseudo gravy infects the room.

My bed is closest to the door. A tray is laid down.

'Like tae see whit'd happen if ah tried that,' says the trolley pusher to the nurse following behind. 'Lyin in ma bed ignorin evrybuddy.'

'Aye,' says the nurse, 'all right for some. Wouldn't have time for it if she'd kids.'

~

The woman in the next bed wakes up after her operation and is transformed into a cyborg of sales. 'You've got your blues, your browns, your pinks ... A selection from the range are in this case, but in the catalogue, see, this entire section – your corals all the way to your crimsons. Every occasion catered for.'

The cleaner who came into our room a few minutes ago with a mop and bucket hasn't had a chance to start using them yet. She's anxious enough about this to interrupt. 'I don't wear make-up that often,' she says, slightly apologetic, 'hardly ever, so it's probably no—'

'Some women – like you, you lucky thing – are gorgeous enough the way God made them. That's why *you'll* be excited by our other products. We're more than just a top-end cosmetics company. In this section,' she says, frantically flicking

145

through pages, 'here! Here we've got everything you need to enhance that face of yours from the *inside*. Natural ingredients, nothing nasty. Millions of women swear by our Perky Lady drink – you've got your beetroot juice in there, your B vitamins, your calcium, your iron, but it's mild, you won't get that metallic taste ...'

A nurse has walked in carrying a bag of fluid.

'That's a lovely eye-shadow you're wearing,' says the multi-level-marketeer. 'What is that? A smokey taupe?'

Ten minutes later (foundation, eyes, blusher but no lipstick) a more senior nurse appears in the doorway. She clears her throat.

'Blame me,' says the pyramid seller, 'but she has such wonderful skin, I couldn't resist. Almost as lovely as yours ...'

As both nurses leave the room she calls after them, 'Come by again, girls. I'm sure I've a wee something here to add sparkle to a night out.'

She falls quiet, but not still. Her gaze lands on me. She reaches over, tosses a catalogue on my bed and says, 'Here, have a read at that, chatterbox. You can circle the ones you like. Not the blushers, though. You don't have the cheekbones.'

All worked up about cancer and I should have been worrying about my flat face. She probably thinks it would have been kinder if I had died, given the unremarkable bone structure.

No one's paying cyborg a salary to lie here. Out of respect for her need to earn a living, I lift the catalogue and place it on my bedside cabinet to give to my mum. She never could resist new slap.

~

146

Somebody sits down near me in the corner of the day-room. I've never met him before. An ID badge clipped to his blazer suggests he must work here. As a psychologist, it turns out. He tells me that he's learned of my situation from the staff but whatever he and I discuss will remain confidential.

After a spark of eye contact from me, he continues, 'Experiencing shock after a cancer operation which threatened your fertility is normal.'

Don't do this.

'I'm here to listen. No therapy if you don't want it. Just an impartial ear.' He waits. Smiles. 'Can you try putting it into words?' Smile. 'Try saying how it feels?'

Pointless, pointless, pointless.

'Everyone has their troubles. Their idiosyncrasies. Even me. It's about managing them.'

If he had a tie on, he'd be loosening it about now.

'There are tools, for inquiry . . . I would like to help.'

A further few minutes spent disturbing the substrate in this manner then he exits to his next victim, leaving me in the murky water. I hate him. I could rip sinew from his skeleton for implying that this crisis – this dissolution of meaning in my then, now and hence – is *normal*.

What does a person have to do to elicit real assistance round here? WHO IS GOING TO FIX ALL THIS?

I kick the chair he sat in. My unshod foot rings with pain. Some guy watching *Bargain Hunt* says, 'Keep it down.' I haul away the chairs between us, growling, 'Why don't *you* keep it down? That shit is on all fucking day in here and I don't moan about that, DO I? Place is full of bloody whiners ... LIKE YOU!' I shout at the pinch-faced nurse who's walking past the glass wall. 'NAE MAN! NAE WEANS! Failed woman? Is that what I am? Well you and all! Compassion's a female quality and you've got none! You're a COOOOWWW!'

The guy beside me turns up the TV.

~

This evening's visitor is Dad. He walks around my bed to the chair. Instead of sitting, he picks it up and brings it round to the other side of the bed, then sits with his back to the internal window. My mother is on the other side of the glass, waiting by the nurses' office. Are we at 'decision time'?

'Car park was pandemonium,' he says.

Their antics have caught my attention. I maintain eye contact.

'We can't stay too long, tonight. We'd like to but we'd best not.'

He looks down. Doesn't explain. I'm being moved somewhere else. They've come to say goodbye before I'm carted off. It's too late. I have messed it up.

'We've been wracking our brains,' he says. 'Can't understand why you won't make more ... progress. Why wouldn't Rhona want to leave there, we've been asking.'

Mum is still waiting for a nurse to become available.

'The only thing we could come up with was that maybe you didn't want to go back to an empty flat.' He reaches for the bag he put down when he came in. The kind someone might take to a gym. Have I pushed him to that?

He settles it on his knee. 'Maybe you don't like living on

148

your own,' he continues, unzipping the bag. 'So . . . ' his voice trails off as he reaches in.

Little ears, then eyes, emerge from the bag. He places the unsure bundle on the bed. Very small paws pad clumsily alongside my leg. After some hesitant sniffing, it lifts its head and finds itself looking at me. Its tiny mouth opens in a meow. Sounding more like a baby bird, it does it again. Dad appears to have abandoned it, so it's up to me to reassure the wee thing. I reach for it and it lets me. Holding it to my chest, I say, 'You're brave, bringing this in here.'

I don't think I've seen a smile like that on him.

'Shift your chair over a bit,' I add, ''cause if the nurse sees this.'

It takes him a few seconds to answer, he's so busy beaming. 'Your mum's keeping watch. What do you think?'

I shrug. Then smile to show I was teasing.

'Don't you think he looks like Bomber?' he asks. 'Soon as I saw him I knew he was for you.'

'How old is he?'

'Eight weeks. Picked him up the other day. We didn't want to move the little man around too much so we've been staying at yours to settle him in. Word to the wise, your mother's getting that look, you know, the one before she rolls her sleeves up.' Having lost many childhood possessions to that look, I know if I want to hold on to the objects I've spent the last fifteen years growing fond of, I should go home.

~

Presumably because I have made the decision to take down the bunting on this festival of depression, I wake with a strong yen for flavour. I can't get packed fast enough thinking of the smoked fish and basil leaves I will buy on the way home.

In the taxi, it occurs to me the nurses could have made more of a fuss.

Eight

Leaning on the freezer door, I'm in awe at the contents. It's never been so well stocked.

'Labels, too. Impressive.'

'You brought out my inner granny,' says Hilary. 'We can't have you defrosting the same thing two meals in a row. Or eating curry at lunchtime.'

'I've eaten curry for breakfast. With you.'

I pull a kitchen chair out to sit. Hilary does likewise, saying, 'I'm not treating you like an invalid, am I? It's so that you can do what you feel like, rather than wasting energy on mundane stuff.'

'I appreciate it,' I tell her. 'Don't let me take advantage.'

She reaches out and tucks my hair behind my ear, the way my gran used to. She knows the doctor signed me off for a month and that most women would have got a week.

Thankfully, the post-op bleeding tailed off in the ward and the cramp-ache in my undercarriage is easing.

'Who else is on the rota?' I ask.

'Believe it or not, Tania put her name down for housework, on Saturdays. Your mum is doing midweek shopping. And Erin is your weekend culture buddy – cinema, theatre, your pick naturally. Oh, and Cyril is the in-house entertainment.'

'The wee guy volunteered? Nice. No guilt about prodding him awake then.'

On cue, the cat hurtles into the room sideways with his tail straight up, spooked by nothing at all, as usual.

~

'Mum,' I say quietly, into the mouthpiece.

She sounds disorientated when she responds. 'Rhona? Where are you?'

'At home. Couldn't sleep. Sorry.'

I hear her covers ruffling and her movement away from the bed.

'Have you got your dressing-gown on?' she whispers.

'And slippers,' I reply, my free hand clasped around bare toes.

'Things okay? You're feeling all right?'

Squatting on the seat of the armchair, in the shadows cast by light-pollution, I try to answer.

'Mum . . .'

'Mmm?'

'What if I can't . . . maybe I'll never be able to . . . any . . . chil—'

'Oh, Rhona.'

Sobs paralyse speech. 'I didn't mean for it . . . all end up . . . wrong . . . Mark . . . wasted . . . couldn't even look after my health proper—'

'Dear Rhona. Darling. This wasn't your fault. Come on.' She has the grace to talk on, while I cry and cry.

'You're better now. That's what matters. And there's *every* chance you can have children,' she reminds me. 'I'd love for you to have a family of your own,' she says, and I hear the smile behind it. 'It was such a pleasure being a mum to you,' she adds.

~

Tania was good enough to take me to the shops (after she'd brought an agency cleaner up to my flat). I should thank her. When I'm off this bus, I'll phone.

It must have been the fluorescence. Or the Saturday bustle.

I followed Tania into Iceland where she started filling a trolley with sealed, rubbery bags and portion-sized boxes. At the checkout, she unloaded them onto the conveyor belt. When I reached for the rectangular doo-da to put between our pile and the pile behind, it just came out, 'But there's nothing here I can eat.' Quietly. So she had to say, 'What?' And I tried to say it again, with my voice breaking, 'There's nothing here ... I can ... eat.' By the end of the sentence I was in bits and she had no idea what to do with me. Neither did I.

Now I'm on the bus and Tania, I presume, is driving home – her boot full of bags and the radio up too loud.

It seems I can no longer be intimate with anything that will not sustain me.

~

Craving time outside is satisfied in the garden of a coastal cottage rented by my parents. I don't venture far from base-camp because my first period since the operation is as heavy as warned.

The upstairs landing has a view of the horse field beyond the track. Gazing on the sun-glossed peaty pelts against an acre of blowing buttercups brings a feeling I don't recognise. A mish-mash of joy and communion.

Annie and Callum join us midweek. The fun goes up a quotient. This easy interactivity; these ordinary delights and irritations of company.

I don't show it, but Friday is spent floored with shame at what a numpty I'd become in the past year. How detached I let myself get. Burrowing into an inflated sense of my struggle, I lost the perspective and benefits of a 'relative' experience. Ouch. Everybody witnessed its zenith. Two weeks as a hospital mute.

The starkness of the teaching doesn't feel great, though at least it's come at a good moment. New rule: be depressive only when others are at hand, so it doesn't have a chance to get its feet under the table.

It had been years since I'd lived alone. I didn't know there was a knack to it while keeping sanity intact. I will return to that flat and find a better way. Just because I don't live with anyone doesn't mean there's no one in my life.

~

When Lizzie couldn't visit me in hospital, she'd given my mum a book of poems, a collection called 'Staying Alive' (lucky we share a sense of humour). I've been skipping this way and that way through its pages since the cottage.

Poetry begins to find me in other ways too, for instance,

from the picture book that speaks to Erin's daughter when she presses different images. Over and over the book says:

a cold drink

a hard brick

a dry bird

a wet bird

a wet cat

It must have been made in America, because it talks to her in a Californian twang or in Spanish.

una bebida fría

un pájaro seco

un pájaro mojado

When she stops playing with it I feel robbed of the voice.

I want to pick it up and press the pictures myself. I wait till she's left the room and then I do.

~

Things I have forgotten to do keep me awake – a website address I scribbled down the other day then never looked at. The fish pie I'm making for Hilary and Gary tomorrow, the prawns I forgot to buy. I must have forgotten to send my brother a birthday card because this is June and he is Taurus.

I forgot to consider motherhood properly before it was jeopardised. Forgot to fall in love with someone I could last the distance with. Would I have the energy for that again?

I've forgotten what it's like to be held. Actually, that can't be true. How could I miss it this much if I couldn't remember? I can feel it like it's happening – the my-back-to-his-torso contact of a lying-in-bed embrace. And if I searched every room in this flat, every street in this city, I'd find no one whose remit it is to share that with me. Is life enough if I am to live without that?

Sex is back on the permitted list, the op was weeks ago. Something else to remember – ask the doctor when this period will end that's been going for more than a week.

~

I reflect on the night-mind and the morning-mind, behaving like they belong to different people.

Morning Rhona could simply switch on her tablet device and browse for eligible hug partners. Yet she has no urge. Daylight has arrived with its good pal, clarity. Men can wait, while she masters the skill of living alone and liking it.

~

We have abandoned our jackets by the climbing frame. Rodeo-riding the wee pink animals on springs, our grown-up weight takes us perilously close to the safety surface but we keep managing to right ourselves.

Tania is laughing so hard she can't get her words out. Her hair is all over the place. Her giggling starts me off again. Eventually, we calm.

'Swings?' I ask. There is more in these muscles. It's a giddying return to form.

'Bench first?' she suggests.

'Okay. Bench.'

Slouching, legs out, toes leaning in, she swigs from her bottle of water and offers me a small, round twist of blue-and-pink paper.

'Bazooka!'

'It was in a tub by the till. Hadn't seen it for years.'

It smells of pocket money. I work on its grainy pulp, not bothering to close my mouth. Watching a small balloon emerge from Tania's pout – it's expanding with each carefully measured exhale. The bigger it gets, the more it resembles a membrane. I study its capillaries till it bursts.

It occurs to me that her spontaneous 'sickie' may have more to it, so I ask how work's been going.

'The job's fine,' she says. 'Except that I can't concentrate on it any more. Not after what happened to you.' She looks at me. 'I realised I have to do what'll bring me happiness.'

What a gift my cancer has been to so many. And I'd be glad – if what she was claiming was true. But we both know she's using my illness as an excuse for her Tania-ness. She'd been bored and getting a job was a challenge. It took a few months but she got one. And then it hit home – she has to turn up every day. Every week. Every month.

'If you're fishing for someone to talk you into staying, bingo – and I've told you this before, so it's not a fib on the hoof – you, Tan, even at twenty-one, were more capable than most of the slumming-it graduates in that car insurance call centre.'

'Jesus, *that* place, underpaid battery humans in cubicles.' She's blowing a bubble, which implodes when she starts laughing. 'Dropping Take That lyrics into the calls.' Tania's helpless again. 'Remember that guy . . . the one who shouted . . .'

The memory has me attempting an impression, '"Oh, oh, it'll take longer than a *minute* girl, to get my car back for good! Gary bloody Barlow, is it? I know what you're doing! And no, luv, it could *not* have been magic. A wizard didn't make my wife's Lexus disappear. Funny, is it? I *will* report you! Not so funny now!"'

She's holding onto my leg, gasping. It takes us a moment to return to the here-and-now. 'Nice try at deflection,' I tell her. 'I'll say it again – you were *good* at that job, and without much effort. Customers loved you. Signing up like lemmings for increased premiums and roadside rescue.'

'Yeah, and when a permanent full-time post came up, they gave it to you.'

Because employers can sniff it a mile off – the staff who might leave at the turn of a mood, giving no notice. The ones without the deferential gene. Throw in a deep and complex habit of sabotaging things when they start going well and, who'd offer a permanent post to that person?

'Have you another job in mind that would make you happier?' I ask.

'Sort of, but I need to research it first. Speak to a few people. And I don't have time to do that when I'm at work, so my only option is to stop working.' And before I can reply, she's saying, 'Yes, I see that now. Thanks, Rhona. Solid advice, as always.'

Priceless. To anyone who inquires it will be, 'I know, but I talked it over with Rhona and she advised me to . . . ' And I can't call her out on this because, like she said, cancer puts things into perspective and does it *really* matter if I get the blame for her packing in her job?

The play area fills with parents and children – letting-out time at a nearby nursery. Order repeatedly bullies impulse; wailing tots have the concept of turn-taking explained by adults crouched at their level. Small bodies run behind swings to cries of, 'Careful!'

Tania keeps talking. 'It was awful, what happened to you, but in some ways you're lucky.'

Because it was minor league cancer? Because the treatment worked? Because I have people around who helped?

'You don't have to worry about this any more,' she continues, waving her hand past the scene in front of us. 'Kids are a lot of hard work. And that's assuming you've got someone on hand who'll penetrate and inseminate – which you didn't.'

I'm struggling to see the silver lining angle Tania's peddling.

'Now that children are out,' she says, 'you're spared the debasement of the "he'll do" dash. God, my sister was at it. So demeaning, watching her date anything with the right tackle. Now she's ring shopping with some collar-unbuttoned-because-it's-the-weekend tragedy who thinks he's marrying for life and is actually being lined up for the living hell of divorce and shared parenting. Everyone else can see it except him. I think she's even convinced herself.'

'Just because this guy isn't your cup of tea doesn't mean your sister—'

'But *you* don't have to worry about hooking up with the last single guy just 'cause you both want kids. You, Rhona, have time to meet the *right* guy, who totally gets you, who you're properly compatible with.'

I could remind her that I still have a uterus and ovaries but she's decided that I'm her sterile heroine. I could also suggest it doesn't have to be one type of relationship or the other ('convenient' with children, or 'perfect' without) just because we're passing thirty-five.

And what's this bitter wistfulness around meeting Mr Right? Tania's the only woman I know who never mentions him.

By the time we've said cheerio and I've dropped in at the doctor's surgery to make an appointment, I'm janxed. My vocabulary isn't even working properly. Ten minutes from home and my legs have nothing left, plus gravity is coaxing pelvic cramp.

A couple of newsagents on this side of the road, though no coffee shops. The sandstone wall I'm leaning against carries on to an entrance way with a square sign hung side-on. LIBRARY. There are bound to be seats in there. Can anyone walk into a library and sit down? No choice but to find out.

When I re-emerge, it's touching rush hour and I'm a bowling ball crashing into skittles after a long, easy glide. The men and women in cars, in buses, on pavements, in Tesco Metro . . . do they know about the hush and helpfulness of where I spent this afternoon? I couldn't bring any books with me, not till I've shown the staff two recent utility bills. I had to read onsite. Poets whose names are poems in themselves, Edna St Vincent Millay, William Carlos Williams. How can I do the daily madness again now I've seen how some get to spend the day? Padded chairs and peaceful hours passing; alone but with each other, too.

It's not a doctor I recognise, so I ask if he's new. He says he's providing holiday cover and his tone lets me know he's tired of answering that question. But he breaks into a smile anyway as I describe the extended menstrual bleeding.

'A healthy flowing period is what you want after a cone biopsy. It means you haven't developed stenosis.'

'Sten . . . sorry?'

'Cervical stenosis. Blockage of an opening. Some people seal up completely as the wound heals. Nothing in, nothing out. But you're open for business so let's not spook you with detail you don't need.'

Bit late.

'A heavy period is not unusual after cervical treatment but, in case it's an infection, I'll give you a course of antibiotics. Swap the bleeding for discharge and itching.'

I'm not sure I like a doctor of my own age, my own social type. The absence of formal awkwardness here is a problem.

'Natural yoghurt on the shopping list. When are you back at work?'

'Week after next.'

'Okay, well make sure you rest before the pace picks up. But don't under-do it either. Idleness plays havoc with your mental equilibrium.'

I'd lamp him for his presumptuousness, if he wasn't right. Making this appointment to discuss my errant lady gear stirred the old anxieties, and their malignance replicated and spread beneath yesterday's mundane pastimes. *How will I ever know I'm okay in a place I can't see?*

Back outside the surgery, it joyrides round my neural highways; worry, worry. Don't let it take hold, Rhona. Talk it out.

Starting for home I phone Hilary but there's no answer.

Can't phone Erin after four o'clock: mum duties.

Is this the kind of problem I can share with Tan? One that's about me, not her. One that's psychological, not practical. I've answered my own question. But I shouldn't keep it in; I know where that'll lead. It'll have to be Tania.

My voice must betray something when she answers. 'Let me phone you back, I'm just parking the car,' she says, then doesn't call.

~

'Hello.' It's a woman's voice. 'Maggie's Centre.'

What will I say?

'Hello?' she says.

I don't have cancer.

'Hello–o?'

'I came along to the Centre a couple of months ago, when I had cancer, but I don't have it now. Barely had it in the first place.'

'It's, um, always good to hear that. Someone making a recovery. Will I pass your news to the team?'

'Yes.'

'Can I say who called?'

'Yes.'

'I'll need your name?'

'Oh. Rhona. Beech.'

'Thanks for taking the time to get in touch, Rhona.'

'I'm fine now. All better. I beat cancer for goodness' sake – I'm beyond fine!'

It's as obvious to her as it is to me. In a softened tone, she says, 'From listening to the people who use our services, it's not always a straight line to feeling better. People can experience difficulties adjusting, after cancer, as odd as that sounds.'

'You'd think cancer survivors would be on a permanent high.'

'Is that how you feel?' she asks, knowing what effect her question will have.

'Not especially. I was getting panicky. Over nothing, really. And I couldn't get hold of my friends. And, I'm trying to be careful not to get too, um, insular. Sorry ... you must think ...'

She reassures me that it was the right thing to phone.

'It's important that I keep talking. I tried not talking. It didn't go well. And I couldn't get hold of anyone. Then I remembered about the woman I met at Maggie's. Before my operation. But I'm better now, other people need her services more than I do.'

'Cancer isn't just physical. A full recovery can take time. I'll look in your file and see who you spoke to.'

~

I've only been in the bath a minute or two when the washing machine starts the eager mechanical squeal of its final spin. Kitchen items tumble from the draining board into the sink and I try not to worry about which ones they might be. When the determined, cyclical straining breaks it is a relief to us both.

The heat and hug of the water ease into my muscles. Perspiration trickles, salty, over the ridge of my lip. Opening my eyes I notice my breasts right there – like sunbathing when you're sixteen. Hurrah for the buoyant properties of water.

I slip my head under to rinse my face. When I surface, the telephone is ringing. Why jump? It'll only ring off as I get there. If it's Hilary, she'll leave a message. If it's Tania, there will be a pause before an unfinished, 'Fuck i—' And if it's Erin, she'll give the phone to Mindy to leave a message – emotional blackmail which guarantees a return call.

My parents don't leave messages but they do phone back in half an hour if they haven't heard from me. That's their current 'maybe she's dead' threshold.

True to form, when I'm securing my dressing-gown round my clammy torso, the phone rings again. I belly-flop onto the bed and reach for the handset.

'It's okay, I'm not dead. I was having a bath.' Dad will smirk. Mum will tut.

'Eh ... hi,' he says. Not Dad. A different voice. 'It's me.' Not my brother. Me who? I don't know any men well enough that they'd phone and say, 'It's me.' Is it rude to ask? *Should* I know that voice?

Oh. I bloody do know that voice! But that 'me' doesn't phone this me any more. Not for a year. Almost exactly one whole year.

I stop lying down. It's not helping. I can't think. I sit up.

'You still there?' he asks.

Answer his question or go for the cheap shot?

'For a while it looked like I might not be,' I say, 'but the surgery was a success. My cancer's gone, they tell me.'

I want him to hear the word cancer and think that I'm joking – laugh, and then stop when he realises I'm not.

I want him to hear the word cancer and think it was the full-on variety. Hear the word cancer and bawl – undignified man sobs which don't happen often enough to sound natural. I want him to be filled with shame, horror, both at what happened when he was no longer there to hold my hand.

164

'Glad to see your illness hasn't affected your sense of humour,' he offers.

Glib? What right has he? *My* drama, my brush with death.

I have licence to make light of it – he doesn't. Not after a year.

Apologise for yourself. Feel bad so I can feel good.

'I thought you might have been more shocked at my news,' I say. 'Everyone else was.'

'Of course I was shocked. Of course I was. It just took a while to decide whether it was right to get in touch.'

'You knew already?'

'Yeah, my mum told me. Word travels, you know what it's like.'

I'd forgotten to think about what the grapevine had been saying about my bad luck; my silence. Hadn't considered their casual catch-ups at fitness classes and petrol stations.

'You've gone again,' he says. 'Have I said the wrong thing?'

I hadn't meant to leave a gap but I like the outcome. I extend it, to prolong his discomfort. He steps in. 'I hummed and hawed about contacting you, after I heard. Maybe this wasn't . . . a card might have been . . . I really don't know what to say. You're not saying much.'

Red. Rag. Bull.

'How rude of me. Sorry. I'll make more effort to spare you this awkwardness you've put us both in by phoning me up. It's only been, let me see, a *year*.'

'You're pissed off. I understand. I don't know why I thought this would be fine.'

I make no sound, no sound, no sound. This man I've been trying to get over for many, many months is now alive on the other end of my telephone – and I'm furious to find that I've made little progress. He's plugged right back into the bit of me he used to commandeer, as though he popped out for a paper and got waylaid and here he is, twelve months later, phoning to let me know.

And if I throw a fit about how long the errand's taking, I might scare him off again but what, just let him get away with it?

Again, his voice brushes my cochlea into my brain.

'I've gone in circles the past few weeks, whether to or not, but then today I didn't think twice. It was easy to dial. One of those moments where I forget we aren't together. Now that we're speaking, it was all back *then*, I see that.'

His turn to pause. But he can't match my silent stamina. 'It was a mistake, Rhona, phoning ... but I may as well say what I phoned to say. I would have helped, if I could've. I'd been hoping things went well, so it's great news about your treatment. Brilliant result. Sorry for any upset. You take care.'

'Don't hang up! Don't you fucking hang up.'

'You're angry. I get it. I didn't think it through properly. We'll just leave it.'

'Give me a second will you? A second. To get my head in gear. You knew you'd be speaking to me today. I had no idea when I answered the phone I'd hear you on the other end. I don't even have a number for you. It's ... unexpected.'

'Sorry.'

'It's all right. Strange ... but all right.' *Hearing your voice again. Like you just popped out. Like you're still the person I know best.* 'So ... um, the blue sofa's gone.'

'What? Big Bertha got the heave?'

'Fraid so. The new one's nicer, though. Mauve.'

'Ah, yeah, *mauve* sounds much comfier. When's the plastic coming off?'

'Oh, maybe never.' *Like twelve months were one moment.* 'The messy students moved out of the basement.'

'No more stinking bin bags in the close.'

'Another bunch moved into the top flat. Tidier, thank God . . . And I've got a—' but I don't want to mention Cyril. Cyril's *my* business. Seems I can only update on things already shared – am disinclined to contaminate my new with my old.

He doesn't get to know. Doesn't get to pass comment.

We'll have to talk about Mark, then. 'How's it going over there? Settled in?'

'I have, yeah. What a city. Folk are so welcoming. Always something going on. I've joined the office soccer, sorry, football team. Ticks all the boxes, pretty much.'

Red. Rag. Bull.

'I'm glad all your boxes are being ticked.'

He waits before he speaks. 'Did you want a response to that? 'Cause I can answer, if you want.'

The nip-nip-naggy woman who has lain dormant for a year says, 'Oh, so now what I want *is* important.'

'To answer your sarcasm, you could have come with me.'

'What could I have added to your new set-up? Except maybe ticking the girlfriend box.' Stop, or keep going? 'But then, if ticking that box mattered, you wouldn't have moved to Toronto.'

'It's immaterial, now' – he's *met* someone – 'but, I did ask you to come.'

'To tag along with a decision you'd already made. Ticking the career box won the toss over us.'

'We've so done this conversation.'

So *done? Are you Canadian now?*

'At least I had something that was important to me, Rhona.'

'That's what I thought I had.'

'Why make me choose you or the job offer?' he asks. 'We could've had our relationship over here. There was nothing in your life that seemed reason enough to stay. A job you weren't bothered about. The only thing you were committed to was us, and you weren't even committed to that because you didn't come with me.'

His voice is getting really fucking familiar now.

'Can you blame me?' I'm squeezing a pillow with my free hand, to help keep my voice sane. 'Hesitating to give up everything for a man who was moving abroad whether I went with him or not. What did that say about *your* commitment?'

'A lot,' he jumps in. 'It was an opportunity. For both of us. Isn't that the point? Grabbing opportunities when they come along? Glasgow isn't the world. Why *not* move to Canada?'

He doesn't give me time to think of an answer.

'Know what? You were right not to move here. It takes a certain mindset to make a fresh go of life and I don't think you have it.'

If I hang up now, the spectacular misjudgement of that statement will occur to him at some point. But just in case, I spell it out.

'Cancer doesn't half hone your ability to make a fresh go of life,' I say, throwing down the phone.

What's the use of the big C if you can't employ it to score a point here and there?

~

I create chaos on shelves looking for a particular pyjama top, discarding each not-quite-right item behind me like a dog digging sand. I say clichés out loud: 'How dare he!', 'Who does he think he is?'

He won't get away with it. I'll write down all the reasons he's a monumental muppet and I shall post them, care of his mum.

Thank God we never had kids! A year in grieving and one telephone call shows it was a lucky escape. It didn't help that we were miles apart during the conversation but that's true of every discussion we had in the year before he went. Hinting left and right about fatherhood yet making no moves to commit.

I was good enough to mother his kids but not marry? Supposed to leave work with no security? He couldn't face up to things. If he'd come at the subject square-on, I'd have told him my position. Soccer-playing tosser. He can stick his phone call up his Canadian *ass*.

The only top left is one I haven't worn for years. And it's nothing like a pyjama. Christ! Christ! Christ! If programming computers in Canada is the pinnacle of his ambitions, I'm better off. It's a job! It can be done anywhere. What's the big fucking deal? You don't feel nauseous and exhausted-yet-manic for a year when you let go of a job.

A relationship, on the other hand ... that is a total investment of self. An act of insanity, is what it is. Why would I even *think* of doing that again? Nothing important in my life?! What does he know about it? What's more important than people – than friends and family and pets?

I can't think of anything.

In the living room, pen end tapping the pad, my resentment becomes more about writing to him than not writing. Why should I spend the next hour of my life writing to *him*? He's had enough of my year. Goddamn.

There's a shortcut out of this. It didn't work the first time but I wasn't ready then.

CD cases hit the wooden floor with the alarming clatter of plastic. A Dusty Springfield 'best of' is swallowed by the stereo. Skipping through to, *It's Over*, I press play and stay with her on every word. I select the repeat button, to make sure I get the message.

~

'Hi.'

'Rhona? D'you know what time it is?'

'Hi.'

'Are you drunk?'

'That is *immaterial* now, is't not? My point is, if Gary was offered job, in Aussstralia, would–you–go?'

'I don't think he'd get enough points for a visa.'

'But if he did, if he was … a brain sssurgeon, then would–you–go–with–him?'

'Em, yes, I suppose I would.'

'You'd give up evrthing and *go*?'

'Well, I would now, yes.'

'Okay, okay, ansssswer this … if *you* got a job in ssstralia, would Gary move? Would he, give up, his whole life, to fit with you?'

'I like to think we have a joint agenda so, yes, he would.'

'He would *not*, n'don't put it to the test. There'sss my advice. A man never puts's career plans aside, for his girlfriend's plansh. His *wife's*, at a push. For th'mother of his child, *maybe*. But for his bidie-in? Never. And if he sssays he would, he's full of shite. They-all-are.'

'Night night, Rhona.'

'Marry him! Sssign a contract. It'sh th'only way to get back, what you put in.'

'The house is in my name, remember? It's Gary who'd be homeless, not me.'

'Good girl. You've gotta think th'way they do. Be all, sssself-centred n'logical.'

'Goodnight, missus. I am hanging up the phone now. One, two, three—'

~

The reveal is imminent – and I don't want this to be mine to deal with. I don't want to be the agent of it.

As the sole of my shoe rises up from contact with the floor, it occurs to me there were other options. A piece of paper and an unlatched window.

This is no choice: wishing to my filament a thing is dead, wishing with every fibre I hadn't killed it.

The worst outcome? The one between. There on the tiles – trying to flee with half of its legs useless, its lower body squashed. One purpose: giving all it has left to getting away. Instinct trying to remove it from harm, though harm stands over it. More harm is the kindest thing.

And my punishment for doing it the first time, blithely, badly, is to have to do it again to this ant, that's no longer out scouting but has entered into survival and is making such a display of it.

My task is to do it consciously, with effort and the intention to inflict death.

Nine

Doing things I won't be able to as of next week, I'm under an afternoon blanket with the TV remote, ascending the channels into a three-digit hinterland. I'm hovering at this melodramatic black-and-white flick.

An anaemic vampire lookalike opens the castle door, and I sense he's a bad 'un, but in the woman goes nonetheless. And she's hanging about, too, even as he approaches her with talons poised. *Why aren't you running?* But as he sinks his teeth into her neck, it becomes obvious.

Who wouldn't want to die like that? By the mammoth fireplace and florid gothic chairs. Claimed. The only cure for a hunger that had no words. A shocked, collapsing shadow cast behind the arching candelabras.

'Go for it, love,' I say, lazily. 'Beats populating cells on an Excel worksheet.'

At an unknown time of the afternoon I'm woken by the telephone. When I've moved my cheek from the patch of dribble on the cushion, I go to check for a message.

'Hello,' says Donald's recorded voice. 'Sorry to disturb you at home. Nothing urgent. Just want to confirm that you have Monday in your diary. Ready for you at this end. Very much so. The temp keeps announcing how many degrees she has but none, it would appear, is in anger management. You might be sourcing a new photocopier. If I don't hear otherwise, I'll assume we're on for Monday.'

During breakfast, my parents ring to tell me they'll be in the area later looking at ski-wear in a fire sale, and why don't I meet them for lunch. *Ski-wear?* I remark on the dearth of fondue restaurants and invite them to mine – I can defrost something. They seem happy with that.

Lunch is a ruse to check that I'm well enough to return to work; that I'm still vocal. It's no hassle to reassure them. I schedule them early to keep the rest of the day free. Thursday late-night shopping.

Throwing half of my clothes on the floor last week sparked a charity clear out. I couldn't fight the urge to jettison most items over a year old. Five bags in a taxi. I won't replace it all but I'll need a few pieces for work and a few bits for fun.

I send a text to see if anyone wants to join me.

Erin's message is waiting when I come out the shower:

If only I could ... Mindy has mumps. Day four in the house. U have fun!

Tania hasn't sent a reply by the time I leave the flat. Nor has Hilary.

~

A narrow scarf the colour of blue glass is tied around Andrea's hairline, keeping her grey bob away from her face. Her smile is as sincere as I remember it, and her habit of taking a moment to look at me when she says hello.

We sit across from each other in boxy armchairs. She recaps our first meeting in the spring, before my operation, asking, 'How are you now?'

'Fine,' I tell her. 'I'm not sure I should be here – taking up your valuable time, without cancer.'

She is quiet after that statement. I don't know whether I'm supposed to continue, so I don't. A few seconds later, she speaks. 'You've alluded to an idea that you're inconveniencing me, though I agreed to see you. If it hadn't been suitable for you to come, I would have said.'

She stops speaking, leaving another space. It's not there for any reason, other than she'd said all she wanted to say. The conventions are different here. But I don't know what they are.

'Have you finished?' I ask. 'That came out wrong. I meant that you could point at me, maybe, or shake a small bell, when it's my turn.'

She's regarding me the way an adult gazes on a child absorbed in solitary play.

'The silences,' I tell her. 'I know they don't need to be filled

175

but it's tempting to fill them. Make stuff up, tell you I hear voices or shoplift, to justify being here.'

'Again, back to the idea that it's not okay for you to be here.'

In the quiet that follows, the point she is making hits home like a smart-bomb. I consider what's detonated in my awareness. I look at her. *Easy for you to say.* Being a survivor is troubling me and, hurrah, now I feel worse not better. *Just as well you don't charge for this racket.*

'What are you thinking about?' she asks.

'About how uncomfortable I'm feeling.'

'In what way?'

'If "being here", as you put it, seems to be a problem for me, what use is it to bring that up? If I knew what to do about it I'd be doing it already.'

My mouth is off on one. My mind wonders why I'm being so petulant. I *asked* to see her.

Andrea takes my nonsense in her stride. 'Describe for me what you mean when you call "being here" a problem.'

It's too late.

Her voice only reaches me in snatches, saying, 'remember to breathe' and 'take a breath, Rhona' but I am not in the same room as the voice. I'm in the swell of a film studio pool, battered and drowning in the storm generated by wind machines.

My crying must last a full minute. Noisy too. She gives me as long as I need to settle, tops up my water glass, asks, 'Can you share what was going on for you there?'

Still feeling disconnected, lacking in oxygen, I do my best. 'When you mention me being here, you say it like it's a given. Like it's something I can rely on; being here, being alive. But cancer's invisible. It's sneaky. The last year showed me that I can't rely on anything. Not health, not boyfriends. I'm not even sure if my friends are in it for the long haul.'

There they are, exposed: the contents of the near-to-bursting suitcase I've been sitting on.

Resting her pen on her notepad, Andrea says, 'In my experience, a lot of people are left with a similar fear, that if it happened once it can happen again.'

'So how do I get myself to believe that I've recovered?'

'Before we skip to the solution, maybe we could stay with the problem a little longer. Can you describe what you were feeling, when you were upset?'

It's my turn to take a moment till I'm ready to speak. I have to sidle around a resistance to revisit the wave pool. If I really don't want to, she won't make me, I know that. While I'm sitting here, I might as well try it her way.

I explain about thrashing around in a film set water-tank, in a fake storm. And the feeling that one big wave is on its way to swallow me.

'When people come to a therapist,' replies Andrea, 'thinking they need answers, they often have them already. They're just not looking from the right angle.'

'Say again?'

She continues, 'Stress and fear and feeling overwhelmed – those emotions start in response to a situation, or a trigger. Like having cancer. But then they can take on a life of their own. They're like the wind machines generating the storm. You can turn off the wind machines.'

I imagine myself back in the pool and someone flicking the off switch. In an instant, there's nothing to struggle against; the drama has dissipated.

'You mean I don't have to feel like that?'

'Correct. Bear in mind, no emotion is wrong. But you can ask yourself, "Does this feeling have anything valid to tell me, or is it a runaway train, a habit I've got into?" You can choose to turn off the hullabaloo and move into a more relaxed place.'

Andrea leaves an assimilation pause, before saying, 'You can *notice* what you're feeling. Observe it. And then choose what to do next. You can *choose* to have confidence in your recovery from cancer.'

I nod slowly in reply.

'Quite an empowering idea, isn't it?'

~

Hilary's response to my shopping invite comes days later, after I've made two trips to town and bought more than I intended.

Sorry! Crazy busy wknd. Ikea flat-packs and family dinners. Spk soon! X

No mention of my return to work tomorrow after six weeks off.

~

Opening the door to leave, I remember my phone is on the kitchen table. I fetch it, noticing I'm easily half an hour early. Enough time for a cheerio to the wee man.

From the living room doorway I can see the hedgehog he shares a bed with but not him. Sofa maybe? Nope. I return to the kitchen. Not there. Under the bed? No. By this time I'm calling his name, 'Cyril. Mr Cyrillus. Cyril-on-the-Wirral.' Until it dawns.

I am standing beside an un-latched front door . . . collecting

178

my mobile . . . how did I forget I had a kitten? Oh my God, oh my God. Has he gone out? Cyril has never been outside. Wee cats his age don't go outside!

I jog up and down the stone stairs as best I can in heels, calling his name, looking behind bikes and hoping no one is trying to sleep.

I can't see him. I can't see him. The idea that he's properly outside is too much. He could have gone under a car wheel already. And been scraped into a bag by a well-meaning driver. And disposed of. There will be no trace for me to find – I may never know what happened to Cyril.

At the main door I remember I have no keys. And that my flat door is lying open. I run upstairs berating myself: *now* I'm security conscious? *Now* I'm worried about my front door?

After collecting keys, I grab tins of tuna from the cupboard, pulling one open and leaving it in the flat, pulling the other open and leaving it in the stairwell. I toss the lids on the meter cupboard and head outside.

If I was a cat and I was small and I'd never been out before, where would I go: the wilderness and freedom of the communal garden or somewhere dark and safe, like under a parked car?

The name calling is resumed. I am frantic in my movements, erratic in my route and I don't know how long to linger in a place before I move on. What if I walk off just as Cyril's getting the confidence to come out from wherever he is? What if I stop here and he's getting further away by the second?

I keep rushing over to the main door to check inside the hallway in case he's found his way back. Why can't I be at the flat and out here looking at the same time? Why can't there be TWO of us doing this? Why is it ALWAYS JUST ME? All the time – ME! From the minute I wake up to the minute I go to bed, THERE I AM.

'WHERE THE HELL ARE YOU, CYR-IIIL!'

'Lost your granddad?'

I hear the voice but there's no one visible. I'm too busy for this. I don't have a granddad. I run down the main steps again to look in a different direction.

'Up here!' There's a head sticking out of a second floor window.

'Sorry,' I call out, 'I didn't mean to wake you, I'm looking for my cat. Sorry.'

On I go.

'Stop! I've got him here, I think, though he looks eighty years younger than his name.'

I jog up all the stairs.

'Oh Cyril! Cyril, Cyril!' I take him and squeeze him nearly too hard and kiss him and cry a bit, it just comes out, and hug him and sit down because I suddenly need to. Then I worry that I've embedded myself in a stranger's home, a complete stranger's day, and I stand to say thank you and goodbye. 'It was my own daft fault, leaving the door … Anyway, thank you so much. I won't keep you.'

'Don't rush, eh, if, you need to catch your breath. Is Cyril okay d'you think?'

'He's fine.' I hold the cat up. 'Very laid back wee thing, aren't you?' I say, to Cyril's unperturbed face. 'It's your mummy who's the loony, hm? Where on earth *were* you?'

'When I got here he was sharpening his claws on the doormat.'

'Sorry about that.'

'It's my sister's mat,' says the guy. 'I won't tell her if you don't.' His tone is conspiratorial. Kind of flirty. He continues, 'I'd passed the can of tuna on the stairs. Something told me I should bring him inside. And then I heard you shouting.'

'I looked everywhere,' I tell him, because I have to discharge the events by replaying them. 'He could have been miles away, I might—' I remember that I'm imposing. 'Anyway, mustn't hold you back any longer.'

'I've just got here. I'm keeping an eye on things. For Nickers. While she's away. Two weeks. Scripture Union holiday. Kid you not.'

He is offering unnecessary information, clipped on, to extend his talking time. And he's grinning like this is the best conversation two humans could hope to have. He's also mocking his sister, so that I'll know he's not in the God squad.

'I have to come and water her plants,' he says. ''cause ol' Jesus would smite me if I didn't bother. I was about to put the kettle on. You're welcome. To join me.'

What's taking place is a wholesome expression of interest. Which would be perfectly normal, except that I am no longer normal. My equipment is dodgy: healthy almonds, damaged pear. Is that not obvious? There *is* chemistry. Do I come across the same as I used to? What was excised: my womb neck not my womanhood?

'Oh Christ!' I blurt. 'Not Nickers' kind, the blasphemous kind. Work. I have work. First day back. Probably late! Excuse us.' The clip-on chat is catching. Dashing along his sister's hallway, I say, 'Thanks again for rescuing the munchkin.'

'Happy to be of help,' he replies, opening the door.

Entering the staff kitchen, Raymond quickly puts down the kettle and pulls out a chair for me. 'What're you having?' he asks. 'Let me get it. You have this one.' He sets a mug on the table. 'I'll make another one.'

'I'll get mine, it's no hassle.'

'Take it, I'm making another one already, see?'

He moves his body aside to give a clear view of the kettle being poured.

'Raymond, I couldn't drink from your special mug. Thank you, though.'

He picks it up, pleased with the busty policewoman whose uniform had disappeared when hot liquid was added.

'Everyone's being so nice,' I tell him. 'Would it be all right if we went back to normal?'

'Sure thing.' He pours the tea in the sink. 'Get your own damn tea.' He smiles. 'How's that? Better?'

'Fantastic.'

'What's fantastic?' asks Donald, coming in with his empty mug.

'Rhona was just saying she doesn't want any special treatment.'

Colour rises up Donald's jaw.

'Excuse me,' says Raymond. 'Calls to make.'

Donald depresses the kettle button. 'I'll be in Manchester from Wednesday till Friday. Bloody County Construction giving Ann-Marie grief every which way. Always the same, the self-made guys. Ask us for help and then they won't be told.'

Have you met yourself? Donald, allow me to introduce—

'You and I are due a catch-up,' he says, dropping his teabag in the bin.

'Yeah, my appraisal.'

'I haven't forgotten what we were going to discuss. Pencil it for a couple of weeks? Once you're settled in.'

~

Andrea asks how I've been. 'We explored some difficult feelings last time,' she says.

No kidding. 'I know you said I could look at my emotional responses, and choose a different one. Are you sure it's that easy? When I think about the time in hospital,' I explain, 'I feel overwhelmed again in seconds. And I'm no more convinced that the cancer won't come back.'

'Remember the breathing exercise we did before your operation,' she asks, 'to help reduce the stress?'

'Yes.'

'That's a portable tool. Practising it could help you to sit with those emotions – allow them to be there, without controlling or resisting. Because when you stop resisting them, they tend to fall away naturally.' She adds, 'You can't control life; only your reaction to it. If you create a space where you're okay just as you are, then it's safe to be aware of any feeling, as a compassionate witness.'

For the remainder of the session, Andrea's slow instructions lead me to a place of restful observation. Steadily, rhythmically, my breath renews itself; it expands to meet each moment.

This in breath.

This out breath.

This in breath.

This out breath.

She offers the suggestion that I can take any problem into that settled space and sit with it; move my breath inside it, become aware of how I want to respond to it. Next she moves me on to utilising out breaths to release feelings of worry or being overwhelmed.

When it's time to leave, I feel like a team of joiners has been round and built an extension on my mind.

How much use will I get out of it, I wonder?

~

Ambling from the train station to where Erin lives, the streets are very quiet except for the gardens, which scream OCD.

She greets me at her front door. 'You told me not to bring anything,' I say, 'so I just brought a teeny thing, for Mindy.' I lift a bubble-blowing kit from my pocket.

'Come through,' Erin says. 'We've been baking in your honour. Making up for not having seen you in weeks.' On a stool at the kitchen counter, Mindy licks cake mix from a wooden spoon. I wipe a splodge from her cheek, saying, 'Hi dolly, how are you? Been busy, I see.'

'I did all of the hard things,' she informs me. 'It's got chocolate chips.'

'Chocolate chips! My favourite. When will it be ready?'

'We can't eat the cake till *after* lunch!'

'That's right, silly me. We might have to eat lunch really fast then!'

'I eated my lunch already.'

'Cheater! Does that mean you get to eat cake *now*?'

'Noooo, it's in the oven!'

'What does the timer say?' Erin asks her.

'Three and three and two,' says Mindy.

'That's right. Three minutes and thirty-two seconds till the bing. We're going to decorate it, aren't we?'

'When it's cooool,' they say in unison.

While Erin puts dishes of food on the table, I explain to Mindy how to blow bubbles through the small oval on the end of the plastic wand. She starts to get frustrated because she 'can't do it'. I steal the bottle back and she squeaks and laughs as dozens of bubbles drift and burst.

'Have another go,' I say, handing back the kit. 'I bet you can do it by the time the cake is cold.'

'It could have bubble icing!' she laughs.

'Yum, soapy,' says Erin, turning the cake halves onto a rack. 'Sit,' she tells me, taking off her oven gloves. 'It's a pick-and-mix.'

'Looks delicious.'

We help ourselves to salads, cheeses and warm bread. Erin quizzes me on who I've seen. I mention Hilary and Gary – that I made them dinner a while ago. Cohabitation suits them, we decide. Erin says that Mindy is starting school next week then, more loudly, 'Aren't you, Amanda-May?'

Mindy wanders out the kitchen door, making effortful blowing noises.

'But she was only born ten minutes ago,' I say. 'School?'

'Fraid so.'

'You get your life back,' I pronounce. 'Bring it on! The advantage of having one.'

'Wasn't by design,' she says, pushing a large crimped leaf onto her fork. 'It just hasn't happened.'

'Oh, sorry, spot the idiot. I didn't realise.'

'Because it embarrasses us. James hates me mentioning it.'

'Only thirty-six, there's time yet,' I say, hoping she never shares her situation with Tania. (*They're such hard work! You're better off with one! Is it James? Is he sterile? Leave him! Take my sister's bloke when she's done with him!*)

The matter-of-fact statements of Mindy's talking book travel through from the other room:

a hard brick

a cold drink

'IVF?' I ask, 'Though it's none of my business.'

'Not yet. James is getting pushy about it and I'm stalling. It's my body that would be taking the brunt. All those hormones. No guarantees at the end of it.'

Erin explains the rigmarole her friends went through – bank loans, unsuccessful attempts, relationship at breaking point. 'Eventually, they took a holiday – a "goodbye to IVF" grieving trip – to make peace with not conceiving and move on.'

'That's hard.'

'I'll be letting Mindy know that young motherhood is a legit choice,' says Erin, 'Why not study or start a career at thirty, when your kids have started school? Wish I'd done it that way.'

'At least you know your equipment *can* work,' I tell her. 'Who knows if mine would hold up?'

Erin asks how I feel about what's happened. I exhale in a half-laugh, half-sigh. 'Not sure, really. It was upsetting to find out I might have problems staying pregnant. But I can't court too much sympathy. Having kids wasn't something I'd decided on.'

'Ever?'

'Hadn't decided *not* to. I just wasn't aching for it. I imagined it happening after a commitment from Mark. The next step. Starting a family. All that bollocks.' Aware of where I'm sitting, I add, 'No offence.'

'None taken – I'm not married, remember.'

"Course. Keep forgetting. You seem so ... *married*.'

'What're you trying to say?' She's smiling. 'More of a rebel than you give me credit for.' She pours water in our glasses. 'Suits us better; that we both stay, despite keeping it easier to leave. Means I need to have faith in James and his choice. Because if you don't trust that your partner wants to be with you, what's left?'

'What if being married was your deal breaker, d'you think James would have done it?'

'To make sure he'd held on to *me*?' Erin's laughing. 'I'd like to think so. But for the sake of making sure he'd had kids? 100%. He'd have married for that.'

Must be a nice feeling to carry around. 'I was never convinced Mark would've picked me, if I'd tested the marriage-or-bust scenario.'

A clutch of bubbles is rising around the doorframe.

'Quick, catch them!' I call out. 'Mindy can put them in her icing.'

~

For the rest of Saturday I don't leave my bed. I'm not sure what keeps me there. Something simply does.

~

Hilary and I sit on a bench by the river. Brunch is laid out

187

between us on the bags it came in: filled bagels, punnet of strawberries, coffee cups. It's a ritual on warm-weather Sundays and this is the first of the summer. We allow ourselves to be charmed by the squirrels, not mentioning that by the end of last summer they became just bloody annoying.

'Sorry I forgot the rug,' says Hilary.

'No problem. We can lie out next time.'

This section of the park is our halfway point, fifteen minutes' walk for each of us.

'I feel like I've hardly seen you,' she says, wiping at her mouth with a brown paper deli tissue.

'You haven't,' I confirm.

'How is it, being back at the office?'

'Work's the same. I think I might be different.' I toss a piece of tomato at a squirrel. It misses. 'Most mornings I could either cry with gratitude that I'm alive and able to work at all, or cry 'cause I might have died but was spared to be a glorified clerk.'

'Hang in there, Rhon. It's only been a week. You'll be firing contestants on *The Apprentice* in no time.'

'I was thinking more *The Secret Millionaire*. Changing lives. Doing something to make the world better.'

'You are a recovery cliché.'

Hilary is a cohabitation cliché, acquiring podge round the middle since her man moved in, but it's safer not to air that. I break a crust in two and give her a piece. We pinch bits off and fling them at scavengers.

'Where's Gary?' I ask.

'Probably getting up about now.'

'Phone him. It's too nice to be in bed.'

'He's got an interview to prepare for. Security manager for one of the unis. Fingers crossed.'

'Time for a change?'

'Standard nine-to-five hours. We thought we'd see more of each other when he moved in, but it's barely made a difference. Which might not matter if it was only the two of us ...'

Squirrels scatter in all directions when I leap from the bench and jump around. 'A bay-bee! A bay-bee!'

The reason we haven't seen much of each other lately becomes apparent. Halting in front of her, I ask, 'Were you worried about telling me?'

'Wasn't great timing, was it?'

'That's very considerate but you're a loony. It's a *baby*. It's the best news ever!'

'Thanks, Rhona. We can tell people now. I wanted to tell you first.'

I sit beside her to share a proper, squeeze-y hug. 'Holy moley. You're actually up-the-duff!'

~

Sunday afternoon and I don't phone anyone to find out what they're up to.

~

At the long postponed appraisal meeting, Donald tells me that he couldn't be happier with my performance. Also, that I'm under no obligation to take on extra responsibilities if recent events have caused me to feel differently.

I tell him recent events are exactly the reason I'm inter-ested in extra responsibilities. I change the word 'stagnating' to 'coasting' before I utter it. As in, why settle for more of the same? As in, I could have died man, make it worthwhile that I didn't.

I remind him how easily I execute my remit. Training as a management consultant is the natural next step. He says we should meet again to draft an employee development plan.

I say, in light of how busy he is, we could do that while we're here. I give him downloaded print-outs from the Federation of Business Consulting.

'They offer an introductory certificate in management consulting, all the way through to a diploma,' I say. 'Home study.'

Donald's thumb pushes paper clips into a pile. Then it picks at a sticker on the front of his diary. He says he won't sanction the diploma, not at this stage. After the introductory course, he'll arrange for me to shadow someone on a consultancy contract. He insists there's no substitute for real-world experience.

'Why not both?' I ask. 'Shadowing *and* diploma?'

'It's a big outlay, Rhona,' he says, worrying an ear hair. 'If a kid asks for a guitar, you book a few lessons and you hire an instrument. If they stick with it, *then* you buy the guitar, or the ice skates, or the unicycle.'

And like the child he compares me to, I leave the room thinking, *I'll show you, you mingy git – just see if I don't.*

The following day I accost him in the stairwell. 'Why not shadowing at the *same time* as I'm doing the introductory certificate?'

'Oh for God's sake,' he says. 'I'm in a hurry here.' *I ain't.*

'Maybe!' he puffs.

And I move out the way to let him past.

A substantial package arrives at the office. I lug it home with me, tearing at its seal on the subway to peek at the first pages.

Aims – to learn the following:
- **The business consultancy role.**
- **The client relationship.**

Show Donald he's a mingy git? Dear, sweet Rhona – not at this rate you won't. Donald, it turns out, knows a thing or two about children and their behaviour. I can't be in the same room as the management study materials.

Having set aside today for Unit One, thus far, the bed has been stripped, the duvet has been to the launderette, the box file in the hall cupboard now contains the paperwork which had amassed on the hall shelves, and all the curtains have been vacuumed with the right attachment.

I'm at the kitchen table with a well-deserved coffee while the big brown envelope waits in the living room.

Actually, Donald doesn't know diddly. This is an essential stage in the process. How can you start a new venture, a new *career*, before you've created the right conditions? To launch in before the time is right would be throwing away good money (which Donald would hate). The study course deserves my full attention and it can't get that till the clutter is gone.

My tablet was on the table when I sat down. I've been idly stroking the screen with my finger – have opened email on autopilot. The inbox appears, showing over 600 messages. Old messages. Clearing this lot will take the rest of the day! I go for the biscuit tin and leave it open on the table.

Tackling them in reverse order, I'm ruthless with the delete tab. *If I haven't looked at it in four years I'm not looking at it now.*

Coming across the dating emails from earlier in the year simultaneously turns my stomach and sparks my curiosity. Progress slows as I click in and out. Oh God, the ones from lechy Bill.i.am.

Re: Crossing the Glasgow-Edinburgh divide

Yup, we could meet up. Meeting up is something we could do. Day or evening suits me. I'm up-and-at-em early (as you can see) so 7am onwards suits fine . . . Early morning is my favourite time for it! LOL

And you haven't even told me what it is you do yet. When we meet up you can 'reveal all' . . . :o)!

For goodness' sake, there are different sites for that kind of dating. And why do web men keep telling me to Laugh Out Loud? If a comment is funny, I'll laugh. If you have to flag up that a comment is funny . . .

Rereading the mails from FerrisBuellerSenior I chuckle without prompting. How would he respond to a reply that's months overdue?

Ten

Re: Re: Mrs F Bueller

Well . . . I don't want to be the one to step out of character, but it wouldn't be right to make an apology as a persona. It has been a while. Apologies. Okay to explain?

Feeble and inadequate reason for going silent – work got hectic. Took on extra duties and totally lost track of social life. Sorry!

I found your emails today during an inbox clearing mission, and couldn't bring myself to press delete. So I've done a little research, and the CatchMe website shows your profile has been active in the last fortnight. Maybe you're still open to missives from strange women, especially if they're grovelsome?

Donald is telling me about a family-run whisky firm which has contracted Muffin Consulting. The patriarch died last year and his surviving wife, Mrs Lennox, has the sense to act at the early signs of trouble. Muffin will be steering a company review and restructuring, starting with the management team.

Donald's just returned from White Cairn's headquarters, a ninety-minute drive from Glasgow, and says he'll be very involved in seeing this one through but Petra will be the lead consultant. Apparently, a woman's 'natural strengths' are required because family business problems are as much to do with relationship dynamics as bottom lines. On that basis, he's decided it can be a starter project for me.

Petra's been told about the shadowing arrangement and my first task is to speak to her about how she prepared the bid to win the contract. When I ask her about it, en route to my desk, she says, 'First, I did a business degree at Strathclyde Uni—'

'Me too!'

'—graduating with a first. Then got an MBA from London Business School and spent several years building my career. *Then*, I contacted Scottish Enterprise, the Mitchell Library, the Scottish Government, the DTI and the Scotch Whisky Association and found out everything I could about the industry – what factors are affecting it, who is doing well, who is struggling, why so. Then I reread my degree notes on family-owned businesses. I learned everybody's names before I met them, shook their hands, presented perfectly, proposed clear means to pinpoint their issues and, finally, I sat down and answered all their questions.'

Throughout her reply she'd kept her eyes on her screen. She opens a drawer to the right of her desk.

'*This* is my file of background material and *this* is the actual document we presented. Other information is in the White Cairn folder in the shared drive. Easiest thing would be to read these and ask me anything you don't understand.'

'Will do. Thanks. I'm looking forward to being involved.' She's facing her screen again. I inject obvious humour into my voice. 'I've done the first assignment for my introductory course, so, all primed and ready to go!'

I'm nodding to the power differential, as in, 'we both know it's there, but it doesn't have to get in the way'. Petra doesn't have the manners to feign amusement. Or turn and acknowledge my existence.

Exclusion. Bitchy game-playing. Also a woman's 'natural strengths'. In my attempt to warm relations, Petra's positioned me as an amateurish twit playing at grown-ups.

～

I grovelled. Tania would never have grovelled. That's why he didn't reply.

～

Petra drives us to Loch Och. Donald sits next to her conducting a mobile call. And I, who never learned to drive, sit in the back belted in, like an amateurish twit playing at grown-ups.

My index fingernail drags over the upholstery weave. It taps on the ringbinder by my thigh. I observe Petra observing the road ahead. Leaning forward, I extend far enough through the gap that she'll be able to hear me above Donald's deep-bucket voice box. 'What's the thrust of today's visit?' I ask her. 'What are you hoping to come away with?'

Thrust? Come away with?

'How d'you mean?' says Petra.

'Em, just, what is the main focus for the meeting, today?'

'I'm not clear what you're asking. Are you meaning *in addition* to what's in the briefing papers beside you?'

She's saying, why are you bothering me? She's saying, why are you so irrelevant? But the point of my question was not to have it answered. The point was to enter White Cairn's headquarters with a connection, a rapport.

The receptionist walks us to the original section of the building along a narrow stone corridor. He knocks on a door marked 'Boardroom'. It's opened by Mrs Lennox. There are hellos and handshakes. 'I'm here learning the ropes,' I tell her, to explain my presence.

'Rhona,' Donald jumps in, 'has been with us for a year and is developing her remit from Office Manager to Consultant. She has a business degree and many years of corporate experience.'

So that's how it's done, when you take yourself seriously. 'Rhona is undertaking her FBC training,' he clarifies, 'and she's keen to contribute to this project under Petra's guidance. And mine. I trust that's acceptable.'

'How exciting for you,' says Mrs Lennox, turning my way. 'We're honoured to be your first case! This is my first time hiring consultants, so we can learn together.'

'Where would you like us?' Petra interjects.

'Same as last time?' Mrs Lennox says, pointing to where the projector emerges from the mahogany. 'The others will be here by eleven.'

While Petra readies her laptop, Mrs Lennox asks if I've been briefed. 'Got the necessary background on us?' she inquires, her expression as soft as her scent.

The potential to answer this incorrectly shorts the electrics in my head. My response is a tremulous grin.

'It wasn't a trick question!' She touches my arm.

'Ha, mm, Donald explained that White Cairn is seeking Muffin's assistance to lead a company review and restructuring,' I say. 'From what I've been reading about the industry, I think you've chosen the right time. The market is there but the customer base is changing, globally, and the excise duty issue – that's an injustice you have to work with until policy on alcohol taxation is brought into this century.'

She's nodding. She speaks, 'It's worth emphasising that the board members are on side. They are as convinced by the timing for consultancy input as I am.' She takes my forearm and a step closer. 'There are other relevant factors, shall we say. And I don't think Muffin can do its job properly without full knowledge. But if the family thought I was discussing its business out of turn, so help me.'

I don't want to encourage inappropriate disclosures. I don't want it to look like I leant on a defenceless old dear. Distract, distract. 'Tea?' I suggest, noticing the tray on the sideboard.

'Absolutely,' she says. 'We'll get comfortable then I can fill you in.'

Marrying Ian Lennox over fifty years ago, she worked beside him to keep the business alive, defending it against wastrel siblings, grasping spouses, cheap imports, dying rural communities and recession after recession. As the mother of the next generation of Lennoxs, she feels entitled to steer White Cairn as if she were blood.

I resist leaping to my feet in a standing ovation.

In the last ten years, she tells us, Mr Lennox, MBE, tried to take more of a backseat but he could never let go completely. Donald is nodding, with 'seen it all before' sagacity.

Ian had wanted to retire so he and his wife could enjoy their remaining time together but his children couldn't be left to their own devices. 'They do their jobs well enough,' she explains, 'but they aren't able to talk properly, not about anything difficult. Maybe they were never left alone to learn how. I'm starting this process while I have their respect and have the energy,' she says. 'If I didn't keep working, I'd become the grieving widow. And we can't have that.'

There's no satisfactory way to respond because other board members have started milling in. I try to catch her eye to offer a smile, in case she regrets her one-way revelations, but she's pouring tea for the arrivals.

When it starts, Petra's presentation feels like an accidental lean on the remote – switching to the Parliament channel while watching *Gone with the Wind*.

~

It's nowhere near dark when we return to the city at six o'clock but I have a winter-like urge to get home and get cosy.

I eat the quickest thing I can make, an omelette, and take off my corporate clothes. I'm on the couch by eight, with my tablet. I order another all-natural moisturiser, having culled my home of chemicals after the health scare. What's happening in the news? What's happening on Instagram? On email?

There, at the top of the list, sits **Re: Re: Re: Mrs F Bueller**. He's replied.

He's replied!

Oh ... unless it's an angry piece of his mind about how dare I wait ages then think it would be fine to pick up the conversation.

It's too late in the day to be shouted at. I'd wait till tomorrow to open that kind of email.

But I don't know whether it is that kind of mail. It could be a lovely message. I'm prepared to risk a bollocking to find out. I click on it. The message starts to open then immediately closes. What—?

I click on the internet icon and a small box appears saying a connection cannot be established. I close it. I click again. Same message. What? Why??

I seek out the router box with its row of lights. Two are flashing. I've no idea if flashing means everything's good, or if it means faulty. And there's zero hope of laying hands on an instruction manual.

I haven't synched any email accounts to my phone either because, well, if I ever lost a job for missing an email during the hours I wasn't being paid to check it, I'd have been glad to leave.

Heading out of the downstairs door, an orange light is twirling on the roof of a utility van twenty yards up the street. Probably knocked a cable near whatever they're fixing.

Re: Re: Re: Mrs F Bueller

Supplicate no more, maiden. Women disappear mid conversation on a regular basis in my experience (and not just online).

Though I've never had anyone get back in touch to apologise for it! For the sheer novelty value, I'm having to reply. Your politeness redeems any earlier rudeness.

Mrs F-rustrated Bueller

Well, it's kind of you not to mind but karma has other ideas. I've been punished this evening by enduring a trial to pick up your message . . .

Got into my PJs after dinner then my broadband went on the blink. I've had to come to an internet café wearing 'square mum from a detergent advert' clothes I pulled on to leave the house (shapeless denims, running shoes, stripey sweatshirt).

But if it makes the picture more appealing, I don't have any knickers on (I just said that to a complete stranger? Dearie me) (though it is my wedding night I suppose . . .)

Ahem, ok, back in character.

Tell me, Ferris, how's our honeymoon? Are we having a nice time?

I surf the net, waiting to see if he'll reply before my cup is empty. My mobile rings. 'I tried you at home,' says Tania, 'Where are you?'

'In a café.'

'Can you talk?'

'Depends, are you going to be on long?'

'What sort of question's that? You're havering 'cause the lonely café geeks can hear what you're saying. Go home, yeah, and phone me.' She disconnects.

Her desire to chat could be the regular, 'I'm bored and

I need you to listen to me' but I sense something more specific.

The Eastern Mediterranean deli beside the café is just closing. The proprietor leans his mop against the wall to sell me dolmas for half price. I'm cross-legged at my coffee table eating stuffed vine leaves from their tub when Tania rings.

'You know how you talked me into giving up my job a couple of months ago,' she says, 'even though I wasn't sure?'

I *knew* it.

'Well, I'm glad you did because it gave me the courage to follow my purpose. I had to tell you first – I'm doing the mad-dash derby!'

'Is that like a vintage car rally across Europe?'

'No! Might not be a bad way to meet fit men, though. Let me write that down. Car rally ...'

'Tan?'

'Sorry, yeah, the mad dash. You know, like my sister did. I'm going to have a baby!'

'*Wha* – hey, wow, you hadn't told us you'd met someone.'

'I haven't. But I want a baby before it's too late, or I'm too knackered, or I need clinics or whatever.'

That was your solution to not liking your job? I hold my tongue. The post-cancer benchmark: does it really matter if Tania suddenly wants to be a mum? No. There's no room for me to speak, anyway.

'When I say, like my sister,' she continues, 'I mean the baby part, not the gauche bloke and the ring part. I don't need to take a man down in pursuit of my goal. Sperm only, thanks very much.'

'A little extra this Christmas from the Winter Boyfriend.'

'God no. No strings. It'll be a one-night job.'

'Have you heard of mother-to-infant STDs?'

'I'm not going for a skanky shagger who's slept with everyone.' – *Isn't that what you're about to do?* – 'I'm thinking younger. Eighteen, maybe seventeen, somewhere remote. Untainted. I get uber sperm for my last-gasp eggs and he gets an older woman conquest to brag about.'

'And your child gets a beautiful "who's my daddy?" story. What'll you tell it when it's old enough?'

'You'll think of something. What else is a godmother for?'

〜

I walk between the kitchen and the living room, forgetting again why I'm making the journey because, honestly, I'm livid. I can't work out why I'm livid. Fuming. I could do damage.

Why've they pegged me as the obvious first choice to share baby news with? Are they insane? Do they give it any thought at all?

The rage goes with me to bed, where I'm awake and loudly tearful. Cyril is deep asleep against my shin.

Have the women I know got nothing else agitating them? Suddenly I can't find anyone who isn't obsessed with having a baby. *Tania* for God's sake! It's like listening to a bunch of friends who've all come back from the same holiday that you weren't on and, what's more, you don't have a valid passport.

I want them to be happy. Also, I want them to retain a full range of conversation topics.

Decision: internet dating is moving on a stage because men have more to talk about.

The tearful insomnia is followed by the arrival of beetroot day. Let's hope it's gone again in four or five. Normal-length periods are a thing I recall with fondness.

~

Mrs Foxy Bueller

Ah my nymph of the no knickers, so many surprises on our wedding night. I know you could see it in my face.

The silhouette of your ample nether regions, gently wedged in the en-suite doorway, your bandy legs echoing your womanly curves. The only sound, the gentle pinging of elastic from your support garments.

The good doctor says there's no reason why I should lose the eye.

Yours now and always, Mr B.

Marital Bliss

As I look into your lone, bloodshot eye over the dinner table for the next 50 years I will have the memory of those magical nights in the Scunthorpe B&B to sustain me. No matter that the Thomas-the-Tank-Engine light fitting didn't hold our weight. What we discover about our compatibility, day by day, never ceases to amaze me. It's minute upon minute of bliss.

Well, 99% of the time.

Oh darling. I don't want to nitpick. If I could find a way not to I would, but I'm helpless in the face of my gender programming. As you know, it is the duty of every wife to start finding fault within a week of her wedding day.

I couldn't ask for a better husband, but in our haste to wed (oh and we did the right thing!) we seem to have foregone the courting period. All those early days memories we don't have – talking in cafés and other crazy acts of romantic abandon.

Am I imagining it? Or perhaps you're feeling it too? Is there a solution to this, hero-of-the-hour? No one ever said marriage was easy . . .

Re: Marital Bliss

Flopsy.

Your concern has sent me betwixt and betwither. Should I have raised this before now? Allow me to clear the worries from your vacant little head so that it may fill again with whimsical musings of flowers and scents, laughter and innocence, stew and dumplings. Oh, I can't keep this up much longer! How's your diary?

Your love trumpet,

Gus

Re: Re: Marital Bliss

Well, hello

Are you really Gus? Then I am really Rhona, who spends Saturdays with a management consulting home study course (us modern wives will insist on keeping our jobs!)

You free for coffee Sunday?

R

Re: Re: Re: Marital Bliss

Hi Rhona,

So you weren't making it up about having extra duties at the office.

I'm taking my profile offline (it was only up there to find a wife). You can email via the private entrance: Fergus.Harrison@col.com

Sunday's out. And Saturday night I'm at a charity ball, an office outing . . . wanna go to a ball?

By the way, it's great this married lark isn't it?

G

~

What business consultancy is:
- **How can the consultancy role be defined?**
- **What are the risks and pitfalls?**

Nope, it's no use. My swotting is done for. I spend Saturday knowing I *shall* go to the ball. Adding to the excitement, my period stopped on schedule.

~

Gus said he'd text when he was in my street. At seven sharp, he does.

Ur carriage awaits, Madam

I hoist my hem away from my heels on the stairs. On the front steps, I scan the street for my carriage – a black cab double-parked, idling. None.

Checking my phone, to find out where he's waiting, I hear my name. A head is craning out the window of a toty half-car, the kind driven by women on their first pay packets, or students. Inside is a grown man, six foot if he's an inch. Wrong and faintly depressing, like carpet in a kitchen.

A heaving surge in my belly – *what are you putting yourself through, and this guy, too? What are you chasing? Let things find you, take them on gradually. A life is supposed to be built from solid things and constants.*

I don't know what I'm doing. This isn't what I want. I don't know what this is.

The passenger door sits open.

And because I can't bring myself to birl on my heel and return upstairs, I swallow back the existential bile and instead, laugh. I don't have the first clue how to make a new life, but I'm alive. No one who knows me knows where I am at this moment. I'm ridiculous, just like him. Crazy or brave.

He's smiling and so am I, but not for the reasons he thinks I am.

~

'His *landline* number?' Erin fist bumps, in a gesture of respect. 'You must give good first date, Beech.'

'It was a free bar.'

'It's a compliment, Rhona. He likes you. Take a moment to let that sink in before you throw him away for not being Mark.'

Erin sips at milky coffee while I fill her in on last night – how funny Gus was, how there was nothing at all wrong with him but I have no idea if I fancy him. None whatsoever. Even having to think about whether I do, or whether I could, blows the fuse on my ability to fancy at all.

When two people hook up by traditional means, it's because

they found themselves in each other's company (in a bar, at a party, in the workplace) and having encountered each other (once, or several times) they became aware of an attraction. Steps were taken to do something about it (tentatively, with gusto, or with chess moves and guesswork).

In contrast, meeting online happens in contrived conditions. In that gauzy, exhausting world, the natural process of being attracted into one another's orbit is circumvented because you arrange to meet *to see if you are* attracted (a brain process, not a body one). I can't speak for the dates but I know I sat there wondering, *Am I feeling a spark or not?* Followed by, *Okay, no instant spark – how many times will we need to meet to see if a spark is possible?*

Ugh. Forcing it. Heeby-jeebies. Not for me. I'd rather be caught unawares. 'It feels like my head is part of a process that should be instinctive,' I say.

'What age are you?' she asks.

'Huh?'

'You sound about sixteen. A relationship might start with lust, Rhona, but that is only part of the picture. Do you even know what it is you want?'

'Huh?'

'Where did you get this idea that your head shouldn't be involved when you meet someone? That's *absolutely* when you need your head. Otherwise you'd go throwing yourself into any physical attraction that came your way. It's great when the chemistry is there, but do you both want similar things? Are you prepared to fight for the same things and let the same things go?'

I imagine Erin's first date with James. Jolly times ...

'Surely it has to *feel* right,' I assert, feebly. 'Like fate has brought you together with the right person at the right time.'

Erin regards me with an expression I've not seen before.

'Rhona, you bring *yourself* together with the right person by knowing what's important to you and sussing out if the guy you've met fits with that.' She continues, 'It's not fate, it's not rocket science – you end up with the right person by not settling for the wrong person.'

And the joy of losing track of time while riding my bike is decimated by learning that I will be sent to bed early for it, because how else will I learn about timekeeping?

Erin McKay's common sense guide to relationships.

Ugh. More heeby-jeebies.

—

Lipari (off Sicily)

Rhonata,

Check it out! I've gone all nostalgic for postcards – did you know they use up more time than texting?

Need to rethink the mad dash strategy … I booked this trip weeks ago, but then my period came late and I've still bloody got it. Could changing my diet have knocked my cycle out? (Goddamn oily fish. Goddamn fruit and veg.)

My first tadpole collecting trip. Like a Victorian botanist. Except I'm bored, barren and can't even get drunk – the chi therapist said vodka would shrivel my ova (is that my eggs?). Three more days of this. From now on, I'm booking at the last minute and staying four days max.

Sobriety plus solitude equals inner circle of hell (make it stop! Ferma! Ferma!)

No Pacino-Garcia sprog for me.
Love Tan (with tan).

Italy looks nice! I text her. **U home yet? PS – did you get tested before you went? That STD thing goes both ways. Spare a thought for the innocent lads of Europe . . .**

~

I sit up front next to Petra, with the nagging sense I've forgotten my booster seat.

'I don't know what it says about interviewing clients in your correspondence course,' she says, 'but there's an art to it.'

I try to remember the course material but my mind is blank under pressure.

'It's more effective for one person to conduct the in-depth interviews,' she continues. 'Emerging themes are easier to spot. When we take questionnaires to the warehouse floor, you can run through a couple. Until then, watch and learn, Rhona. Watch and learn.'

She really does say that.

Glancing inside the folder at today's itinerary, it's full. Every hour, on the hour, Petra has an interview scheduled with a member of the management team. I will hover close by while she interrogates: Mrs Lennox, both her sons, one of her nephews, a niece, the eldest Lennox granddaughter, and the husband of her only daughter (an at-home mum with an equal shareholding).

When we arrive, Margaret Lennox asks us not to narrow our focus. 'Let them ramble. We don't want to miss anything important.'

Petra reveals her teeth; her version of a smile. 'We'll cover as much as we can in the hour available,' Petra says. 'Talking of which.' She looks at her watch.

'It occurs to me,' says Margaret, 'that if you and Rhona divide the interviews, that allows *two* hours with each of us.'

'The sche—'

'No one ever learned anything by watching. I certainly didn't. Rhona, you can interview me.'

This turn of events is not my doing but I will pay for it.

Petra hasn't moved.

'I'm sure Rhona will manage,' says Mrs Lennox. 'Ask Lauren across the hall to photocopy any paperwork we might need.'

Eleven

Starting up the front path I can hear their voices so I bypass the front door and go to the side gate, where I can knock and be let through. Getting closer, I make out my dad's voice, saying, 'She's fine.'

'If she's fine why's she coming here?' Mum says. 'On a Saturday?'

Through the wooden slats I see her bang something down on the wrought iron table on the patio. Several birdfeeders are lined up beside a hefty bag of seed mix.

'What *time* did she say?' asks my mum (in a voice more suited to the news that all flights out of a disaster zone are about to be cancelled).

'She said she'd phone from the station when she wanted picked up,' he tells her.

'Will she be wanting lunch?'

'Does it matter?'

'I don't know if I've got enough in!' she fires back, then states, 'Ask her straight out, when she's here. She's not to leave today without you asking.'

'Asking what?'

'If she's all right. Why else would she be coming here? On a Saturday morning? Just be matter-of-fact about it. "Do you have secondaries?" That's all you need to say.'

My dad exhales and tells her not to be so daft, adding, 'If something like that was going on, Rhona would have told us.'

'You think so? She didn't speak at all the last time. Not one word.' My mum has started to weep. 'Oh I can't bear it, I–I could not go through all that again.'

My dad puts his arm around his wife's shoulders and with his free hand, he wipes below his right eye.

'She's fine,' he tells her, gently. 'Maybe she just wants some company.'

'Oh Phillip!' My mum is wailing now and he probably doesn't realise why, but I do. A lonely daughter is worse than a cancerous one. *Thirty-five years old and no husband,* she is thinking. *Where did we go wrong?*

~

'Toast's burning,' says Hilary. She is pouring tea and doesn't see my hands laden with items from the fridge: butter, cheese, jam, milk.

'I know,' I say, 'I can smell it. I'm not . . .' I stop, unable to finish. 'What's it called when you don't have a sense of smell?' I ask, as she's pulling the tray away from the grill.

'Em . . .'

'I was going to do that sarcasm thing,' I explain, 'when people get something pointed out to them that they already know. "I can see it, I'm not *blind*", "I can hear it, I'm not *deaf*".'

Hilary is doing a very good impression of being deaf.

'I can smell it,' I continue, 'I'm not ... without a sense of smell. I've no idea what the word for that is. Smeaf?'

Hilary finishes putting Marmite on her first slice and begins putting jam on her second. I suspect she'd be putting both on the same slice if I wasn't here.

'Hil ... there's no word for not being able to smell is there?'

'Or taste, that I can think of,' she says, taking her plate and mug with her into the hallway.

When I go through, she's cosied-up on the settee: mug, plate, bump. I arrange myself into a shape that fits the remaining space. We stare and crunch as the programme comes on. In the absence of anything better, we're watching a documentary called *Insanely Talented*, about famous people who were also criminally insane.

When anything graphic is shown, I reach my hand across to cover the bump's eyes. At the advert break, Hilary asks, 'Enough?'

'Yup.'

'Taxi time?'

I carry the plates to the kitchen and phone a cab, knowing it'll take longer to arrive on a Saturday night. The kitchen window faces the street. Hilary sits with me while I wash up.

'Getting dropped off at Trampoline?' she asks – a joke which amuses her every Saturday.

'Of course,' I reply. 'You're just jealous you can't come too.'

'Say "Hi" to the handsome bouncer for me.'

'Will do,' I reply, breaking into some moves, 'if I'm off the dance floor long enough.'

Her giggle rings off the high ceiling and hard surfaces.

'You *should* go one weekend, Rhona. Go with Tania. Have fun. I'm fine on my own when Gary's working.'

'I know you are. But isn't it nicer having me? Anyway, Tania's ... busy.' I lean down to hug her shoulders. 'If I wasn't watching telly at yours, I'd be watching telly at mine. I've no urge to be out.'

'What's happened to the Rhona zing?' Then (à la Marcel Marceau) she opens my bag and looks inside, shrugs, then lifts the edge of the tablecloth and looks under that, shrugging again in defeated amazement.

'Je ne sais pas,' I tell her. 'C'est un mystère.'

'Are you still tired?' she asks. 'A wee bit? You seem well. A few months ago you were skinny as a dog's wet leg but now you just look normal.'

I take up a Marcel Marceau shovel and make the action of digging a hole.

'Healthy, I mean,' she says, laughing. 'Like your old self. Beautiful. Gorgeous! STUN–NING!'

At that, I stop and rest on the handle, smiling.

Hilary adds, 'Doesn't the, um, experience, make you want to go out and grab life? Say yes to it all? Be a Secret Millionaire *and* a social glutton?'

Do I have to play a role for everyone? Can't I just be Rhona, who got better?

I answer her, 'Perhaps life isn't remarkable because of the stuff we spend our time doing. Perhaps life itself is remarkable.'

Hilary lays a palm on the rise of her abdomen.

I can present evidence of my aliveness, if that's what it takes. 'You're forgetting, I took a punt on a stranger and went to a ball. And I'm doing my consultancy course. That's excitement enough for me,' I offer, almost grasping the truth of the statement as I'm saying it.

～

The car drives slowly up the street you think the party's on and then slowly back along the other way. The driver shouts at you all to, 'Shut it!' and you do; rolling the windows down and staring hard at the passing flats as if your eyesight can enhance your hearing.

You don't want what will be said next to be said because you can't get the mood back once you've killed it. But of course someone's going to. 'We're not gonna find it.'

Nooooo! 'We'll find it, we will.' You know how close you are.

But your certainty's being sucked from under, like sand at the tideline. Face it, you won't be going to a party.

You think it might end you, to assimilate this disappointment into your unfulfilling existence. The following night, you run into some folk in the video shop; people from the other car, who had the address. You ask how it was and they say it was shit. So shit they only stayed an hour. You smile. God does like you. He was doing you a favour.

As sure as this fiver needs to last till Friday, there'll be other parties.

～

It's less frenetic on the inside of the pavement, away from the hasty weaving of commuters. I saunter in defiance of how much these partners and parents are needed some-where else.

I pass the glazed front of a wine bar with plenty of people inside. Thursday is nearly Friday, after all.

At a window table, a couple holds aloft colourful drinks in a cheers pose. They look like the over-the-top cocktails we order when someone from the office has a birthday … being held by Petra and Raymond.

I walk on before they glimpse the uninvited. Must be Petra who's celebrating. She's from the breed of woman who will stop making eye contact with you for days at a time, with no reason given, letting you know she's taken against you that week, or is actively scheming behind your back. One who feels no compunction about making her target's day unpleasant. Doles out nastiness as if it's acceptable, everyday currency. As long as she's winning, who cares? Believes that everyone was born to jig to her tune, and doesn't know how to sacrifice for someone else (unless there's something in it for her; praise for her efforts or her well-turned-out children).

I've moved around enough to know that every office has an un-sisterly conniver and, if you're unlucky, a whole pack. Their antics can be amusing to watch (controlling every interaction with the turn of a mood), as can their outfits – too glam for work wear and textbook on-trend.

Raymond is harmless enough, he turns up every day for the mortgage payments. Petra's in it because of her high-achieving, heart-of-Teflon, hurt-soul, pathological competitiveness.

What am I in it for?

~

Rhona,

An email from Turkey, so you know where I am.
Sensible. See? I'm thinking like a mum already.

Spent the last two days steeped in hot, blue,
geothermal pools . . . completely alone.

Got this deal to Pamukkale, then headed off to a
remote town for the 'mission(ary)'. Took me a while to
realise that the commotion at the marketplace wasn't
over a bargain on a stall – they were freaking out about
my exposed knees and arms. I got the first bus back to
civilisation.

An escape plan is hatching. Meanwhile I'll console
myself with how beneficial the hot springs must be
for my reproductive organs. Mineral therapy is like a
detox, right? Wherever I end up next I'll be ripe for
impregnation!

Lots of love,

Tan

PS eh, DUH! to your testing question.

~

The woman ahead of me has her hood up but I know who she
is. I recognise her jacket and the horsey gait is a giveaway (a
side effect of long, strong legs). I jog a few steps to catch up.

'Hey!' I say, clasping her by the shoulders.

Her torso jerks free as she lets out a yelp. Lashing her arm
out behind, it lands on my breastbone and she rushes away –
at some speed for a pregnant lady. I pick up my pace, calling
after her, 'Hilary! Hilary!'

Stopping by the railing of the monument, she turns to face me. She swipes her hood from her head. 'For God's sake, Rhona!' Her eyes transmit rage. It knocks me off kilter to see a face that usually loves me, not loving me.

'I thought you were about to attack me!'

Will you like me again if I make you laugh? 'Of course I wasn't going to attack you,' I say. 'I was only after your purse.'

'What a bloody fright!'

'Sorry if I scared you. I got excited when I noticed it was you.' It had felt like a double bonus – running into Hilary on a trip out of the office. Her eyes haven't mellowed. In fact, they look raw with tiredness.

'What are you doing here?' she asks.

'Stalking you.'

My humour's impaled on the railings. There's an agitation to Hilary's features and she's not speaking . . . Oh. My intuition was a step ahead. Apparently I uttered what she was thinking.

I give her the real explanation before I have time to decide whether I should bother. 'I'm taking a scenic route back from the dentist. A drizzly park is better than the bus. Wet jackets and wet windows.' I shudder.

Wilfully neglecting her side of the conversation, she pulls her hood on and makes a show of adjusting it to keep the rain out.

'Got time for a quick coffee?' I ask.

If she'd answered straight away I'd have believed her. But it takes her a moment to think of something.

'Gary's mum's coming round after work. She's buying us the pushchair. We're going to browse online.'

'No worries,' I say.

Hilary manages her first smile, the straight-line kind.

'Saturday night?' I ask her. 'We could have a Netflix binge. Anything you've been wanting to see?'

She's already in motion. 'I have to get going,' she says.

If it wasn't the first time it had happened, it might be easier to absorb: Hilary has given me the brush off.

~

Rhona,

Fertility window was still ajar so flew straight to somewhere less sunny, to prevent premature wrinkles (I'll be a geriatric mum but have no plans to look like one).

Chi therapist has recommended avocados for my insides and outsides, and also ... something else ... nope, can't remember.

Have landed in Jersey to discover that all the guys look so British. Visualise 'man from the Boden catalogue'. OK, perhaps not that repellent but still, I had my heart set on an exotic babbie.

Lonely love,

Tan

~

Margaret Lennox telephones Petra to say that dishing out questionnaires to production employees was dehumanising. Raymond and I attempt to look occupied with our work. Having started the call on speakerphone, Petra is too embarrassed to take it off now.

We hear Mrs Lennox saying that her distillery floor isn't the high street on a Saturday and her workers deserved proper interviews. To her credit, Petra was able to explain that paper capture does have advantages. 'Workers with less influence can feel empowered by anonymity and often express more freely than they would in person.' Petra estimates the cost of interviewing a hundred staff. There is a lull from the speaker.

'We need to meet at least some staff from that section,' says Margaret. 'The impression given so far of "us" and "them" is awful.'

'You're quite right, you're quite right,' she says to Margaret, with a shaking head that says anything but. The agreed solution is focus groups, which should allow us to meet forty per cent of the workforce face-to-face.

This'll be one long week, I think, in the passenger seat the following Monday. How wrong I am. If day one is anything to go by, the next few will be a delight.

Opening the door to the first arrival, Petra greets him, saying, 'I won't tell you my name. Don't say what yours is! I'm meeting you all for the first time. We'll wait till everyone's here to do names.'

The guy looks confused but goes along with it and makes his way to a seat. 'Whatever you say, Petra,' he mumbles.

She looks amazed, like he might actually be psychic.

'It's there on the PowerPoint.'

She flicks the projector off, angrily, on her way to answer the door. 'Don't tell me your name!' she says, ushering in the next employee. 'We're doing that bit together 'cause it's a new group. I won't say who I am, we'll wait for everyone.'

To say the guy adopts a puzzled expression is putting it

politely. She offers him tea. Picking up the milk jug, she asks, 'How much for you? Just a little? More?' He isn't answering so she says, 'I'll give you a Petra measure, shall I?'

Doh!

She should be letting me do the tea or the door (or the introductions) but she's insisting on doing them all, to remind me that it's *her* focus group. When the door is tapped again she opens it fully. 'Come in, hi, I'm Petra.'

Is it wrong of me to enjoy it this much?

~

By Saturday afternoon, I haven't heard from Hilary. She answers on the second ring. 'Hiya,' I say.

'Rhona. I was expecting it to be my mum.'

And if you'd known it was me, you wouldn't have answered?

'I'm just seeing if you need anything brought round. I could get it while I'm out.'

'We did a big shop this morning,' she says. 'Gary was off last night.'

'Sly sickie?'

'No. He's trained a couple more shift-leaders, to split the weekends. The new owner at Trampoline is on top of the family-friendly stuff.'

'Nice change for you.'

'A day job would be better. He is looking, though.'

'I won't chat long. When's good? Seven thirty?'

'I'm shattered, to be honest. Haven't stopped all week. Probably be in bed by nine.'

Like a Saturday prime-time Gladiator with a gigantic cotton bud, she has rebuffed me. 'That's early!'

'It's pretty normal for me these days.'

'You could tell the truth, Hil.'

She says nothing, while she decides whether to. 'Truth about?'

'You're not going to bed at nine,' I assert. 'You just don't want me to come round.'

'I'm in bed at that time quite a lot,' she says, and I can hear she's losing patience but I don't care, because I'm right.

'Except on Saturday nights,' she continues, 'because you come over and keep me up till eleven so I'm wiped on a Sunday.'

'How do I keep you up?' I squeak. 'It's always me who suggests phoning a taxi.'

'What am I supposed to do? Turn round at eight thirty and say, "Still here?"'

'Is it that much of a chore to see me?'

'Every Saturday night it is, yeah.'

I've never heard Hilary speak to anyone like this. I hate that it's happening with me. 'I thought you liked the company,' I say, blindly, 'while Gary's out.'

'Sometimes,' she says. 'But maybe not as much as you do,' she adds, with sleeves-up roughness.

Who is this? We're on the same team, aren't we? 'What's that supposed to mean?' I demand. But I don't want her to answer. I want this conversation to stop.

'I'm saying, I can't be your whole social life!'

'You're not my whole social life!' *You won't be any of my social life from now on, cow.*

'No?' she asks. 'Who else are you hanging out with?' Righteousness emanates from the receiver as she lays down these cards she's been holding to her chest.

I reply to her question, though she makes no space for my words. 'I've been very busy with work, y—'

'After your, your . . . illness, you went out and about for a while,' she says, 'but then, I don't know, you stopped, and it's been ages since you bothered your arse to socialise with anyone except me.'

I'm reluctant to reveal any fondness for her, knowing she has none for me. 'I like hanging out at yours. You're my closest friend.'

'Yeah. And I live with Gary. And nag nine-year-olds all week. And there's a baby coming who'll need me every waking minute. I can't handle you needing me as well.'

'I–I was trying to give something back, for the help you gave me.'

She's silent but I know she's still there. 'You don't have to pay me back,' she says. 'I'd have done anything to help you get better, we all would. But the convalescent period is over. We can't keep making allowances for you because you weren't well.'

'Am I asking you to?'

'You had a hard year and now you're scared of . . . something. You come round here instead. Truth is, I feel like I'm being used and this bump is using up everything I have. You need to find something that's yours, Rhona.'

Has she been on the phone to fucking Toronto?

'You're right,' I tell her. 'Who'd stay in on a Saturday night? Your social life might be gone forever. Not mine. I'll bloody go to a club tonight. Maybe start a ferocious coke habit while I'm at it.'

'You do that,' Hilary says. 'Knock yourself out.'

223

~

I exit the flat but not to a club. I walk, propelled by this almost tangible air; thickened and tinged pink by the sun setting on a clear, close-of-summer day. The end of the lighter evenings. The end.

I make it to the far side of the park before dusk is over but I don't attempt to make it back the same way. Pissed off I may be but not mental. On the main streets, pubs have belched smokers onto pavements. They sit outside contained by flimsy barriers; oversized segments of my nephew's toy-farm fence.

The sky should be all-the-way dark for the last leg home but a high moon turns this familiar travail into a stage set. The dome of a corner tenement juts into sepia, a row of broadleaved trees glows almost orange behind school railings, and what scant cloud there is slips along like backlit silk.

I'm not saying it's magical but no one could say it's not out of the ordinary, in this place where the sky is most often a marble slab and streetlights are relied upon to get us wherever there is to go.

Why hasten, when I can lean against the granite balustrade to see platinum peaks on the busy river moving closer, closer, closer, under, away? Tracking a piece of silver-lit debris with total attention as it travels towards me induces a woozy in-time-out-of-time sensation: standing here, feet planted and simultaneously bound in the pace, the weight, of the water.

I can only be water until my vision hits the bridge rail and then, abruptly, I am Rhona.

A burst ball: watch it, watch it, with it, with it – gone. Piece of plank: with it, with it, am it, am it – gone.

Water-time is fundamentally different from bridge-time and repeatedly arriving back in the latter is a suffering I can tolerate only for so long.

I leave the river but it doesn't leave me. Not fully. Meeting firm un-flowing bitumen, foot after foot, I carry the river – its effortless momentum, its sureness of direction.

Until there is too much competition on my senses. This shop, now this bar, now another. Cars idling in a queue at the red light. Diesel vapour. The acrid orange night-sheen. And all these other lost sods, sliding along like holograms.

~

After breakfast I call Tania, to see if she wants to come to the seaside with me. She tells me she's still in her clothes from last night. The reason she'd answered her mobile was because it was in her trouser pocket.

'I thought you weren't drinking?' I say.

She has already hung up.

I phone Erin to ask if she and Mindy want a day out.

Nobody answers.

I conclude that this day trip is one I will take on my own. Into the bag: apple, MP3 player, book and scarf, because it's always windier at the coast.

Two train journeys later, I land that first bright footstep onto sand. Then another after that; it goes on this way for an hour.

Up at the back of the beach, sizeable driftwood shapes have come to rest at intervals. The sea has bleached and polished them to the bones of nearly recognisable creatures. They are plenty big enough to walk along – these nature-made play-ground toys – with arms out for balance.

Sitting on one offers vantage of the sand and the bobbing water beyond. Figures in anoraks walk the beach, picking up something to throw for the dog, bending to greet someone else's dog.

Beyond the human tideline, fleet-footed shore birds rush along the wet, reflective sand like hot droplets on a non-stick pan. From their static bodies you wouldn't know they were responsible for their own motion. Not like the pronounced, bobbing walk of the crows back at the harbour wall.

Crossing the beach road to find a café, I'm stopped by a window display that couldn't exist where I live. What category of shop does it herald? There are tins of shoe polish, a mannequin in a sequinned jumper, wellies that stop at the ankle, boxes of instant noodles and a pile of football annuals, 'REDUCED'.

Seeing the annuals, my impulse is to go in and buy one – a jokey present for my football-daft boyfriend. *What boyfriend?*

The tears start but I don't surrender; I breathe.

~

Stopping to buy veg after work, I find the small greengrocers is jammed with people. I'm hungry, though, and can't walk away from the ingredients I need. I end up loitering at the doorway while I decide, making everyone else's experience harder. Among the fliers on the noticeboard my eyes catch today's date and dart back to it. A poetry event in the basement of a local pub ... I look for the start time ... A solution coalesces. I'll eat dinner there and listen to some poetry. It's only round the corner. I can be home in five if it's weird.

Tell me again, I want to say to the first reader, *about holding your wife's hand in bed till you both fall asleep. About the deal you made to always say what you think, because one day you'll be dead.*

Tell me again, to the second reader, *about the sound of your own blood pumping under hand-cupped ears. About your land-locked affair with the sea.*

Stop telling me, to the next, *about the kitten your step-mum locked in the cellar, letting you think it was gone. About the games that other children didn't have to play.*

When the last reader takes the stage, my attentive ear is spent: an out-of-condition muscle. She announces she's brought only one poem. *Phew.* It's not by her, it's by Morgan somebody. She starts. It's a poem about God. *Excellent, I don't need to listen.* Soon the last line is out, uttered and it's too late to hear all that led there. Damn. *Start again.* She doesn't. Maybe it's fine. Maybe I heard the lines I needed to:

'God only told me one thing
hard finger in my chest
live.'

Twelve

Donald sends me an invite to a meeting with Petra, to discuss her stage one report. It's up to me then, to ask Petra if I can have sight of the document – with inadequate time to read it through.

'White Cairn's not in the worst shape I've seen,' says Donald. 'Far from it.'

'Agreed,' Petra says. 'Management team members fulfil their remits, reflected in the health of the figures, but these are not easy times to be a UK producer, especially of luxury goods. To stay afloat someone will need to be at the helm.'

'I'm thinking the same,' he replies. 'Management *has* to adapt to the absence of Margaret and her husband. If we identify a new main player to have the last word on decisions, hold the overall vision – is that all that's required?'

'I think so, if he, maybe she, is helped into the role by leadership training,' Petra says, 'and good backup. If division directors recruit well at deputy level, they won't need unrealistic expertise themselves.'

'There's common sense in that family,' Donald adds. 'I believe they'd support a recommendation to appoint differently from now on, limiting the younger family's involvement to those with a useful specialism, a proven skill set.'

'Exactly. Like Margaret's granddaughter, who studied risk management.'

Mention of the granddaughter brings to mind something I didn't see when I glanced through Petra's report. 'There was an issue Eva alluded to, when I interviewed her,' I tell them, 'that I don't see highlighted in the stage one review.'

Petra carries on talking about who should be designated Chief Exec but Donald interrupts with a raised palm and a nod my way.

'Me? Okay, well Eva's uncle Arthur, Margaret's youngest, has responsibility for marketing.' I'm clause-ing my way to the nub of it. Who am I to discuss this man's life in shorthand? 'Eva gave the impression, as did Margaret, that he'd been given that role because it was seen as the least crucial of the directorships. Assigned to him when marketing was more of a fun add-on, back when whisky sold itself. It was heavily hinted that Arthur's spent the last thirty years drinking too much of the stuff. There's concern in case his next-in-command ever leaves, because she's the de facto head of marketing.'

'That's not in my report,' says Petra, 'because as a *professional* you would never record a matter of that nature.' She looks to Donald for vindication. 'And it's easy to solve. The guy's fifty-one. We'll recommend that White Cairn pensions him off and promotes from within. End of.'

End of.

The answer-machine relays a message from Hilary. The second this week.

'Rho–na. Pick u-up . . . Rho–na. Are you ignoring me?'

'No,' I say to the machine. 'If you can't get hold of me it's your own fault. You are no longer my whole social life.'

I think through the things I've been doing lately.

Monday – two-for-one meal deal in town with Erin. She couldn't believe we hadn't seen each other in a month. I could – it's what happens when one of you has a child and the other works nine-to-five. Mondays are good for her because James is home early to babysit. She made me pencil in another meal for a fortnight hence. I was happy to.

Tuesday – badminton. First time in years. The sports centre near the office does a drop-in. I didn't embarrass myself but I might not go back. I was drawn to the sound of the aerobics session in the other hall; the beat and bass of high volume, mediocre dance music.

Tomorrow – Martin from work has given me spare tickets for a play at the Terminus which opened to great reviews. I'm taking Mum.

~

She is a beacon of lilac cashmere between vast concrete walls and iron piping. Maybe I should have thought more carefully when deciding who to bring. Oh face it, there was no one else. Small mercies; Martin had only two spare tickets so Dad stayed home.

It isn't a play so much as three men naked in a cage,

emotionally tortured and no dialogue to tell us why, just a soundtrack as loud as an air-raid and as terrifying. Parts of the actors are visible in strobe lighting: this one's bleeding shoulder, that one's pronounced calf muscles, the other's genitalia.

'Best thing I've seen in a long time,' is Mum's verdict, knotting the belt of her raincoat. *Sadly, yes*, I conclude, making my way home.

~

We wait in our foyer for Donald, who left his phone on his desk. We're heading to a meeting at White Cairn. In her report, Petra has made a recommendation to remove Arthur Lennox from his post as Marketing Director. Has Margaret Lennox brought this on herself, by hiring us to poke our noses in? I don't think this is the outcome she'd had in mind. If it was, she could have done it herself, no?

Petra is whistling along to the reception muzak like she's trying to pass an exam in it.

'Are you prepared for Margaret's reaction to your suggestion to sack Arthur?' I ask her.

The whistling stops. 'Why should Margaret *react* to a sensible solution?'

'Because Arthur's her son and you're asking her to sack him.'

Petra lands her gaze on me. 'Mrs Lennox is paying us to solve the problems she, *they*, have been avoiding. You heard her say that yourself.'

Not in so many words. 'I also heard her recount how White Cairn has dealt with all manner of challenges, always with a high regard for workers' welfare. Can't we offer her something more in line with the company's ethos? If they were the sacking kind, they'd have sacked him already.'

'It's a correspondence course in social work you should be doing. What is the guy? Over fifty? Totally acceptable time to retire. He'll still be a shareholder getting dividends. He won't suffer.' This from the woman who would turn up daily and give a hundred per cent even for no money because doing so defines who she is. Without a platform to feel superior she'd disintegrate.

Donald emerges from the lift.

In the back seat of the car I wonder what will happen to Arthur Lennox's drink problem when he's not required to be somewhere every morning.

~

Aerobicisers spill from the hall to become a tarrying throng in the corridor. I progress at the collective pace – who could hurry with thigh muscles this spent? Emerging into the sports centre's entrance hall I'm aware of sweat on my face as the new air meets my skin.

I'm bumped against by someone arriving at twice the speed I'm leaving. 'Sorry,' I mutter, shuffling on.

'Hello,' says the body.

Turning to see why it spoke, I recognise FerrisBuellerSenior. 'Don't tell me,' he says, ' . . . Rhona! Isn't it?'

'Yes, Gus, it is. I must be more forgettable than you.'

He adopts a deliberate swagger, saying, 'Can be hard to remember names when you go on so many dates.'

'Having a rare date-free evening, Bueller, or is she waiting for you in the motorised sedan chair?'

'A night off from the ladies to maintain my physique.' He is stroking the desk-job curve of his stomach. 'What's your excuse for being here on a Friday night?'

'This is how I spend my Fridays. I have rediscovered aerobics.'

'Won't meet a lot of guys that way, I imagine.'

'Not too many. Is that why you exercise, to meet women?'

'Strictly in-and-out again, that's me,' he says, ' . . . of the sports centre I meant, not the women.'

Gus's ears are going puce. 'I'm rarely in this place,' he says. 'I play squash usually, further west, but the courts are flooded. Came here for a go in the gym.'

'I was thinking about you recently,' I tell him, which happens to be true. 'I was thinking about your hair.'

He regards me askance.

'Don't panic, wasn't having a weirdo wank about your barnet,' I tell him. 'I was remembering the internet dating, and how you were the only date who still had his hair.'

'Coincidence. So were you.'

We banter beside the plastic foliage till it becomes apparent that we're enjoying ourselves – to the point where keeping each other back any longer would be tantamount to acknowledging interest.

There is a lowering of gazes, an adjustment of bag-straps, a 'Right then,' a 'Run well,' and thus, we part.

~

Rhona,

This is like catching up on the gap year I never had. And it would have been cheaper doing it on one of those inter-railing tickets. Sending this month's email from an idyllic Greek island. I could phone, but you'd lecture me on safe sex.

Decided to look less touristy, so I'm pretending to be here on business – sourcing speciality items for a deli chain in Scotland. Stroke of genius ... I've been welcomed into shops and shown around vineyards and olive groves by the owners' well-mannered sons – the generation which learned English at school (if I didn't loathe emojis I might put one here: a thumbs-up or an aubergine. They both apply. Winky wink.).

I'm extending my ticket.

Tania Pickering,

Senior Buyer, 'Deligael'

PS I'm giving people your mobile number as 'head office' – just make something up if anyone calls.

Don't give anyone my mobile number! Seriously! I text, after seeing her email on Saturday morning. **For that, I'm leaving you a long voicemail about condoms.**

~

No number shows on the screen and when I answer the call, an emphatic female in a language I don't know rages at me, not stopping when I say, 'Sorry, I don't understand.' And, 'SOR-RY, YOU HAVE THE WRONG NUM–BER.'

I end it the only way I can and hang up.

When the phone beeps again by the subway's ticket machine, I drop my coins with a line of lively supporters at my back. Having wondered in the past what kind of person drops money and doesn't bother to pick it up, now I know.

I read the incoming text: **Still thinking about my hair?** He kept my number, after going to that ball.

Hard, metal brakes lament from the depths and warm, dank air pushes up the escalator – my cues to descend two at a time, rather than wait for the next train. But there'd be no signal down there. I lean on the wall by the turnstiles.

Don't think you've clinched it with your productive follicles. It'll take more than that. At least a hot-air balloon ride and a star named after me.

~

Jamie Lennox, White Cairn's Finance Director, is praising Petra and Martin for their global markets strategy. He shakes our hands as he leaves for his meeting with Scottish Development International. When the door has clicked behind him, Donald looks over at Petra and Martin. 'Well done you two.'

His comment creates awkwardness with Margaret still here – exposes us as different to her, here for the money, doing a job.

Margaret wants to summarise ground covered by Muffin and what stages are left in the process. She wants a timetable for implementing changes and a date for stepping down as Executive Chairwoman. 'I turn seventy-five in December,' she says. This is a lady who's ready for retirement. This is a lady who has earned it.

'We can roll out the Board restructuring as soon as you like,' says Donald. 'As our report stated, their positions are well-defined already and we recommend Jamie for Executive Chairman. We want to give that role more teeth so there'd need to be training, in London probably. Or America. We could take Board members through a preparation period, to get them used to a peer becoming their boss. But they'd each remain boss of their designated area.'

'Except Arthur,' says Margaret.

'Employees have to be fit for work,' Petra explains. 'No company can carry an under-performing employee, not even a family-run one.'

Margaret expects more from us. I know she does. Petra's proposal is too simplistic. It doesn't take account of the aftermath. Arthur may not be coming to work any more but he'll stay joined to these people as a son, a brother, a father.

Say it, Rhona.

'As we know,' I begin, 'employees will often under-perform in roles that don't suit their skills. You can't do your best if you're not playing to your strengths. But employees often cling to positions they don't like because no one offers them an alternative – we all prefer to be doing something than nothing, yes?'

I have Margaret's smiling gaze, Donald's anxious attention and Petra's furious glare.

'What do we know about Arthur?' I pose. 'In the brief times I've spent with him, I've learned more about whisky-making than I knew there was to learn. And I remember it because of the way he explained it. I've also been entertained by his anecdotes of the Lennox ancestors starting out in business.'

236

Donald needs to make it look like he has sanctioned this, planned it, even. He backs me up.

'Arthur is your classic bon viveur,' he says, 'an enthusiast and a natural raconteur. What he doesn't know about whisky-making you could fit on a, a . . . '

I take my topic back. 'I could understand if there was reluctance to air the family history in public but perhaps enough time has passed since the 1800s to talk about the early days of White Cairn – the skulduggery, the colonial exiles, the illegitimate children, the sibling rivalry, the government bribery – people love that stuff! Have you seen the genealogy programmes on TV? Celebrities are lining up to unearth the least redeemable characters in their families.'

Margaret is nodding. 'Arthur takes a great interest in Lennox family history,' she says. 'He and his father were documenting it before Ian died.'

'It's easy enough to find a replacement Head of Marketing.' I'm on a roll. 'But the kind of insider knowledge Arthur has is unique. He would be an asset for the Visitor Centre. The personal touch. He might need managing, he might need support, but he can still be used to good effect. Make him part of the tour, the tastings, the presentation.'

Seeing the enthusiasm in Margaret's face, Petra wants a piece of it. 'He could link to the whisky elite, too,' she says, 'doing events for specialist audiences.'

Margaret resettles each side of her cardigan over her bosom, saying, 'This is a suggestion I can take to the Board. Leave it with me.'

'Sure,' I say.

Donald clears his throat. 'Certainly,' he says, re-establishing the pecking order.

We have given her back her son. No one likes to think they have raised a useless child.

~

On the subway after an evening haircut, I look forward to the bit of telly I'll watch, the cup of tea I'll make. Stepping off the escalator and out into the night, I reckon it'll be ten minutes till my pyjamas are on. In the stairwell, I remember Cyril exists and wonder which room he's lying in: whether he'll get up when he hears my key in the door. In the bedroom, my clothes are off and re-hung in the time it takes for the kettle to boil.

Flicking through the channels, it occurs to me to plug my mobile into its charger. Finding it in my bag, there's a new message:

There's already a star named after ur anus. No wait, that's a planet. (That word will never not be funny 😊)
It depresses me, MrsB, to think that aerobics is the highlight of your weekend. Could I take my bride out for a meal?

My stomach tingles as I read it aloud, slowly, to the cat. 'He kept my number in his phone, did I tell you that?'

Gus's text had been sitting, unopened, since 5.44 p.m. Nearly three hours. Fantastic! I've managed to come across as nonchalant without having to try. To keep him waiting longer could be unnecessarily calculating, and make him think I'm not interested. I start pressing keys.

Not as much as it depresses me, Bueller. YES. We could celebrate our 3 month anniversary on Saturday.

Let's wear full wedding outfits. I want it to feel as special as our big day!

I review what I've written. Does it convey a balance between easy-osey and interested? Hardly. Upper case letters? Deciding which evening? Hey Rhona, why don't you dial the landline number he gave you when he was drunk, and reply that way?

Nice idea to meet up. Wetherspoons? To remind us of our big day.

Crediting his initiative. It's ready. Am I sure? Yes. Am I? Yes. Send. I watch the message fly off the screen. I re-read his message then read my reply. I'm satisfied. I plug the phone into its charger.

On TV, two panels of comedians comment on recent news items. It's just noise. Has Gus read my message? Is he smiling? How long will it take to compose a reply? Maybe he'll wait three hours, because I did. No! I didn't do it on purpose. What if he waits three hours? What if he doesn't reply till tomorrow?

I'm aware of wide blades turning faster and faster and can feel the rising swell of water. I sit up straighter, place my hands on my knees and breathe in. And out. And in. And out. If he doesn't reply till tomorrow, he doesn't reply till tomorrow. If he doesn't reply at all, he doesn't reply at all. I will respond to the situation when there is a situation to respond to. For now, I am breathing.

The wind-machine blades slow to a stop and I'm back on the couch. Bliss – the tea, the TV, the repartee. My phone beeps.

Perfect. 8pm. Saturday. Wait outside though. My one eye doesn't see too well in mood lighting.

Bless him! My turn.

You can take my arm, if that helps. It's been detachable since birth.

Send. Wait. Beep.

Thoughtful as ever. See you Saturday, outside W's on Jamaica Street. Now, time for beauty sleep? Goodness knows we both need it.

Does that need a reply? A wee one.

C u Saturday, zzzzzzzzzz

With that, I switch off the phone.

In the morning, there's a message waiting.

I hadn't forgotten your name at the Sports Centre. I pretended, in case you didn't know mine. Wasn't possible to forget you.

~

Rhona,

For God's sake, how hard is it to get pregnant?
Beetroot day came, after taunting me with its lateness.
I was sure I'd been seeded with a gorgeous wee Greek.
Alas, nae bun in this oven.

I'm working through my grief at a day spa in
Edinburgh. Midweek offer on GroupDeal. The
masseuse said that my cycle was probably knocked
out by the travelling and changes in daylight levels
(apparently the amount of sunshine entering your
eyes affects your menstrual cycle. Why didn't you
tell me that?)

If travelling the globe is interfering with my fertility, I'll

240

have to try something else. Do you think they offer 'room service' here, or does that only happen in films?

Why am I emailing you from Scotland?

Phone me,

Tan

~

With her mouth full of pasta, Tania says it's too wet to hit the shops. I'm up for it because the rain has kept the crowds away. Tania is adamant; she doesn't want to ruin her shoes. I tell her she should have worn different shoes. She says I should stop raiding my mum's wardrobe.

I'm careful not to start a conversation about what we're each doing tonight. My connection with Gus is too nascent to mention. Nothing might come of it. He might not turn up. Or maybe he will. The anticipatory tingle in my stomach leaves scant room for lunch.

'No good?' asks Tania, pointing to my plate.

'Not as hungry as I thought.'

'Imagine what I'd be putting away if I was eating for two.' She goes on to make a joke about being hooked up to a nose-bag. I wonder if she needs to talk about this in more detail.

'I notice you've not been away anywhere since Greece.' She goes a little pink. 'More trouble than it was worth, that nonsense,' she says. 'I've come to my senses, if you can believe that.'

'Hallelujah,' I say. 'Sicily, Turkey,' I break into laughter. 'The whole mad plan. You having a kid? God help it!'

'I've decided,' she says calmly, and directly, 'to go to a fertility clinic rather than traipse around the globe.'

'Oh, well, that sounds like a better plan. Yes. Get your equipment checked . . . mm.' To change the subject, I say that I'm happy to shop in the rain myself (in case she hates me and needs an 'out') but Tan says she doesn't want to go home yet (still likes me!) so we settle on the cinema.

She looks for local listings on her mobile and suggests a film about a couple in the final, agonising throes of their relationship.

'Next!' I take her phone. 'What about this?' From the blurb I quote, 'Let down by modern life, he embarks on an epic trek into the wilderness in search of a more honest way to be human.'

'I think we know that's not happening,' she says, taking her phone back. 'In rural France,' she reads, 'the new doctor takes lodgings in the home of the village undertaker, with hilarious consequences.'

'That'll do, yeah?'

'Yeah.'

Two hours later, the credits disappear into black and we have a hard time moving from our seats. Afternoon-snooziness has assailed us. In the abandoned auditorium we have no choice but to stand and discover our upright selves, like foals. Tania goes slowly towards the bathroom while I flounder to the main doors, taking my phone off silent. There is one voicemail message.

'Hello wifie,' says Gus's voice. 'Enjoy yourself at keep fit last night?' His tone is breezy. 'Checking to see you're still on for later. Haven't changed your mind.' A seed of panic sprouts behind my ribs when he suggests I might have lost interest. I want to be there. I want him to be there, too. 'I'm here pressing my velvet cummerbund and for all I know,' he's saying, 'you're off seeking an annulment. Our marriage was never, technically . . . you know.'

Cheeky! It has to be a short text because Tania will be back any second.

Been in cinema. See you 8. Looking forward to it.

When Tania hails her taxi, there's enough time to descend into TK Maxx and resurface owning a dark red blouse with split sleeves and a deep neckline.

~

In the lull after ordering espressos, Gus moves the candle aside. 'This is going well, isn't it?' he says. I'm about to agree when he jumps in with, 'Thanks for turning up. There's always that fear of being left standing.'

'Never occurred to me that you wouldn't show.' My tone is leg-pulling. 'Thank *you*,' I add, 'for leaving the cummerbund at home.'

He smiles across the table. To break this beam of attention I say, 'Full marks for booking this place. I hadn't known about it.'

'Seriously?' Custodial pride emanates when he calls it his family's favourite Italian, and lists the many occasions marked here.

'No engagements . . . ?' I inquire.

'No . . . *sey*,' he says. 'You're the only cyber-wedding anniversary I've celebrated here.' He puts a hand on top of mine. 'There wasn't enough time to organise a hot-air balloon ride. Sorry. But what Italian dinner would be complete without a serenade?' He's signalling to the waiter.

I put a grin on, hoping he didn't notice my initial spasm.

The waiter arrives with an emphatic, 'Enjoy!' His junior side-kick appears ... laying down two espressos and a flaming pancake. Gus is laughing heartily.

I slowly reverse whistle. 'There sits a man playing fast and loose with his chances of a second date. Hair or no hair.'

He squeezes my hands inside his, in a baby-voiced pity gesture. 'Ohhh Whona ... it was there, I took it. Forgive me.' Chortle, chortle.

'It's not an apology if you're still laughing.'

He has kept eye contact. 'Do you think if our first date hadn't been at a corporate ball, we'd have made it to a second date?' he asks.

I consider this for a few seconds, trying to recall our first meeting. What else was going on, who was I? Homebody Rhona: Saturday nights on Hilary's sofa.

'I don't think it was going to a ball that spoiled it,' I reply. 'I think it was the internet thing.'

'You liked the emails. Was the real Gus a massive disappointment?'

'I mean internet dating in general. The mechanics of it. It's too artificial. Arranging to meet people and then having to *think* about whether I fancied them or not. I kept drawing a blank. My head was drowning out my intuition.'

Watching him nodding in sympathy, noticing his level of interest, the strong curves of his mouth – I'm wondering what was wrong with me at the ball. 'When I spurned internet dating,' I say, with turned-up sultriness, 'it seems I threw a babe out with the bathwater.'

'You bet your sweet aerobics ass you did.'

'Although ...' I move invisible specs to the end of my nose

244

and peer over them. 'I don't remember you phoning me after the ball, Fergus Bueller.'

He takes a few seconds to reply. 'At the end of a date you get a vibe from a woman, about whether she wants you to contact her again. I wasn't getting 'call me' signals when you got out the car.'

'Sorry about that. I did enjoy myself.'

'Me too. No matter. We got here in the end.'

Taxis aren't the easiest environment for couples who're barely acquainted. Not sober, anyway.

In bed, I have to fall asleep against the excitement of all the kisses I know I will be getting.

~

I'm home without any of the provisions I went out for. Metres from the Co-op's doorway I'd caught sight of Hilary and Gary packing bags at the cash desk and instead of going in, my reflex response was to retreat; turning off the main road to walk home the long way.

Now it's sinking in: I avoided saying hello to a heavily pregnant best friend.

Why? Because ... I don't think she sees me that way any more. I'm not sure where I fit in her new world order.

~

Pushing sheets into the machine, I hear my mobile ringing and run to find it. 'Wotcha,' I say, in my best Essex.

'How's you today?' he asks. 'Lazy morning?'

'Not too lazy. Blitzing the flat.'

'I'm here with the paper and bacon-butties. But I was playing squash for an hour.'

'I haven't made it as far as the shops, yet,' I fib. 'What can I have for lunch?'

'I'll courier a full English. How's that?'

'Perfect. I'll set the table.'

We laugh, giving this getting-to-know-you humour more appreciation than it merits.

'Anything planned for later on?' Gus asks.

'Nothing much.'

'I know you were at the cinema yesterday but I wondered if, eh, you fancied going again? It'd be good to hang out before the weekend is over.'

Bless him.

'How about bowling instead?' I suggest. 'There's that place beside the multiplex.'

'Hey, that's an idea. I can watch you from behind while you launch the ball.'

'If I can do the same.'

~

Gus steadies his body around mine to demonstrate a better way to release the bowling ball. 'How cheesy is this?' he asks.

'Now one of us needs to lose our balance,' I answer, 'so we land on the floor on top of each other.'

He's laughing. With his hand spanned over mine, he says, 'Yup, then we'd stop laughing at the same time, stare at each other, and hesitantly move in for a kiss.'

'Voilà!' I turn round. 'The condensed romcom.'

His eyes are studying my expression. He leans forward and we kiss.

Thirteen

I spend all day at work on Monday with that candy floss feeling; the *I have a special someone* sensation, *and I wonder if he's thinking about me?* It's a reality shift: I no longer inhabit the world solo. How quickly I moved from one state to the other. Relationships, it would appear, are like riding a bike. Or is it falling off a horse?

I endure the hours I have to, until we can make contact.

After dinner, I wonder how to play it. Phone him? Text him? Wait for him to text me? If I muscle in on his wooing by taking the initiative, will it put a dampener on it? Why hasn't he been in touch today?

Jeezo. Listen to yourself.

Breathe in. Breathe out. In. Out.

We like each other. He's been reliable about making contact; there's no reason to think otherwise. And if he doesn't get in touch? I'll cross that bridge in a day or two.

This nervous energy should be put to good use. A walk.

I start out under a broad, blank sky with a large, low-hung moon. Deciding on the longer route, I take the steps from the main road to the path by the river. I stop to watch a heron, statue-still where the water is rocky and rushing. It knows what it wants and it knows if it waits it will come.

One sudden stab in the water. Dinner.

I daunder alongside the wall, strolling towards the next stairway that accesses the road. Up on the pavement I meet Tania's sister, Bryony, and we chat for close to half an hour. On my return home there's a new text.

I'm around, if you wanna speak? Hope you're enjoying your evening ☺

Could be too late for talking. We haven't established our habits yet. I reply: **Just home. You free any night this week? You could come over to mine. I'd cook and introduce you to Cyril.**

His reply arrives.

Lovely offer. Wednesday or Thursday? I'll bring wine.

Which kind does he prefer?

He's not fussy, no breeding. Wednesday, 7.30?

I add my address details, and he sends: **C u then Lebowski. X**

A couple of evenings later, Gus arrives with wine *and* flowers. After we eat, he kneels beside the stereo commenting on my CD collection while I hurl cushions.

～

Petra's away on a detox holiday – 'cleanse while you cruise' or some such (it sounds physical, rather than emotional, in its

248

focus unfortunately) – so it falls to me to accept the invitation from Mrs Lennox to her annual Ladies' Charity Lunch. It's at a hotel by Loch Och, where arriving by helicopter on the lawn is a regular occurrence. I accept specifically so that I can tell Petra about it.

I suss that Muffin must have been sent a ticket for a table which hadn't fully sold, because the others are dripping bling. I'm trying my best with the women sitting on either side but it feels sacrilegious to make small talk while eating this food. It's almost sacrilegious to eat it – the care that has been taken, the flavours, the plating; Scottish-caught sashimi, confit pheasant terrine with samphire, whisky mousse in a sugar-glass beaker, coffee with petits fours.

Afterwards, we move to a room where seats have been arranged in rows. Margaret takes the stage. She thanks us for coming and adds, 'A show of thanks, please, to the Ladies' Lunch committee members.' Margaret lists the efforts that made today possible and describes how the money raised last year was spent. We watch a piece of film about a self-supporting community in Rwanda, comprised of women subjected to the horrendous extent of the crisis.

'Running a successful whisky firm is a privilege I never take for granted,' Margaret says, 'but it's not a product I can donate to those in need.'

There is vocal amusement; a release of discomfort and guilt.

'I *can* donate my time, however, and my business skills and my chequebook. Last year, you ladies gave almost fourteen thousand pounds. So there are women in Rwanda who have a second chance' – her voice is cracking – 'at a good life. When I met them they asked me to pass on their appreciation.'

Another minute or two of film is shown; warm eyes and smiles to camera, monologues of self-worth regained, hope in life renewed, skills learned. 'They think you are angels. In my view, we're just luckier, with surplus to share. I think we all know who the angels are.'

At this point Mrs Lennox welcomes a Scottish radio personality to the stage, to get the auction started. By the final bang of the gavel over sixteen grand has been raised and I'm the owner of a limited edition print that cost £165.

I don't want to stay and make polite chat; what could we say that would be apposite? What words would cover it? I won't slip out without saying goodbye to Margaret. I must thank her, pledge to her fund, be near this woman who knows what she's doing and why she is doing it.

'No business today!' she says, her forefingers forming an 'x'.

'Wouldn't dream of it, just came to thank you for the sublime lunch. And learning about your charity work has been very—' I'm not sure how to express it. If in doubt, continue anyway. 'Those women are . . . after what they went through . . . if they can get up every morning and smile, the rest of us have no cause to moan. Ever. I'm ashamed. Where do they get their strength? So . . . dignified.'

'Yes, that does come across when speaking with them.' She lays a hand between my shoulder blades. 'What's that old saying? Flourish where you're planted? Don't feel bad, Rhona, if your life is easier than other people's. You were born where you were born. Just remember to be thankful, that's all. And offer something back whenever you can.'

～

I can't focus on my study notes because the stereo keeps pulling my attention away, but the remote control is on the table and Cyril is asleep in the crook between my tummy and my tucked-up legs. Reaching with my fingertips, then loosening off my shoulder joint and reaching further, I am able to press the standby button. Such relief ensues I can't understand why I didn't do that an hour ago. The room is an oasis of silence – a reminder that here I am, on a Thursday evening, body conducting the processes it always does to maintain life, in the company of another creature, whose body is doing the same thing.

This is how we are spending our lives together, in this moment, on this aubergine sofa, in the mustard light of these low-energy bulbs.

Cyril must really trust me, to be so out-for-the-count. Am I ever that soundly asleep? When I wake in the morning, dusted with dread and turning over a Pelmanism spread of dream scenes (a train trip with people I knew at school; hiding in a house from a gunman in the garden; a job interview I forgot to prepare for) I doubt I could have looked dead-to-the-world with that going on.

Cyril's fur is rising and falling; a full breath to one of my in breaths. I match the speed of his breathing but it's unsettling and I have to compensate by taking a long, deep inhale, which is so settling that I have to do it again.

Slow in.

Slow out.

Slow in.

With each cycle, the space inside my head expands until there is nothing but space.

Slow out.

No mind, no me. Only a vast tract of sand, repeatedly claimed by a wave then exposed again on its gradual retreat.

~

Petra is refusing to mentor me in future, for undermining her on White Cairn when I was only supposed to be shadowing. Donald is reluctant to upset her further.

I tell him it's fine, I got the experience I needed. 'I'm ready for my own project.'

Donald says I can deputise on the next small contract he takes on – once County Construction has been successfully completed. It needs a close eye.

'But that could be well into the new year!' I point out. He's looking gleeful. Why is that something to be pleased about? Several months of standing still.

'How would you like to start the Management Consulting Diploma?'

Petra can cause as much strife as she wants if this is the pay off – five grands' worth of training.

'Donald, you surprise me. Thank you very much.' For the next two years my Saturdays will be spoken for.

'You pay two k, I'll pay three?' he suggests.

My eyes narrow.

'One k, four k?' he tries.

Narrower still.

'We can sort out the course fees later. Go ahead and sign up with the FBC as soon as you want.'

~

Wandering round a Whistler exhibition at The Hunterian, Gus suggests going for a drink. In the pub, he offers to show me his place because it's only around the corner. On the way there he announces he has no resident pets, parents or kids to introduce me to. I tell him it's his CD collection that I want to meet; that it's payback time. He takes his smartphone out of his coat pocket. 'This is my CD collection.'

'How dull.'

He holds it high while I try to grab it. 'I think you'll find it's beyond reproach,' he says.

Afternoon gives way to evening as we talk, entwined on his couch; sometimes exploring contours, sometimes kissing.

'I can't be bothered queuing for a table tonight,' he says. 'Shall we phone for a takeaway?'

'Who could think about food at a time like this?' I ask, dramatically.

'I know it's only six thirty,' he says, 'but it'll take a while to arrive. Saturday night, after all.'

'What *shall* we do till it gets here?' He smiles but doesn't say anything.

'What do you think,' I ask, 'is it time yet?'

'For what?'

'You-know-what.'

'Don't take this the wrong way,' he says, 'but you remind me of my nephew, the way you come out with things. He does that and he's autistic.'

Is there a right way to take that? 'Well, from the little I know,' I reply, 'people with autism dislike physical contact. Which doesn't apply to me . . . ' I am walking my fingers down his shirt buttons.

He's resisting the bait.

I stroke a finger over my own top button, undo it, then let my hand drop with an exaggerated sigh. 'It's not quite the same,' I declare, 'ripping my own clothes off.'

He scoops me towards him, grunting with comedic ravenousness in my clavicle.

～

Gus returns from the bathroom and pulls aside a curtain. 'What a morning,' he says. A back view of his body reveals squash-playing gluteals and a level shoulder line. 'Not a cloud.' He climbs into bed.

I get up, draw the curtains fully and quickly rejoin him under the duvet. These are the days I made the effort to get better for. This is the weather that nullifies all that came prior. I must be smiling because Gus says, 'Somebody likes the autumn sunshine.'

I turn his way. 'Somebody does.'

I will tell him what happened to me, last April, maybe in a couple of weeks. When the moment feels right. 'Want to get outdoors?' I suggest.

'Not right this minute,' he says, linking his fingers into mine and bringing his body closer.

～

Donald and I walk up the stairs together. 'Good weekend?' he asks.

'Family stuff. My brother came to Glasgow with his son. We'd promised him a trip to the Science Centre. First at the door on Saturday morning. He was that excited.'

'I'm sure your nephew enjoyed it, too,' says Donald.

I laugh before I can stop myself. 'You're getting better at the humour thing,' I tell him, with slow approving nods of my head that would infuriate anyone.

He sighs hard onto his fingernails and polishes them on his breast; a mime of triumph I haven't witnessed since school.

'What about your weekend?' I ask.

'Same as you. Family. Did I tell you Vicky's pregnant? A happy accident. Her parents were so delighted they arranged a lunch.'

'Congratulations! That's great news. It means Chesney will no longer be *the one and ooonlyyy . . .*'

'Dear oh dear,' he groans. 'Better get used to that, I suppose.'

~

At weekends we end up at whoever's flat is closest but Wednesdays have developed a pattern – mine two weeks ago, Gus's last week, mine this week. Having to keep this place tidy all the time is a small price to pay. When will we let our respective messes show – a month from now? Less?

Gus probably has no hidden mess. He's a gorgeous creature – phones when he says he will, holds my hand when we're walking, plays me songs he thinks I'll like, cuts me off with humour when I stray into pompous or precious.

I worry that my friends are thinking, *Rhona's in selfish 'new boyfriend' mode.*

Andrea's words resurface. I observe my breath and the limitless space it seems to arise from.

Choose again: Hilary disappeared into her impending family. I've not missed a scheduled meal with Erin. And Tania has never suffered from lack of female company.

They're fine, I'm fine.

The idea that Tania is fine won't hold: it's over a week since she sent so much as a text. I phone her. She doesn't answer. She doesn't call me back. I can't remember her going without an audience for this long.

On the way home from work, I stay on the bus and get off near her flat. She buzzes me straight up, no questions. Have I been worrying over nothing? She's standing at her front door in her pyjamas, holding her purse. She'd thought she was letting in a delivery.

'Hi Tan!' I say, overshooting my 'this is perfectly normal' pitch. 'I missed my stop. Found I was practically at your front door.'

Tania begins crying. Keeps crying, cries hard. I have to intervene; guiding her towards the living room, then the sofa. Her crying isn't stopping. I will retrieve props to interrupt it – something to drink, a tissue to offer. I'm bringing these through when the buzzer goes. By the time I've paid the driver and put the pizza box in the kitchen, Tania has arrived at a more peaceful place. She smiles, palely, with her feet tucked up under her and a tissue crushed in her hand. 'It's nice to see you,' she says.

Whatever made her upset must be pretty major. Dare I ask? Is it any of my business? 'You don't have to talk about it, whatever it is,' I say. 'I'm here though, if you want to.'

Tania's hair can't have seen shampoo for three days. I'm guessing her pyjamas have been on for the same length of time. She reaches a hand over to grasp my coat sleeve. 'I had my appointment at the fertility clinic,' she tells me. 'They did tests. An *ovarian* assessment. Investigated all my—' her voice thickens with emotion.

I steel myself; silently rehearse my most sympathetic voice.

'There's NOTHING wrong with me,' she howls.

I pat her knee gently a few times. She doesn't know what she's saying. It's safer to keep quiet until she starts making sense.

'I'm in the top ten per cent for my age bracket,' she says, over her sobs. 'I can have babies. Tons, probably.'

OK. That's a definite piece of good news. Now I'll join in. 'That's great!' I tell her. 'When do you go back, to start the process?'

'I don't *want* plastic babies,' she says with impatience, like I'm slow. 'I don't want rubber gloves or test-tubes or transplanted embryos. I want a real live penis and whole weekends of sex!' And she is off again like a factory klaxon.

~

Thank you, I text at lunchtime.

Thank YOU, he replies.

Ten minutes later, Gus texts again: What are we thanking each other for?

For coming along at the right time and bringing your own special magic with you.

Aw, you're welcome. It goes with me everywhere. Like my hair.

For the record, if ur thinking about disguising the grey – hair dye is for women. Touch ur mop with a bottle and I WILL trade you for a baldie.

Wasn't aware I had any grey … thank you for bringing your own special autism with you.

257

Eek! Swept up by urge to be appreciative and end up insulting! Am sorry.

Gotcha! If you asked me to perm it I would (not) my cherub. I'd name a star after you too but somebody got there first . . . Andromeda (Google it).

It takes seconds to bring up results on my PC.

I might come across as vacant, but do have a morsel of general knowledge. A whole galaxy just for me? When are u bringing the bolt-cutters, Perseus?

I'd come now if I could. No rush to use them, though, just handy for after . . .

When my mobile rings a minute later I reach for it and whisper lustily, 'Unchain me, Perseus!'

'Sorry to phone you at work,' says Erin's voice, 'but I'm sending Hilary flowers and need to know if you want to chip in. Tania's going to. I can put your names on the card. It's better than three bouquets taking up their whole house, I thought.'

Eh? No! When you don't speak to pregnant people they go and have their babies? Hilary has a baby. 'What did she have?'

'Hm? Oh she's not given birth, she's only thirty-four weeks. She's been signed off on maternity early 'cause she's not been feeling well.'

Oh God, when you don't speak to pregnant people they go and get ill and don't tell you so you can't help when you really should then your friends phone you at work and you can't ask for the details because you're under office rules where social lives go on ice for the time that you're here.

'Definitely, put my name on the card and text me how much I owe. How long till she does have the baby?'

Erin decodes for the uninitiated. 'Forty weeks is considered full term.'

~

I spend half of the evening wanting to dial her number yet I can't. Each time I'm close I imagine her shouting at me again. It was bad enough the last time when I hadn't done anything wrong. She's got reason to shout at me now. I should have returned her messages weeks ago when she was trying to make amends. Thank heavens for technology and the coward's way out. I compose a text saying that Erin called me and that I hope she's feeling better. I offer to help if she needs anything.

There's no reply.

~

Gus won't let me order coffee, and asks for the bill instead.

'Why are we walking by the Clyde in the dark?' I venture, ten minutes later. 'I'm not doubting your self-defence skills, dearest. Just asking.'

'There's something I want you to see.'

'Beer cans? Broken lighting? My whole life flashing before my eyes?'

'Are you still talking?'

I fall quiet and turn my attention to possible exit routes from the walkway. Gus's hand is keeping mine warm. After another couple of hundred yards his body weight steers me off the path and we emerge into the car park of the Armadillo. It's full to its corners with cars. My guess is we've missed the start of whatever gig he wants to go to. We become Lilliputian the closer we get to the entrance where 100 feet of glass stretch up to a vast, canopied roof-peak.

The foyer is sparsely populated and audible in the background is what two or three thousand people in the auditorium are enjoying. Being led a few metres to one side I nearly point out that the desk is over the other way, but then I remember that would be talking. Gus rests a hand on my shoulder and strokes the smooth wall with his other one.

'This is one of mine.'

Baffling.

'I built it. Laid the bricks. I'd show you the others but we can't go through without tickets.' He turns to me, putting both arms over my shoulders. 'Not bad, eh.'

'It's exceptional, for a Client Relations Manager.'

'I wasn't always this boring.'

Before he was boring, apparently, he was a contract bricklayer working for six months every summer to fund his winter obsession, snowboarding.

'My actual boyfriend built the Armadillo?' I reach up to smooch him.

'Your actual boyfriend used to be pretty rad.'

We're swaying in an unashamed display of affection when the aerobics-favourite that's my mobile ringtone interrupts the moment. I fish for the phone and hand it to him. 'Flash mob!' I make an attempt at street dance, with a serious face, till the ringtone ends. Gus is shaking his head as we reconvene. 'I wasn't always this boring either,' I laugh into his chest. He cocoons me inside his unzipped jacket. 'I'm confiscating this phone until you're no longer a danger to yourself or others.'

On the way back to his flat, I get the long version. How snowboarding was first included in the Winter Olympics in 1998 but Britain didn't enter a team. He'd placed high at the World Championships already and was desperate to compete. He tried to keep going till 2002 but couldn't fund year-round training. Pushing thirty, he had a hard talk with himself and applied to uni instead.

When we're home he offers to show me the young Gus in action.

'Oh my God, let me look at that!' I grab the tape.

'You have to put it in the machine to watch it.'

'Very funny. You've still got video cassettes!' I examine the black plastic oblong with the dimensions of a book. 'It must be ten years since I held once of these. Freaky.'

He twitches his upturned fingers, requesting it back, then slides it into the machine. I'm treated to an overdue reminder that watching your man do what he does best is the strongest aphrodisiac around. It's a miracle we get any sleep at all.

~

My desk phone rings mid-morning. It's the secretary from Hilary's school.

'Miss Marshall said you'd be able to collect her things. A few odds and sods she wasn't able to gather up the day she went home early. We've boxed it for you. When's convenient?'

I take a late lunch hour plus some flexi-time to get to Elmwood Primary while the office is still open. I'm hoping the secretary will be like a sitcom character whose job requires the utmost discretion but whose personality can't help blabbing.

She isn't.

261

I find out nothing about what's wrong with Hilary.

When she opens her Staff Only door to push the box my way, I reassure her that, 'It's okay, I'm fine, I can manage,' and six minutes later I'm back at her sliding window asking to call a cab because there's no way I'm making it all the way to the bus stop in these shoes with this thing.

I wait on a plastic chair in the corridor learning about 'Where Our Food Comes From' courtesy of a yard of sugar paper pinned to the wall with magazine pictures stuck on.

'Are you the new badminton teacher?' asks a boy sitting opposite.

'Eh, no, I'm a friend of, eh, I don't work here, no.'

'Oh,' he says.

It was such a random question I have to ask, 'Do I look like a badminton teacher?'

'You've got a box of badminton stuff.'

Sure enough, protruding from one corner is the handle of a badminton racquet. He's wearing gym shorts and poking out from his school sack is the handle of a badminton racquet.

'Ah, this stuff isn't mine,' I clarify, 'just collecting it for someone. Waiting for a cab.'

'Hm.' He kicks at the chair leg absently with his heel.

'I'm waiting for my mum. Badminton's cancelled 'cause the teacher's off sick with a baby but I wasn't here last week so I didn't know. Had tonsillitis. I was just getting the hang of it. Now it's cancelled.'

When the taxi stops at Hilary's the curtains are closed.

I lay down the burden on her porch.

~

I come to a stop at the open door of Donald's office. His comb-over has fallen away from his head as he sits bent over some paperwork. 'What's our staff policy on volunteering?' I ask, sitting down.

In one well-practised motion he sits up while smoothing his hair across his scalp. 'What's our whaty?'

'Thought as much. Corporate–community links are something we ignore at our peril. These are socially responsible times.'

His mouth muscles poise to deliver speech but he doesn't get the chance.

'Communities don't happen by themselves,' I tell him. 'They happen when good people give up their time to offer something back. How are the kids supposed to put down their knives and pick up racquets unless someone makes the effort to book a hall?'

'What kids? What are you talking—'

'A whole generation of youth could be lost without people like us making the effort to go out there and sow seeds for their future. And they've got a lot to teach *us*, too, the kids do. A lot.'

'What?'

'Take Chesney! Do you think he'd be where he is today without all the advantages he's had in life?'

'Possibly, he's quite a determ—'

'No! Precisely. He would not. I knew you'd back me on this, Donald. It's typical of your big-hearted management style. The kids will be so pleased that it's all settled.' I stand up.

'What's settled?'

'Me, leaving here at three o'clock every Tuesday.'

'To go where?'

'To take the badminton club at Elmwood Primary,' I say, exiting the room.

He's hollering after me, 'Since when was Elmwood a deprived school? Chesney went to bloody Elmwood!'

'*That* is discriminatory,' I call back, retracing my steps and leaning on the doorframe. 'Kids are kids wherever they grow up. Prejudice like that is exactly why we need a volunteering programme. I'll do a memo to all staff.'

'Do a . . . ?'

'No one bothers to read emails anymore,' I reply.

'There are only four of us, Rhona. You'd be better standing in the middle of the room and speaking in a loud voice. Which you do quite often as it is.'

'Shouting, Donald, is threatening. Seriously, we need to get you on a soft skills course. I'll source one for you,' I say, pushing my shoulder off the wood.

~

The school's Head says yes to the idea immediately. The phone call ends with an instruction to report to her office fifteen minutes early on Tuesday, bringing my passport, my birth certificate and a recent utility bill.

After work, I head to the bookshop to look for a 'badminton basics' manual. I want to make sure my lingo is fresh and that the rules haven't changed in the eighteen years since I was any good.

~

Gus is reclined against the pillows, resting his wine glass on my naked hip. My head settled on his chest gives us full vantage of our lower halves.

'My only internet date with hair,' he says.

'We should make a website,' I murmur, 'in praise of the pubic triangle.'

'Gorilla thatch dot com.'

'No, something tasteful. Black-and-white abstracts. I'll model and you can take the photos.'

He puts his glass on the cabinet and tucks his arms around me. 'Then everyone would know my girlfriend has a lady-garden.'

'No faces showing. Hang on, d'you mean you'd rather I didn't have one?' I ruffle my fingers over his coarse hair. 'What's this?'

'I'm a bloke.'

'Sure are. The kind who prefers women to look like girls, or dolls.'

'Easy tiger. That's quite an inference.' He kisses my shoulder. 'You remind me of the magazines I stole from my dad. I spent many happy hours looking at women with pubic hair. It's gorgeous. Even on hypocritical women who trim theirs.'

'Because I'm not a complete barbarian.'

He tickles my ribcage till I scream, 'Enough!'

'So,' I double-check, 'you love my *Joy of Sex* body?'

'I do, I totally do. I haven't shagged anyone with fur since, eh, what was that nurse's name . . . ?'

I punch his leg.

'You're super sexy, Beech. I forgot how erotic it is. I love it. 'Cause I love you.'

~

Last week, I wouldn't leave Tania till she promised to meet me this Friday for a drink which, I explained, would involve her getting showered and dressed.

All credit to her, she has turned up. Her eyes are back to normal. I won't start into the heavy stuff again unless she does. She greets me and it isn't mentioned.

Not long after the alcohol kicks in, it is. She thanks me for my unannounced visit and for sitting through her incoherent drivel (her words, not mine). It turns out that prior to Tania's appointment at the clinic, her sister had announced she was expecting a baby with the editor-of-academic-textbooks. The happy couple sat in Tania's kitchen holding hands, oozing a noxious blend of shared elation and shared trepidation. The experience had haunted Tania before, during and since her clinic visit.

'I still haven't fathomed what my mad dash was about,' she says. 'But when I saw that pair, I knew it wasn't motherhood.'

I could hazard a guess what her mad dash was about. The fact she barely knew her parents. Some category of chaos meant she got dumped on her grandparents (and Bryony on an auntie, because no one had the resources to raise both). Her grandpa died when she was young, and her granny when she was seventeen. Maybe her whole life has been a mad dash towards (or away from) something. Whose wouldn't?

Tania takes a gulp of Pinot Grigio. 'Dewy eyed at the prospect of giving their whole lives over to the welfare of a thing that's going to need them *all* the time. For *years*. Who'll turn round aged eighteen and hate them for their efforts. Too real ...' Tania takes another swig. 'Far too real ... I like a challenge, you know that. I'll fight whoever I have to for better plane seats or a last-minute wax but those rewards are instant. I'm not patient enough to parent. Who was I kidding?'

'You're over-analysing,' I tell her. 'You don't have to be sensible and straight edged to have a child – having children *turns you* sensible. It takes care of itself.'

'Not always. Not to Courtney, or Kerry, or Whitney. I don't want to bring forth a new generation of twelve-steppers.'

'What about that hot boyfriend you're going to be having filthy sex with,' I remind her. 'He might fall in love with you, might beg you to have his offspring. Do it. You'd make a great mum.' I've changed my tune. The Friday-at-five glow, where all is well in the world and we each have the potential for everything.

'No, Rhona, I wouldn't. I've seen the light. We don't have to pretend any more.' Tania's wine glass hangs bloated and bulbous in her hand. 'Hey, maybe you wouldn't make a great mum either except now you've got a convenient reason not to look at that.'

The glass raised between us says, *Come on then, square go.* She was ready to swing the conversation spotlight away from her. But to make it about me? What have I done?

I breathe in. 'You've been sorting through a major issue lately. I know you were upset but you don't need to take it out on the rest of us.' My intention was to leave it at that but it doesn't happen. 'If you paid attention to anyone except your-self,' I add, 'you'd know I'm *not* infertile. I had an operation on my cervix, that's all.'

The base of her glass has a violent reunion with the table. 'Stupid me, jumping to the wrong conclusion. But turning into a headcase was a pretty big reaction to a small operation. How was I supposed to know you could still have kids?'

I don't have to listen to this drunk talk.

'Hey, Rhona, maybe that *hot man* you're seeing will fall in love with you and *beg* you to have his offspring. Have you discussed babies with Gus yet?'

I'm picking my bag up from the seat, reaching for my coat.

'Nope? Didn't think so. We'll never know what kind of mum you'd make 'cause you're avoiding it altogether. I can see that much.'

I'm standing up, fumbling in my bag for a note to fling on the table. I won't be in debt to her.

Erin approaches the booth, wafting the smell of outdoors as she removes her coat. 'I'm having what you're having,' she says, thinking I'm headed to the bar. 'What have I missed?' She sits down.

I glower at Tania.

I'll let you tell her, shall I?

I elbow through drinkers to the door.

～

I look forward to Tuesday afternoon at Elmwood and after the first ten minutes, the kids aren't shy. Competitive sport brings out the best and worst in their natures. The challenge is to ascertain the right way to coach each one. Some like instructions straight out. They want every suggestion I have that'll improve their play. Others need several compliments before mentioning anything constructive and God forbid if anyone overhears – they go crimson or sulk.

At break time we revert to our usual selves and sit around sharing tangerines and being goofy.

～

On Wednesday Gus meets me straight from work. We go for something to eat in a pub that is also a comedy club.

We laugh at nearly all the same moments but there are some things he finds funny that I don't.

Fourteen

We're outside, it's evening and the wine glasses catch reflections of hanging lanterns on the restaurant terrace. His gaze never wavers. He seems happy that it's me he's telling his story to. When the plates are cleared I sense his relief that, at last, there will be no more interruptions to being able to focus on each other.

He tells me that he's been offered a contract in a different city. But he'll only go if I want to go with him. He says that his company pays an allowance for spouses, so it won't cost anything.

I flit between full immersion in the experience and wondering how it can be happening. We're married? I ask myself. This perfect creature married me? This love, this security and care, is a forever arrangement? It's not a feeling I know but it's one I want to let in. My phone starts ringing. I apologise and tell him I forgot to switch it off. It keeps ringing. My phone. Keeps ringing. My phone is ringing. It's the middle of the night. Rhona, your phone is ringing!

I prop myself on an elbow and reach for the receiver. 'Rhona. It's me, can you—'

'Hilary? Are you okay? Where are you?'

'Waiting for an ambulance. Feel awful. Can't get hold of Gary. Will you keep trying? I need to hang up now. You'll meet me at the hospital?'

'Yes. Yes.'

Hope she heard my reply before the disconnect. Don't think I need to do things in same order I would on normal morning. Can't think which elements of getting ready aren't essential.

Not the baby. Not the wee baby. Give me cancer again if it means Hilary and the baby will be okay.

Taxi. Need to get to hospital in taxi. Phone. 'Can you make it fifteen minutes? Not any sooner than that, I need to get clothes on. Thanks.'

Time check. 2.10. Jeans, top, boots. Hair up. Face splash. Teeth brush, barely. Bag. Coat. And? What might Hilary not have had time to remember? Tissues. Pack of Caramel Wafers. Might need them. Jesus. I don't know. Money. Cash in purse? £17. Taxi and coffees. Mobile. One bar of charge showing. Marvellous. Try Gary. Scroll. Gabrielle. Gillian. Where's Gary? Why have I never taken Gary's number? Low battery, no net searching. Find phonebook. T, Te, To, Tr, Trailways, Trampoline 0141 3— Christ! Phone. 'Hilary? Oh. Outside. Thanks. Just coming.'

Keys. Careful. Quiet. Neighbours. Air. Cold. Steps. Door handle. Seat. Springy.

'The Southern, please. A&E entrance.'

Driver. Question.

'I'm fine. It's my friend.'

Driver. Question.

'Not sure. False alarm, I hope.' Voice wobbling.

Driver. No question.

Mobile. Directory Inquiries. 'It's a nightclub called Trampoline, in Glasgow. Yeah, and text me it. Ta.' Connected. Ringing. No answer. Doesn't anyone sit in the office during club hours? Wait for answering machine to kick in. No answering machine kicks in. Maybe Hilary's got hold of him by now. His shift will end soon. He'll get a phone signal outside. Phone-able by 3.15.

Hang up. Preserve lone bar of charge.

Red traffic light. No cars. Delay. Pointless. Delay. Coloured light inside the museum's turrets. Late pedestrian. All-night petrol station.

Entrance. Purse. Tenner. Tip.

'Thanks.'

Cold. Automatic. Slide. Bright.

~

I explain to the man at the desk that my friend told me to meet her here. I give him Hilary's name, mentioning the ambulance. Reminding me I'm not a relative, he tells me he'll have to confirm my identity with Ms Marshall. He suggests I take a seat.

There are only half a dozen people, so it's easy to find a chair that has an empty one on either side. Survival instinct: avoid sitting next to someone who might have something.

I send Hilary's phone a text to tell her I'm here, with no idea if she'll see it. When I join her, I'll do whatever she requires of me. I'll phone people or I'll let her do it. Go with her or stay put. Get her coffee or not get her anything. Hold her hand or sit out of the way. Do the right thing or the wrong thing. I can be leaned on or screamed at.

Poor Hil. She hates hospitals.

Looking at the clock on the wall, it's 3 a.m. already. If the man at reception had anything to tell me, he'd call me over. It's fruitless to pester him.

At 3.05, I feel there's no harm in asking. 'It's a secure area,' he reminds me. 'You'll appreciate that we can't let you through until Ms Marshall has vouched for you. As soon as she's available, I'll get back to you.'

I know there's no point in asking why she's not available. I know he wouldn't tell me. My only frame of reference for this situation is TV hospital dramas. I try not to picture Hilary being helped under each arm from a room of intensive care incubators, where there was nothing more that could be done.

I reclaim the same seat – only two people are still here. Rush hour must be over. Rush hour. Work. I am due at work in six hours. Hilary has asked me to be here so I will be here until Hilary says otherwise. Maybe I should telephone the office, in case I can't nearer the time. I could call Gary again, too.

On the way out, I wave at the man behind reception and point to my phone, to let him know where I'll be.

It's as dark as it was an hour ago. I dial the office. When the answering machine stops talking, I say that I'm at the hospital with a friend, that I might come into work after lunch, it depends whether I get home for a sleep. I say I'll call again when I can. I'm accessing 'call history' for Gary's work number when the phone dies in my hand. That's that.

273

The pre-dawn air creeping around my limbs awakens impulses in my muscles to set off – for where, I don't know. *There has been enough sitting*, they say to me. *Sometimes you have to sit*, I tell them, *even when you don't feel like it*.

The cool air starts whipping grit and a streak of car park is lit like daytime. There's an unnameable noise like all hell. I want to run but I don't know which direction it's safe to run in: I can't discern the source of the noise. It's above me. I move further under the porch but not all the way back inside. Within the thrumming well of wind I hear a rhythm. The beat of rotors. Beyond the roofline of the entrance, at a speed I wasn't expecting, a helicopter sweeps away. Taking a doctor somewhere? Taking a patient somewhere else?

Such urgency in the between-time hours and till this morning, I knew nothing of it.

Back in my seat, waiting at the edge of the emergency I can't attend, I make eye contact with the guy at reception. This doesn't provoke a response. My hope of a false alarm scenario cannot be sustained. But that doesn't have to mean the worst. What is stacked in their favour? This hospital houses Scotland's Children's Hospital. It's world class. If they can't do it here, it can't be done. Hilary's strong, she never catches anything from the kids she works with. And if it's taking this long, there must be stuff to do. It's not a lost cause.

In this library quiet, I silently address the authority which decides such matters. I tell it that I don't know how it works up there, but anything goes wrong tonight and it's got me to deal with. There is no version of events in which losing either of them could be okay. None.

Someone drunk has come in and is hassling at the desk. I

turn to see. He isn't drunk. He's Gary; his urgent voice modulating as he tries to explain why he's here. 'My partner came in an ambulance. Hilary. Marshall.'

I almost rise to approach him – intuition keeps me put.

'We've been expecting you, Mr Buchanan. You need to go up a floor. The stairs are on the right, just there. Ask again at the nurse's station on Level One. They'll take you along.'

Gary holds his jacket closed with one hand as he runs. His free forearm lunges at the stairwell door. I don't bother speaking to the man at reception on my way out.

Emerging, the daylight dimmer-switch has been turned up a fraction and this continues to happen as I make my way home along pre-active streets.

～

Gus sends me an email at work.

Wanna get away tomorrow night? Here's a few links to hotels, all within two hours' drive. Let me know which you prefer. And I checked the weather. Clement in the east.

I forgot to contact him yesterday. I was a space cadet because I'd been up all night. And today I've been thinking about Hilary. All I could do was leave a message on both her phones.

I reply to Gus's mail, suggesting we speak later to discuss the idea.

When I get home there are no baby-related messages. I phone Gus. It goes to voicemail. Friday night is his squash game with a pint after, so I hang up because now I have time to think before I speak.

Do I want to go away? I want to get hold of Hilary – or her mum, or Gary.

In my address book, there's no number for Hilary's mum. Who might have it? My mum? She phones back twenty minutes later. It was in an old address book which she found in a handbag she hasn't used for years. It seems the 'no hoarding' rule applies to everyone else in the house but her.

~

Gus comes round at midday with a deli bag of lunch items. Again, I tell him that we could still have gone away and he looks at me, like, *You are kidding.* He asserts that we can go away anytime. He puts the bag down and leads me to the living room. When we're comfy, he says, 'I still don't really know what happened.'

I describe the middle-of-the-night phone call and waiting in the hospital. I tell him what Hilary's mum told me: Hilary was signed off work with pre-eclampsia at 34 weeks. During week 36 she woke with a thumping headache, blurred vision and her limbs were fitting. The only cure for eclampsia is birth so the hospital staff delivered a tiny wee boy. Hilary's weak and they're monitoring Eric. She's hardly held him yet. There's nothing more to tell. And if there was, I'm crying too much to tell it.

~

On my next visit to the badminton club, I'm struck by the emptiness of the space where children spend most of their childhoods. School buildings are different to offices. They are hard surfaced, single-glazed, comfortless and two tones of colourless.

276

And Elmwood is one of the better ones. Particularly today, harbouring sunlight at angles in the corridor.

Another school comes to mind: Denburn, the one that contacted Muffin twice about consultancy input, the one that I researched and emailed to Donald before my surgery. Before shadowing Petra on White Cairn. Imagine what that school is like.

On the bus back, a woman a few rows behind is singing. Not like, 'I'm pissed and you all have to listen to me.' More like she's heard a song she liked earlier, and today's been a good day, and she's from the kind of family who sings aloud as easily as it snarks. The sound sends a mellifluous pulse through my skin; it generates palpable well-being. I settle in.

We pass a garden with a topiaried evergreen shaped like Santa. A ripple of amusement travels up the seats. I must remember to tell Mum and Dad I saw that. She'll ask what kind of tree it was; he'll say, 'Santa looking rather spruce, was he?'

~

Gary phones my mobile around one, to say he has managed to persuade Hilary to leave the hospital later. Just for an hour or two. He wants her to eat something decent. He thinks she's more likely to go through with it if she has a reason, i.e. me.

During his call I'm in a lunch hour queue to buy tickets for Scottish Ballet's Christmas show – my annual gift to Lizzie. I dial her number as I'm walking to the office. 'Will you see what you can do online?' I ask. 'I'm heading back to work so that I can leave early.'

'No problem. I'll text you alternatives if the 22nd's sold

out. Anything else I can do, don't hesitate. Huh,' she reflects, 'buying my own Christmas present. You're as bad as John.'

~

At the office, I type,

> Hey Donald,
>   Advance notice that I'll be sneaking out the door a teensy bit early today (but I do sacrifice most Saturdays for the Muffin cause).
>   Shall we bust out of the kitchen and have our monthly catch-up 'exeat' tomorrow? Raymond's in Edinburgh and Petra's on jury duty (whatever they did, they don't deserve that). We shouldn't be cooped up in here. I'm seeing a pavement café. Audrey Hepburn and Gregory Peck. You can be Audrey.
>   One o'clock? Scarf and gloves?

~

Crossing the road, I see Hilary inside by the window. Something about her is different. Her facial muscles have reset. She has entered new territory.

When she stands to greet me, we end up in a long hug. 'So good to see you,' she says, with intensity. Sitting down, she's becoming effervescent at her release; brimming with things to say and animated as she says them. 'There are countries not far from here where people's own homes smell like this. Can you believe that?' Aromas come into focus: brewed coffee, sweetened butter, sautéed garlic and seasoned meat, slightly charred.

Aware of how much I've missed her, I end up clasping her arm. 'Oh Hil, how *are* you? How's Eric?'

The light that had flared in her eyes fades. 'Can we not talk about it right now?' she asks. 'I'm awful for saying that, aren't I? Gary's "time off"' suggestion is taking hold.'

'You're not awful. I don't need to know anything.'

She reflects for a second and says, 'Gary has a practical way of approaching things ... it's good, we have a sort of routine going. It's been intense, the whole situation, obviously, but manageable. Just short of being exhausting.'

'What use would you be to anyone if you were exhausted?' I ask, realising it sounds fatuous.

'Indeed,' she says, posh-voiced. 'Nervous fatigue is *the* number one enemy of the competent housewife and I'd have no business indulging in it.'

'Well, quite,' I concur. 'Decided what you're going to order?' I ask, scanning a menu.

'All of it. It's too good.'

'Why don't you order for us both? Same deal for dessert.'

The thing she wants most, for some reason, is avocado.

When the plates arrive, Hilary picks slippery, green slices from my open sandwich and puts them with her pile of fusilli and pesto. She slides the chicken and bread heap towards me, which I neaten up before biting in.

'Good choosing,' I tell her. 'Happy with yours?'

She gives a thumbs-up, her mouth too full to form words. In a pause between forkfuls, she says, 'What's news. What have you been up to?'

Bobbing my head for comic effect, I reply, 'Is it *awful* not to talk about me right now? The "time off" thing has *really* taken hold.'

She puts her hand over her mouth to prevent pasta falling out. I'm only half joking, though. Does she need to know I've had a boyfriend for five minutes? The dropping sun is washing our window-table in beery light. Hilary has acquired an angelic aspect. I'd take a photo but that would look weird. I gesture beyond the window and we observe the effect of the lowering sun as it catches the closest tenement building, burnishing the sandstone.

'I was a piece of work a while back, on the phone,' she says.

'Maybe,' I reply, 'or maybe I'd been a drain you didn't need, hanging around your house every weekend.'

'You're weren't a drain. Well, slightly, but only because I was so tired. Rhona, nothing prepares you for the tiredness of pregnancy and motherhood.'

'You've done incredibly well, Ms Marshall.'

She transmits suspicion.

'Seriously. So much changed for you in a short space of time and you got on with it – never moaning about a partner on nightshifts, or a hard pregnancy, or budgets. I'm in awe of you. I am,' I say, descending into self-consciousness.

She wears a *'What planet are you on?'* expression. 'I wasn't that unruffled,' she says. 'The pressure was getting to me before Gary got this job offer. I don't want to go back to work full-time but on his wages I'd have had to. I probably took it out on you.'

'Gary's starting a new job? Tell me more,' I say. 'But not in too much detail – wouldn't want to keep you up past 9 p.m. You might fall out with me.'

She laughs and sticks two fingers up at me.

When we've finished eating she goes to the counter,

returning with a take-out bag. 'Portion of lasagne for Gary. He's better at doing nights than I am. Poor guy.'

'You heading there now?' I ask. 'I'll jump in the cab with you part way, then I can walk back. Burn off that toffee pudding.'

'It'll take more than a wee stroll,' she says, engorging her cheeks with air to imply obesity.

Our taxi slows to a halt at a junction. There's a couple waiting on the pavement to cross. It takes me a second to recognise that the guy holding the woman's hand is the composer of red-and-black, cut-and-pasted emails. 'He was one of my CatchMe dates,' I tell her, nodding my head towards them.

'Did *any* of your dates have hair?' *Just the one I never mentioned.*

'Well, the internet must have worked for that guy,' she's saying, "cause he's got himself a chica.'

Chuffed as I am for him, something in me has to shake off the fakery of his assiduous communication. Leaning towards the window, I wave at him, mouthing a surprised, 'Hellooo!'

'I know what I'm doing,' I tell Hilary, and I kiss her with enthusiasm (just to the side of her lips) before turning back to mouth a coquettish, 'Call me ... ', my hand representing a telephone.

That'll give them something to chat about before the film starts.

~

On the way home, I stop in at a deli to inquire about deliveries. 'Yes, we deliver,' says the server in a tinsel-trimmed apron, 'until 8 p.m.'

I give a violin-worthy spiel about my friends' situation, culminating in a request to deliver a couple of 'specials' to

Hilary's home address, at eight in the evening, for the next week, perhaps phoning her mobile first to check that someone is home. His hesitation is assuaged by my offer to pay for those meals upfront, including a tip for the driver.

It feels like the least I can do, in fact, the only helpful thing I can do: making sure they both have decent meals and ones that are portable.

I'm almost home when my phone rings. Gus's number. I forgot – it's Wednesday. We arrange that he'll come to mine tomorrow, instead.

～

By late on, Gus hasn't mentioned Hilary and Eric; cautious, no doubt, in case it upsets me. I want to let him know it's okay, that I'm no longer fragile. I tell him Hilary was looking well yesterday, when I get up from the table with the plates. He points to my brother's Christmas card, pinned to the fridge door, saying, 'James Whistler, eat your heart out?'

'A Callum original. They must have scanned it.' I hand the card to Gus.

'Signs of early promise. Captured all the elements here, of the classic snowman.'

'I'm only a godmother for the super talented.'

'I didn't know you were a godmother,' he says.

'I'm David's only sibling. Who else was he going to ask?'

'Less of the modesty. They probably asked because they could sense you'd be good with kids,' he says. He puts the card down. 'I can sense it too. S'obvious.'

Not this conversation. Isn't it supposed to be the woman who sneaks a route into this conversation? 'Why? Because I remind you of one – your autistic nephew?' I laugh, hoping to divert the topic with banter.

'Partly,' he says, deliberately deadpan. 'Also because you're fun company. And caring. And beautiful . . . on the *inside*.'

We enjoy his well-timed insult. I hold his hand across the table, brush it softly with my lips and say, 'You're beautiful too,' hoping to divert the topic with sex.

He kisses my hand in return and says, 'I didn't realise how much I wanted to be a dad until my last relationship ended. It took me longer to get over the fact we hadn't had kids than to get over her.'

'Did you try having one?' I ask, fishing for information on his fertility, hoping for the worst.

'Not with any effort. We weren't particularly bothered. Until the opportunity was gone. Then I was very bothered. Gets worse with every birthday. I'm forty-four. I don't like the idea it might never happen.'

I do a thin job of hiding my indignation.

'A Big Ben body clock doesn't really match the Ferris Bueller alias.'

'How d'you work that out?' he asks. 'Ferris was in love. He took risks, he grabbed life. Ferris had a lot of life to pass on.' He's laughing.

I put my wine glass down. 'Back in a sec. Bathroom,' I tell him; the only option left to deflect the topic.

~

At midday, I send a quick message to Hilary's phone:

How are you holding up? Hope everything's good today. Love, love, love to you and Eric and G. xxx

~

Donald's espresso is brought to the table. I've set the scene, summarising my diploma modules and how well the course is going, telling him about the residential weekend next month. Then I thank him for the badminton afternoons at Chesney's old school. And remark that even a well-managed school can't afford to pay for extra-curricular coaching.

'If Elmwood is one of this authority's best schools,' I say, 'kids at other schools are in trouble. I mean, think about Denburn. Remember when they asked for our help? I can understand why, now.'

Donald ceases nodding to allow the small cup to meet his pursed mouth.

'It's been on my mind again, Denburn,' I say, airily. 'So much so, I contacted the head teacher to offer consultancy services.' I force a grin. He will go along with me if I make it appear as though this is a done deal.

'Think about it, Don. It's great experience to supplement my diploma training. You don't have to let me loose on any big-money clients and a school that really needs help will get it.'

Don't give him time to respond, go in with the guilt.

'I couldn't help thinking about those kids getting a second-rate start in life because the staff, who want nothing more than to teach them, don't have the resources to do it, because they're pedagogues, Donald, not money managers. It's not their fault they're rubbish at that bit. Teaching is a *vocation*. Unlike profiteering. Teaching is the closest thing to the clergy I can think of.'

Too much? Not enough?

'You've got two children, nearly. What example do you want to set them? Daddy only cared about money? Or Daddy cared about people, about adding value, about teaching men to fish. Okay granted, Chesney's probably ruined already, but the one that's on the way – that kid could be a really nice person, it's up to you.'

Get back on point.

'If Denburn is a successful project, which I know it will be, I'm going to specialise in third sector consulting. Everyone should have access to high quality business advice. And Muffin should be offering it. I want every pound I am paid, every pound I free-up in an organisation, to translate into more meals for the elderly, or more staff on a youth project, or better wages in a recycling initiative.'

If he varied his facial expression, I'd have some idea whether to stop or keep going.

'And you can't sack me because I looked into it and . . . you just can't.'

I put my grin back in place.

He slides his cup and saucer aside, leans forward and lifts his specs to his crown. 'I'd have to be a real prick to say no to that,' he says.

～

On Friday, Gus texts to see if we're on for Saturday afternoon. I text back saying Hilary has asked me to come for visiting hours that day.

Hilary has asked no such thing.

～

The schmaltzy movie which dominates this pre-Christmas evening exerts the mind control its makers intended. *Christmas is for family and friends! What grudge could matter more than harmony at Christmas??*

Okay! I GEDDIT! It's a curse on my future happiness to continue on bad terms with Tania. It's not that I haven't wanted to make contact. Being busy let me bury it, until this Disney dressing-down.

I know why she slung opprobrium at me in the bar, splashing our table with it. Because, on the rainy afternoon we ate lunch and went to the cinema, I told her that the idea of her having a kid was crazy. *God help it*, I said.

She let that go for weeks. I deserved every drop of drunken hassle. *Right back at ya'*, she was saying.

What kind of mother *would* I make, when I can't be supportive of those closest to me without condition? Can't trust them to manage their own lives.

When I dread producing a Christmas meal unaided? And have set aside the whole of Boxing Day to recover.

What do children need? At least a mother who can handle an incubated start. Perhaps worse. Would they get that from me?

I'll be thirty-six in a blink. Having a hurried baby after that would feel like grabbing something, anything, off a Christmas sale rail because the shop is shutting in five minutes and it's the last chance to save a few quid on an arbitrary item I wasn't feeling the lack of.

A purple, wrong-sized skirt can be returned to the shop in a rational mood. A baby can't be handed back when you're thirty-nine and in another zone of exhaustion and self-neglect (perhaps also resentment, and maybe depression thrown in).

If I don't need a child for *me*, who am I having one for? A child wouldn't know if it never came into existence. For a partner, then? No. I can't offer myself as a vessel for a man who wants children so badly his eyes leak tears at the fact it hasn't happened yet. If my partial cervix couldn't deliver, he'd leave – to fulfil his longing. This is common sense pain avoidance. Erin would be so proud.

I won't stand in the way of Gus having his own kids.

I don't have to cling to this man.

There'll be a guy out there for whom children are more of a take-it-or-leave-it prospect. That's the kind of someone I can stay with.

~

Visible lives of others spoil my trip to the Co-op. Is it so hard to pull a curtain of an evening? When the bulbs burn it's time to close the blinds. I don't want to see your square-shaped, squalid, inside spaces. Ugly-hung laundry on handles and heaters; on brown veneer door tops. I am assaulted by your tat; by the slovenliness of your modest, mismatched innards.

A wide open home is the man who says too much on a first date, before I've had time to decide if I like him and will, therefore, forgive shortcomings.

This is too much of all of you.

Even the tidy rooms trouble – the vile-papered feature-wall, co-ordinated cushions, supermarket wall art and nothing else, nothing at all, but neatness – the terrible wounds of someone who needs a high level of order, plainly displayed.

And the worst of it? The Christmas trees. Their near-holy presence ascending these facades – as if the tenements are advent calendars and the windows are squares for each date; and the squares that have been opened reveal Christmas trees. That's how I should have felt, protruding into my bay window. Proud among the rest. Tapered and gleaming with the tiny lights of love he had strung me with.

~

If I learned anything this year, it's that two days of my own miserable company are plenty. Heed the warning signs. Re-enter society. Navigate the tricky territory.

Hi Tan. I'm not getting in touch just because I watched a sentimental xmas movie. Okay, yes I am. Apols it wasn't sooner. You have every reason to ignore me, I deserve it. I am a mouthy ignorant madam. SORRY for what I said. I miss you. Want to meet up? It would be good to talk about Hilary & Eric.

~

Ordering three Proseccos from a passing waiter, Erin resumes her full flow, '... never encountered such navel-gazing as you two, honestly. The short answer? If it happened you'd get on with it, it's what people do. But until you get your acts together – naturally, by adoption, with a turkey-baster – you can get all the practice you want helping the rest of us.'

Whilst Erin continues talking, Tania reaches across to squeeze my forearm, mouthing, 'Sorry'. She rolls her eyes behind Erin and we smirk as we sit to attention.

'Mindy has no available grandparents,' says Erin. 'They're either still working, dead, or in the Algarve. So I see your roles as crucial. James and I agree that Mindy needs a range of adults around, growing up. Aunties – do you mind that word? Aunties are her extended family. And uncles.'

'It's an honour to be included in Mindy's social development programme,' I say.

She shifts her face away in a faux huff, saying, 'Fine, if you don't want—'

I've sidled in, shoulder to shoulder. 'I *am* touched, *we're* touched, that you think we have anything to offer. Maybe I could give Mindy career advice, I've sampled enough of them. Tania can do the stuff about puberty and teenage boys ...'

Rhona! Why test it so soon?

'Heeell ye-ah,' says Tania, mouthing me a kiss. Phew. 'Chips?' she suggests. 'Who's with me? This auntie is hungry.'

Erin insists on a proper dinner so, instead of moving from bar to bar, we stay put, talking our way through two courses. Cutting her meat, Tania almost whispers, 'You're sure I can be a good influence in the life of your only daughter?'

She's expressing the same chuffed disbelief I was sheltering. The surrounding hubbub seems to curl in on itself and a kernel of warmth in my chest grows slowly till it's swollen beyond my body. I taste the certainty that I must do my best with whatever circumstance I find myself in, letting go of the circumstances that no longer are. Ones that never were. And any that never could be.

I can choose what I want – but I must start from where I am. This moment, the ever-rolling now, is where I have influence. Tania is snapping her fingers at me.

For the rest of the evening, we empty ourselves of everything we've been wanting to say to each other about the one who isn't here. What she's been coping with, what Eric's been through and what, if anything, we can do by way of help.

Fifteen

Back in September I'd decided that the way to get through Christmas Day this year was to host it. With two days to go, I'm questioning that wisdom. But I'm in too deep, there's nothing I can do, except carry on checking the to-do lists for different rooms and the shopping schedule (which grocery item, from which shop, on which day).

My brother's family is staying at my parents' and when I'm not over there building Lego with Cal, I'm at home, making cranberry sauce, oatmeal stuffing, trifle and a misshapen centrepiece of twigs and pine cones.

The day itself goes smoothly, because Mum and Annie anticipate (in collaboration?) what I might (and do) overlook. They come with a giant roasting tin, with pouring cream, butter dishes and experience.

None of them knows about Gus; he hasn't been mentioned

yet. So when my mobile rings while loading the dishwasher and I ignore it, I don't have to answer any questions.

~

I didn't think post was delivered between Christmas and New Year. I thought the world stopped.

The envelope is not firm – it's not a late Christmas card. Small mercies. There's nothing sadder. A Christmas card's task is to arrive in time for Christmas. When it can't do that right, I want to pick it up with tongs and drop it in the bin. It's addressed to The Occupier. Who is this from? The letter itself is printed and there's no signature, just an email address.

Hello Occupier,

I'm trying to contact a resident of the building I met last June. Did you lose your cat called Cyril? I'm the guy who found him. We didn't swap numbers at the time. I should have been quicker off the mark.

I thought maybe I'd run into you again but no joy. I can't stalk you (LOL) because I don't know which floor you're on. And I can't ask my sister about you because she's not really the type to confide in (but if any of you see her at the bin-store, don't mention I said that).

I'd like to keep in touch, kitten lady, if you would. I'll be watering the plants over the Xmas break. Fancy coffee?

cp80@ntconnect.com

PS Keep Cyril away from the TV this week, he might pick up tips from Steve McQueen. Watch out for small piles of earth around your flat.

Hmm. Keen or what? It's only taken him six whole months to get in touch. It's obvious to me, if not to him, that he's been reflecting back on his year because he's single at Christmas. He's spun himself a sentimental tale casting me as 'the one who got away'.

I won't be sending him an email (though he'll get a few from the students on the top floor). Even if I was desperate enough to be a months' later afterthought, it's hardly the right time. I'm not even replying to my own bloke. Why would I reply to this guy?

Ignoring two men at the same time – Tania would be so proud of my progress.

~

Clematis the colour of a winter solstice sun-up covers the trellis around the hotel entrance. Mum stands before it, her nose in the flower heads. 'Mm, wonderful. Vanilla.' She turns to face us again. 'How does nature do that, Phillip?'

I wipe pollen from her earlobe.

'How can different plants have similar scents?' she asks. 'Clematis and vanilla. Gorse and coconut.'

'Let's ask that on the garden tour,' he says, steering her towards the glass doors.

By dinner time, I don't remember anything the head gardener had said as he led us round the Victorian-faithful grounds; probably because I couldn't hear him. I was deaf from the precious sunshine. I'd loitered on the fringes of the group to enable older people to get in close. Mum frowned with concentration as she scribbled in a notebook and Dad walked slowly beside her, wearing her handbag. Adorable. When the tour ended, I think I was more disappointed than anyone.

My parents are discussing the wine poured, trying to discern the flavours noted on the wine list.

'I don't get blueberry. Do you get blueberry?' Mum asks.

'Vanilla! Coconut!' Dad contributes.

'They're not in the description.'

He winks at me.

I'd already mentioned to Mum on the phone the reason why I was taking them away for new year. Do I need to say it again here? They came, didn't they?

The memory of her sobbing by the lined-up bird feeders comes to mind. We might be cradling silent fears and it's time to interrupt that cycle. I raise my glass in the direction of theirs.

'A toast. To you two.'

Confusion morphs into anxiety on Dad's face. 'It's not our anniversary?'

'Chill Phil, it's not your anniversary. It's a thank you toast. Last year . . . can't have been easy for you both and I forgot to say thanks properly, for putting up with me and helping me when I needed it.'

'Nothing to do with us,' Dad says. 'Cyril did the hard work. We just phoned you a couple of times.' The jokey card; it's his way.

'Ah, but you gave me Cyril.'

Mum isn't smiling. Still holding her glass aloft, she appears pensive, steeled for something.

'Now that I'm *better*,' I emphasise, '*totally* fine again,' I squeeze her free hand, 'I wanted to show my gratitude. This hotel for garden lovers was perfect.'

'We didn't see any of those on the tour,' Dad says. 'Where were they?'

I head-back laugh. Mum missed the wit because she was taking in my speech. She's making small, chuffed sounds. She starts, 'Isn't this a wonder—,' but her shoulder is grasped by a tanned man in a silver jacket. 'Madam!' he exclaims.

'Monsieur!' cries a woman in a split-to-the-hip dress who grips Dad's arm. The spotlight has found them and my parents stand up because they're the type not to make a fuss in front of strangers (cheering all the louder because they weren't chosen). Tango music starts, clapping diners keep time and for the next few glorious minutes my parents are pulled, marched, turned and bent backwards by Windermere's finest off-season entertainers. Dad gets into the spirit and puts his hands, theatrically, on the lady's yellow satin bum.

'Oi, Phil! Keep it clean!' I shout, while she repays the gesture and his face turns plum.

~

When I exit the sports centre after aerobics, Gus is leaning against his unmanly car by the kerb, basking in a cloud of his own breath. Looking beautiful.

'Nice hat,' he says.

Neither of us moves to hug the other.

'You actually suit yours,' I reply. 'Must be why you're so good at snowboarding.'

'Because I look all right in the *gear*?'

'Yup.'

He's containing an impulse to step closer. 'Thought you might need a lift home,' he says.

I catch a searching look behind his smile; doubtless he can see the evasiveness behind mine.

We pick a pub where it won't matter what we're wearing. Near the start of the conversation, I come out with, 'I don't want them. I've never wanted them. I'm not built that way.' Which is only half a lie, since the spring.

Gus isn't ready to discuss the issues making our union unviable. He wants his righteous five minutes about how disrespectful it was to excommunicate him over the festive season. How hurt he felt. I can't argue. But I don't see how I could have done the right thing by two people at the same time. How could I cater to his needs *and* mine?

He says all he wanted was a phone call. He would have understood. He had a present for me. He'd planned things for our time off. He didn't realise Eric being in hospital had affected me so badly but did I have to shut him out completely?

Was he listening when we sat down? I tell him it wasn't about Eric. It was about the conversation we'd had *after* the conversation about Eric.

I'm having to force myself to engage in this. First week at work after the holidays. Aerobics. I just want to be at home, in the shower then having dinner, yet here I am in a wood-panelled pub telling my internet boyfriend that six months before I met him I had surgery that could preclude motherhood.

'Rhona,' he implores, 'I don't want you because you can give me kids. I want *you*, first and last.'

That's the flush of new love talking, overriding what's important to him. 'When your last girlfriend moved out,' I remind him, 'you grieved kids more than you grieved her. I heard you say it.'

'Aye, because our connection was long dead. We'd nothing left. But if you walk away, it's not children you're denying me, it's *you*. Don't deny me the best woman I've been close to.' He looks down at his near-finished beer. Swirls it. Takes a couple more seconds to raise his eyes. 'You've redefined what being with someone is for me.'

I make the gesture of 'a little bit much' with my thumb and forefinger.

'Listen. It might sound like romantic shite but it's true.' I take one of his hands. 'Sorry for disappearing before the holidays. I'm ashamed of how selfish that was. Not being able to provide you with the kids you desperately want freaked me out.'

'I don't care about kids.'

'Yes you do. And you will. It's what happens. A relationship settles into banal and people revert to type. New partners say they want what the other person wants, just to keep that person. But deep down they want what *they* want. And it causes all sorts of hassle when they remember.'

I know there's more to this, though. I know, now. I tighten my hands over his. 'You can't choose me,' I say to him, 'because I wouldn't even be trying for kids. It's not that we *might* not be able to have them. We won't have them. Not just because of an operation. It's the timing. If you'd caught me a few years ago, on the updraft, this'd be different.' Opposing polarities keep our gazes locked. 'My goodness, we'd have been such a force.'

I have to lift my hands away to find a tissue to sort tears and snot.

'We are, Rhona. That's us.'

'Let's not be in a pairing that ends up defined by what it missed out on, what it doesn't have. I could be thirty-seven when it happened. Thirty-eight, thirty-nine. IVF maybe. My window to embrace motherhood has passed. Not yours, mine. It's not for me any more. Even if I can have kids, I wouldn't. That's what I've realised.'

Despite this appearing like the say-everything moment with Gus, there's something I won't say. Understanding my position is enlivening. I'm at liberty to make the most of whatever else is on offer. And that adds up to elation. How can I say that out loud?

'Sorry,' I whisper. 'I'm sorry. I should have said something. I didn't know, before.'

He's sitting back against the leather-effect padded wall.

'Your silent treatment pissed me off. But, I get it. Those kinds of insights don't arrive out the air. People need to get tangled up with each other, to find out about themselves.' Gus draws his thumbs across the moisture on my cheeks. 'Life is messy.' He's trailing a finger down my face. 'It was nice getting messy with you, Missy.'

~

Saturday is never-ending and totally fucking tedious.

The transition back to single is not as seamless as the change in the other direction.

~

When Tania said she knew what her strengths were, she wasn't making it up. Erin and I do nothing except arrive at the allotted time.

Gary knows, of course, and the nurses are in on it. 'Look out the window,' they have been primed to say at 11 a.m. Hilary's face crumples in laughter when she sees three demented women waving from a limousine sunroof. Canapés and champagne have been laid on for the drive to a country spa which normally has a two-month waiting list.

'You're our hostage for the next eight hours,' Tania tells her.

~

Hilary and I emerge from the twin massage room and recline onto loungers. Erin and Tania go in the door we came out. Tchai is poured for us.

'How's Eric doing?' I ask her. She tells me that he'll be coming home after the weekend. I squeal and make her clink tea cups. She settles back into the chair. After a minute or so, she says, 'When Eric wasn't developing properly in the womb, wouldn't grow enough, I thought I was a crap mum for him. It should have been a happy time but it got more and more stressful.' A tear slides down past her ear. I don't think I'm meant to speak at this point, I think I'm meant to listen.

'If I hadn't phoned that ambulance—' She stops. 'We came quite close,' she continues, 'to not having him, or me, any m—' Hilary's crying cuts through her sentence. I take the space on her lounger, placing an arm around her till her breathing becomes normal.

I offer her a tissue from the box on the table.

Dropping the bunched up paper into the wastebasket, Hilary says, 'I've got a vacancy for a maid of honour next summer, if you're free.'

'Aaaahhh! Congratulations!' I throw my arm back around her. 'If you come up with an alternative job title and a decent dress, I'm in.'

~

Boxercise is predictably stowed out with January enthusiasts. The instructor is taking a while to get round all the pairs. In a back corner, Tania and I have gone rogue, attempting to skip inside the same rope.

She drops the handles to the floor with no hint of sweat. Her mysterious powers. *If you find things so effortless, how come you don't do more?*

Unrelated to anything, she asks, 'Remember when you sent that long message to the text-pest guy, by accident?'

'I remember when *you* sent him the draft he was never supposed to see, yes.'

She tugs her second glove on using her teeth. 'What if you could have texted it to a neutral third party instead?'

She jabs me while I'm still securing my gloves.

'Ow! Why would I have sent the message for the annoying guy to someone else?'

'For your self-respect.'

Jab.

'Ow!'

'And for money.'

Jab. Jab.

'OW! No one's shown you how to use those gloves. Desist, you mad pugilist.'

She bounce-steps back and forward, her face full of attitude, sending pretend punches at me.

'Does Muffin work with start-ups?' she asks.

You know where I work? You've taken an interest?

'Depends,' I tell her. 'Muffin works with whoever will pay

them. Personally, I only work on projects that contribute something to society. Why?'

Her hands fall to her sides. 'Honestly, I think I'm slightly psychic. My new business is *all about* helping society.'

I'm scared to ask, but she's telling me anyway, that she's starting a premium rate phoneline and text service. *Because I'd mentioned you'd were good in a call centre ten years ago?* I'm getting more scared. Sexy talk? Tarot readings she can do in her pyjamas?

Once she's shared details, I'm wishing I'd thought of it. Basically, she said, when a person has an urge to text or phone someone that they probably shouldn't contact (an ex, a ghoster, a person they fancy who doesn't fancy them, their married lover, their boss after 8 p.m., family members when drunk, the list goes on), they can message Tania's service instead. All the closure or satisfaction of sending the text, or leaving the voicemail, with none of the fallout.

'That, Tania my girl, is a concept whose time has come.'

Her face creases briefly as she tries to take on board the compliment.

'Digital communication and human nature don't mix,' she states. 'It's been with us twenty-plus years and still we haven't mastered it. Most folk have zilch self-control when it comes to phone buttons.'

Jab. Jab.

OWW! But I won't let her know she's hurting me. I am toughening up.

'Instead of expecting miracles from people's willpower, I'm bringing the solution. There's a charge for every text and voicemail the service receives. But, you can't put a price on your dignity.'

301

She jerks back a couple of times when my fists play close to her face. 'What's the name of this new emergency service?' I ask. 'Don'tDial ... CallCurb ... DignityDial ... ?'

'Decide that later.'

'... SafeStalker? Your next question is going to be about money. I can't lend you any.'

She's popping two quick fists below my shoulder but I deflect her hand on the third, slapping a left hook on her ribs.

'Keep your money,' she wheezes. 'There's an investor – one of the WBs earns stupid sums from online poker, big league. He's fed up with women hassling him after a couple of hook ups. All I need from you, Beechy, is business advice.'

'I'll help you,' I tell her, ''course I will.'

'You'd have free access for life,' she adds, 'So we know who's getting the better end of this deal.'

～

Marge Simpson is quite a way ahead but still discernible within the jogging crowd. Lisa and Bart struggle to keep up. It's our own fault. We've been blethering too much.

Each sponsored kilometre takes us closer to the price of an infant-cardiac-something-or-other for the maternity unit (in vests promoting an adult premium-rate phoneline, which doesn't feel wholly appropriate).

～

Beyond the shade of the courtyard it is blood warm, the temperature of life. The air is a blend of Mediterranean scent: lantana, oleander, honeysuckle. Flower heads drip over the curve of a low wall.

302

The swimming pool isn't a rectangle. I know the water will be very cold, though the air is not. There are steps at the side but I jump, to get the shock over with.

It is sudden on my skin. Wiping wetness from my face and eyelids I see everyone is there, on the concrete rim, waving and wishing me luck. I am waving back.

Where am I going?

The surface is calm and chlorine blue. It accommodates me.

I don't pay much attention to my strokes. After a while, I decide there's no point in wondering how much further it will be: if I adopt a steady rhythm, I'll get there.

Arms out, breath out; arms in, breath in.

The end comes into view and I've no idea how many minutes, days or months I've been swimming. The prospect of no longer having to swim is interesting to me but that's all. It is no effort to stop.

Walking from the poolside on to the grass, my towel is hot and soft and waiting.

~

A woman dashing for the subway doors reaches them just as they're closing. Her limbs recoil wildly with an accompanying, 'Wooeeaah' before she is eclipsed. The vision is so brief, I wonder if I saw it at all and the mania of it sets me giggling.

I should have been getting off about now but the outer circle is closed. I've had to take the inner circle and go round the long way, through places I've never been to, like Cessnock. It must have been something in its day, to warrant an underground station, but I can't imagine what it is now because not once in conversation, ever, have I heard anyone say Cessnock. While having these thoughts I'm weakening my cardboard ticket between my fingers and rolling it into a tube.

At every stop I glance up to check if it's mine yet.

'Land ahoy, Cap'n,' says a man's voice.

I've been holding the tiny tube to one eye and looking through that. *Fuck.*

'Daydreaming,' I manage, mortified.

'Ticket origami – or tickegami, to give it its proper title – is the best way to get through an extended journey,' he says, passing me a small cardboard plane; basic model, the kind a four year-old could fashion.

'Nice,' I say, turning it, to examine it thoroughly.

'Give it here a second,' he says.

He takes the plane, bends the tip of both wings upwards and hands it back, saying, 'Last minute adjustment for take off.'

'When's take off?'

'When you've spotted land, let me know, and we'll launch it in that general direction. Oh wait,' he says, taking it back again, getting a pen from his pocket and writing, SEND HELP on the wings. He returns it to me.

'May I?' he asks and I hand him the tube. He puts it to his eye. 'My God!' he says, too loudly, 'That's amazing!' Steady on, son. But I realise the outburst is not for my benefit. We're playing 'the emperor's new telescope'. He leans in and speaks in my ear, 'Someone on this row will roll up their ticket now and look through it. Fiver.'

'Make it a double vodka and you're on.' Where did that come from? Too late. Said it now.

He shows me the time on his watch. 'Two minutes,' he says. We face away from each other, glancing along the row.

He elbows me. 'Red handbag,' he whispers, 'black coat.' Sure enough, a woman is raising a rolled-up ticket to her face. He holds my forearm as we watch her, watch her . . . tackle an itch at her hairline and then lower her hand.

'Boo,' he says. 'Keep looking.'

I lift his wrist. 'Sorry mate, time's up.'

'Already? Okay, make it three min—'

'My stop!'

I pick up my bag, stand, realise I'm still holding his aeroplane, turn round to offer it back and he's standing up too. 'Quick!' he says, shoving me towards the door.

We take the escalator up in silence. It's kind of awkward. Of course it is. We don't know each other. That stuff on the subway – what was that? Part of me wonders whether he got off the train to honour his bet and buy me a drink. I admonish that part of me. He got off because it's his stop too. Don't turn it into more than it is, Rhona, and for God's sake don't speak.

'You lost,' I say, 'fair and square. Where are we going for that drink?'

We're at the top of the escalator now. We step off. He moves to the side and faces me. 'Plane,' he says. Unbelievable. He's turning me down *and* he wants his shitey aeroplane back. I hand him the tickegami plane and start to walk away.

'Hey.' He touches my arm.

'Cross your fingers,' he says, facing into the escalator canyon and sending the cardboard aeroplane into the air.

～

Had I been released from a sensory deprivation chamber I could tell you, stepping out the door today, that winter is coming to an end. The leaves aren't on the trees, it's not warm, but barely perceptible signals speak of impending spring; the vibrating quality of the air, the glazed blue porcelain overhead.

The traffic is in that brief lull after rush hour. Those minutes when, if you wanted, you could walk up the middle of Great Western Road. Spires stand out from the sky the way they can't against summer's hazier blue. One slows my stride on the bridge; pronounced edges and angles in relief. I look around for other stone trees in the urban canopy, counting seven. I can picture their street level locations. I often bear myself by them without realising.

I'm still looking up as I gather pace and that's when I see the moon hanging high: a chalk smudge. I'm hijacked by a smile. The sun is finding my neck, and the moon – too pale to make itself properly known – is there if I want to see it. I read too much into the fact that I'm heading out this morning under the auspices of both.

I exhale. I take a step. I inhale.

Acknowledgements

Organisations to be thanked: The Scottish Arts Council (now Creative Scotland) for a generous Writer's Bursary, 2009 • Hi-Arts, for its encouraging Work-in-Progress report, 2010 • Creative Print Publishing, for short-listing the book for its Women's Fiction prize, 2011 • Cargo Publishing, whose team made the book's first outing so enjoyable in 2014.

Publications which accepted extracts of the work: *Clockworks* (Short Run Press) • *Gutter Magazine* (Issues 3 & 9) • *Reading the Waves* (Editor: Linda Jackson).

People who commented with care on sections, or full drafts: staff and students on the Glasgow MLitt, 2007–8, especially Mary Paulson-Ellis and Pippa Goldschmidt • Kay MacGregor, the first test reader • Polly Clark, a supporter (anonymous at the time) on the awarding panel of the Scottish Arts Council, and a wise voice on her Fielding Programme at Cove Park, 2010 • Reviewers at youwriteon.com, and the

Hookline Novel Competition, circa 2010, sincere in their desire to read the whole thing one day.

Others to thank: the experienced nurses of the Gynae-cological Cancer Team at the Beatson West of Scotland Cancer Unit who donated time and medical knowledge, 2009 • The Chartered Management Institute for its informative website (managers.org.uk), circa 2011 • Ronald Turnbull, Sara Sheridan and Elizabeth Reeder, for advice in 2013 • Staff of libraries, festivals and shops; thank you for promoting the book because you enjoyed it, and for promoting reading in general • Team members at Freight Books (in 2015, Cargo was bought by Freight, which liquidated in 2017) • Creative Scotland staff (Jenny Niven, Sasha de Buyl et al) and Freight authors, especially Merryn Glover, for pooling ideas, information and support during the liquidation • The Society of Authors for its excellent advocacy and advice • Duncan Lockerbie for patiently fielding e-book queries and deftly navigating Kindle • For website services (katetough.com): Damian Reilly's design talents and Shaun Phillips' hosting • Readers, every single one; you made the hard work feel worthwhile • Friends and family who tolerated my disappearing act during writing phases • Kenneth, for being 100% a fan to the last, for being a true comedian, and for providing the fisherman anecdote (and 'the roll in the kitchen' joke, and …) • Elspeth, for introducing me to libraries when very young, and for access to her bookshelves laden with gems (a few of which I 'forgot' to return).

Formal credits: When Rhona Beech attends a poetry event, themes alluded to arose from memorable readings by Tom Leonard, Eveline Pye and a third poet, content to be anon-ymous. The final poem in the scene quotes from 'The Stone

Bible' by Morgan Downie, from his collection *Stone and Sea*, reprinted with kind permissions from Morgan, and Colin Will at Calder Wood Press (and thanks, Babs NicGriogair, for reading it) • Rhona Beech has an email correspondent called FerrisBuellerSenior. Elements of that communication were donated, with permission.

Aside from those already mentioned, this novel exists in your hand due to: Helen Sedgwick, who made so much of it happen (as a freelance editor, then as MD of Cargo Publishing) • Mark Stanton at The North Agency, whose unbound-by-convention outlook could see what others hadn't (and who noticed that the novel's main character had accidentally left her name behind in a different KT story) • Clare Smith at Little, Brown, for her enthusiastic 'yes' and her incisive editorial super-powers.